Kiss
Of
Death

A Lee Truelove Novel

ROBERT SKUCE

Preface

The night was quiet now with all her roommates working or studying late into the night. That's why we chose tonight to save this helpless, sinful child. No distractions or witnesses. Tonight, it was just the three of us alone so that we could save her. Nobody to interfere with what must be done. As she slipped on her white housecoat grabbing a towel and soap, she was humming a classical tune that we had heard before. It was her nightly routine. She thought that her nightly routine of soaking in the tub was cleanliness, but we knew all her little secrets and not everything she did in there was wholesome. We slipped into one of the other rooms and waited. At times like this you must wait for the best moment and setting. Timing can be everything and we had this night planned down to the second.

We heard the water tumbling into the tub and we waited even though the excitement was overwhelming. We had planned this night over and over until every detail was perfect and it should be executed just as perfectly. Even the day was special. It was our anniversary. Ironic how on our rose anniversary we are saving Rosie, but she wouldn't understand the meaning. The bloodhound would though. He would remember the meaning. Rosie was humming that same song endlessly. If only she knew that the next song she sang was going to be amongst Angels. Through the little crack in the door we could see her body as she slowly undressed. She was vain about her body and enjoyed the idea of being watched by those around her. It was a flaw in her character. One of many flaws that existed and those who took the time to truly see her, took advantage of it.

We stepped closer towards the door. A low squeak rang out with each step we took. From the little crack in the door we could see her smile and slip under the white foaming suds. Her eyes sparkled as she tried to determine who was watching her. After a moment, she lifted her body up just a little higher allowing her nipples to poke through and an even bigger grin filled her face. Such a naughty child she was and now we would punish her.

Opening the door her smile disappeared as she whispered, "What are you doing here?" She dropped beneath the water whispering, "You can't see me like this!"

"Don't worry Rosie. Remember I said I would save and protect you always."

Her lips quivered as she whined, "Yes."

Pulling the knife from our pocket, we whispered, "Tonight's the night we save your soul and release you from your body."

CHAPTER 01 – BRUNO

My father once asked me when I stopped being the man he admired. I guess I should have felt something when those words left his lips, but I didn't. I didn't even know how to answer him because the man he admired was weak and empty inside. A yes man, so eager to please those around him or too obedient to stand up for himself. There was always something missing though. A void that couldn't be filled no matter how hard he tried. That version of me was slowly choked away until the weakness was removed. The victim was murdered, leaving behind the predator that now lives inside me. That's when I decided that I needed change and a hell of a lot of it. I didn't abandon my family, I just walked away, but you can't truly ever leave your family. Family, like destiny, isn't something you run away from. The best you can hope for is that you can hide long enough to be able to choose when you face them, rather than let them hunt you down. My name is Bruno Norcross. It's not a powerful name like William or Arthur. No, unlike every other man I know who were given a strong name based on a cherished uncle or great historical figure, my dad named me after his childhood dog. Yes, I was named after the oddest-looking creature ever. I was named after a Borzoi that was left behind and my father claimed it as his own. I am sure he loved it dearly and his happiest childhood memories were playing with that mangy mutt, but that is exactly how he treated me my whole life. I was treated like the family pet. I felt more like a flea bag kept out of obligation, not love or affection.

It took me some time to start building my new life. You know how it is, an uneducated small-town boy living in the big city for the first time. No job, no real skills and no money. Those first few months were cold and lonely, but I knew that life had to get better. It sure as hell couldn't get any worse. It was the first time I had ever been more than 30 minutes away from where I was born and raised. It was the something exciting that is for sure. The sweet taste of freedom. It took me even longer to build a life here, but I did it.

I am in homicide, so most of my work life and a big portion of my personal life is seeing, thinking or investigating the worst of mankind. I am the one that makes sure that the world hears the victim's stories and that their pain is not forgotten. I am not complaining mind you. Some of us are meant to live in the sunshine while others, like me, are meant to stand in the darkness with our gun in one hand and a flash light in the other. I chose to chase killers and it's the only thing I really know how to do. Hunt and catch monsters.

I don't know why I think of my child hood every time I get called to a crime scene, but I do. When I was a kid I would stay up watching those late night 50s black and white horror movies then run to my room and cocoon myself under the blankets, telling myself that those raggedy blankets were magic and that they would protect me from the unknown. Under my blankets vampires, demons and zombies couldn't touch me. It was the lie I told myself so I could sleep at night. The lie that helped me sleep through the night without the fear deep inside keeping me from closing my eyes. I still have a habit of cocooning myself under the blankets, but I am no longer lying about it protecting me against the monsters lurking in the shadows. I have seen too much to let myself enjoy such a child like fantasy.

I could see the familiar orange flashing lights all the way down Sandwich street. It wasn't that common to have yellow tape and two cars parked outside a crime scene twenty-four seven like you see on TV, but this wasn't exactly a common crime scene either. Most murders that I had seen were committed out of passion or crime related. Usually their story was easy to read. Most times even the greenest rookie could put all the pieces together like a jigsaw puzzle, but then there are the other ones. The ones where you needed to get knee deep into the shit storm and keep digging deeper. Sometimes you had to dig so deep that you were choking on it just to find a direction to run to. Today was going to be one of those days. I hated these days the most. My first Sergeant told me that you had to be emotionally detached in order to do this job, but after fifteen years, I still couldn't pull that off. I am not sure if that makes me weak or strong, only that no matter how hard I tried, I could not detach myself from it. It was even harder when I see that the victim had all the possibilities for a great future. Possibilities are just like dreams. All you needed to do was chase them and want them. Seeing them snuffed out always made me question life. It always made me wonder if there was really any balance in the world.

I pulled up behind the cruiser surprised that there was nobody in sight. Usually there would be someone marching around stopping the nosy neighbors from sneaking a peak. As the saying goes, loose lips sink ships, and it's always the neighbors that do it. They see more then they even know and the important details slip out. Generally, the smallest details lead to the important parts. The cold dampness hit me as I opened the car door. The swoosh of the cars passing by threw a second gust of cold slapping me right in the face. Welcome to November I thought. The air was always freezing in November thanks to the damn great lakes and the constant wind. It wasn't that hard to spot the place. Even if the front door wasn't wide open, the collection of bikes and scattered garbage all over the place revealed that it was filled with university students.

The street was busy and the cop cars taking up the one lane didn't help matters. All the traffic heading towards the

Ambassador Bridge for the USA wouldn't make managing the crime scene any easier. People headed over to Detroit for Thanksgiving would make it damn near impossible on a normal Friday night let alone a damn holiday weekend. Some twit in a beat up red Toyota actually honked his horn for me to move out his way when he passed. Damn idiot must have missed the flashing lights from the cars beside me.

"It's a mess Bruno. it's the worst thing I have seen in my whole career and the sarge said this one had to belong to you." I looked over to see Logan Lupus, pale faced, holding his flash light in one hand while the other hand lay clenched at his side. The worst crime he had seen in his whole career. What all ten seconds of it? Hell I had underwear older than his whole career. He hadn't been carrying a badge long or working homicide for more than six months yet and he was already acting like this was front page news.

Of course, I knew that this had to be important for Charlie to call me in on my day off, but it couldn't be all that bad. "Where is Lassitor?"

Pointing past a chain link fence towards this narrow tilting shack of a house, he said, "He is inside the house with the coroner. Demanded that nobody else steps inside until you got here. Said that this time there couldn't be any fuck ups. That this time you were in charge all the way."

"This time?" Before I could say another word, Logan shrugged and jumped into his car. I guess they had him standing outside for too long and the coldness was stronger than his curiosity. When I was his age not even minus forty could not have stopped me from being right dab in the middle of things. I was always knee deep in the shit since my first day on the force. My nosy side was enough to get me noticed and getting noticed pulled me deeper into things. The only question now was the fuck up something I did or something somebody else did? With Charlie it could really go either way. I just hoped it wasn't one of those, 'here is what your screw up caused' incidents. A few had managed to get off Scott free because of my screw ups in the past and I just hoped that this wasn't one of mine. There was always too much guilt in seeing the results of your mistakes. I had only seen it once and it still haunted me. It was a domestic abuse case and I forced him out of the house when I should have kicked his ass all the way to a holding cell. I tried playing the part of good cop letting him leave and believing his promise that he would go someplace far and sleep it off. He came back that night and smashed her so hard she died of a blunt force trauma. That one was on me. Her name was Judy, like the actress, and she had the bluest eyes that sparkled when she was alive. The last time I saw her though, they were dull and empty. Some images you just don't forget and those empty hollow eyes are like a ghost that I can't ever stop seeing. She was only thirty-one and another one of life's possibilities. A possibility that I refused to let go of and to fade from my memory.

I made my way along the green plastic covered chain linked fence. At least the crime scene had a readymade perimeter to keep people out. Of course, the stream of water flowing off the lawn onto the street was probably washing away any evidence that might be left behind. Turning, I made my way up the walk way towards the dull painted two-story house turned into mini-apartments. It was one of those box houses built in the early twenties. The city was filled with many of those odd yet unique looking houses. This one had a narrow porch on the front with a tilted floor and pealing white paint that was probably lead based. Like too many houses in this part of the city, the walls were rotten and I am sure that the vines climbing the walls were holding the place together. As I climbed the steps I could feel the wood beneath my feet bow and bend under my weight. If the wind wasn't so damn strong and howling as it passed by my head, I was sure that the stairs were creaking and screaming would be very loud.

I slowly made my way to the open door. There didn't seem to be any forced entry damage. Of course, that didn't mean that this wasn't some kind domestic violence, just that the door wasn't kicked in. One of the terrible parts of my job is knowing the numbers. The statistics for Essex county are one in four women face domestic violence. Most never call or press charges, but the number is right there. Five women in Canada die a week from it and no matter how hard we try, it's a never-ending cycle. I ran my hand along the door frame as I entered the house.

The front door led right into the living room. It was common for this type place. Small narrow rooms because there truly wasn't much room for anything else. There was a stained beige corner couch and two metal end tables with wire like legs. Yard sale furniture is common for university students and the city is filled with them. Scanning the room there was no sign of any kind of violence or fighting, just your standard messy college house.

"Good you are finally here," Charlie snapped as he bent over walking down the narrow stairs. The low ceiling made his 5 foot 3-inch frame look gigantic. "You won't find anything anywhere except in the bathroom Bruno and you definitely will want to see this." I stepped towards the narrow slat boarded wall and headed for the little stair case. I wasn't exactly thrilled with the idea of having to crawl up the winding narrow stairs. When you are 6 feet 4 trying to walk up these stair cases makes you feel like you are crawling through a tunnel and you think with every step that you are going to kick your teeth out. I grabbed hold of the two by four post feeling it move forward with just the slightest amount of pressure. As I walked up, Charlie's cold voice rang out, "It's happening again and this time I want the bastard caught." Following him up the stairs I wondered what the hell he was talking about. Generally, I would ask, but I assumed I would get my answer soon enough. Every crime scene told a story and seeing it firsthand without any other interpretation was always best. Somebody once said seeing is believing and I was about to see the whole story first hand.

Charlie entered the bathroom and loudly bellowed, "Clear the room." Slowly two men walked out of the door. They looked like they had too many thoughts inside their minds. There have only been a handful of times that I can remember silence at a crime scene and both times involved kids and were bloody. I couldn't help, but think, "Dear god don't let this be a murdered kid." I struggled with kids. Again, the possibilities seemed gigantic and the wasted life unbearable.

The first thing that hit me was a soft flowery scent that lingered in the air as I stepped through the low arched door way into the little make shift bathroom. I say make shift because it was like an afterthought. They just tucked it along the side in the only available opening there was. Stepping into the little room, on the left side was a small little off-white porcelain sink with a shattered mirror above it. The dim light added a spooky aura to the dark feeling of the room. The word "Ugly" was written in red lipstick right across the cracks of glass. The way it was written, it was supposed to resemble blood, but tests would confirm it was heated up lipstick.

Charlie bellowed, "See it's happening all over again," as he pointed towards the broken mirror. He stepped next to the claw foot bathtub and stared down in silence. Sighing he gripped his hands and muttered, "He is back and this time I want him. I want him so bad that I can taste it."

I knelt down beside the tub. This wasn't a pretty sight. A petite twenty something tattooed blonde's legs dangled over the edge. There was a fresh tattoo of a rosary on her ankle. It was a simplistic classy looking add on compared to the flashy colored ones that covered her arms and legs. I had seen that exact tattoo before only it was on a different leg, but the circumstances were the same. I never quite understood its meaning, but it still had to have some kind of meaning.

Seeing the leg dangling over the edge reminded me of Callie. God only knows how Charlie was keeping it all together since it brought back a trunk load of emotional baggage. How does a father handle being reminded that his daughter was not only a street walker, but also tortured and nobody really noticed? We hadn't found all the pieces then or maybe he was still honing his craft.

Red bloody water pooled on the floor around the tub running through the cracks in the tiles like little streams. Along the walls were splattered blood stains that reminded me of rain drops on a warm spring day. The blood ran down the wall leaving little trails as it made its way to the floor. Her hands were handcuffed to the legs and based on the deep gashes that were dug into her wrists, she must have tried to fight. Everybody fights when the carving starts, but it's always too late.

The size twelve-foot prints circled the tub like a predator, but those steps never lead anywhere or at least not yet. There was always a small hope, but hope doesn't catch a killer. It just teases you until frustration kicks in. It was like running a race with a torn hamstring. No matter how hard much time you spend in the gym you can't compete with the other competitors.

I stood up and scanned her body. She was a beautiful petite framed creature, but the sheer number of tattoos stole it from her. They were flowers and bugs. He loved naughty tattooed woman who he saw as ugly. The profile always said that he must have been raised by an overbearing mother who abused him, but there was never any real proof of that. There was never truly enough evidence left behind to prove it.

A soft boyish voice says, "The coroner unit is here."

"They can wait," Charlie snapped. "Tell them we need five more minutes." I didn't have to look back to see that Charlie was flinging his hands through the air.

"But Sarge.."

Charlie screamed, "Give us five more minutes. Bruno needs to see everything as he left it. Don't you get it? This sick bastard always gets away. If he slips through our fingers again we have to wait another long five fucking years." Five years minus a day. He was early this year.

Charlie was emotional with good reason. Too emotional to help me and I needed a clear head to truly see the hidden signs. There was always a hidden message left behind if you looked hard enough. Charlie was still snapping at everyone who came within a heartbeat of the room. He wasn't solving this crime; he was reliving his daughters murder all over again.

Calmly I whispered, "Charlie stop it."

"Bruno, we need to catch this guy. We need to make sure this is the last one." He was slapping his fist into his hand muttering, "I don't care what it takes. I want him in our holding cell."

"Charlie go get coffee and let me finish. I won't miss any details. I promise you if he left something, I will find it."

"Bruno, I need to be here. I need to see this through."

"I know, but I need you to step away so I can find it. You need you to step away from this. I will keep you informed of every step I take. If there is any possibility of solving this case, I will do it. I swear Charlie no rock will be left unturned."

Charlie glared at me as he stood there with his hands in his pockets. "I can't walk away from this."

"Charlie you can't be involved. You must be a bystander, not a participant." I was delicately trying to tell an old friend to fuck off and let me do my job. How do you tell a father that his daughters murder didn't count right now? That a stranger's murder took priority? "Go grab a coffee and let me do my job." I watched him walk down the stairs. As he vanished from sight, I just listened to the hollow clumping sound that echoed from each step growing distant as he did as he was told.

The baby-faced cop smiled, "Damn the sarge is taking this one personal."

"We all should. This isn't just a murder." I said as I turned away. I knew he was left feeling dumbfound, but he would figure it out soon enough.

I went back to the body. On her right cheek was the tell tale sign he had visited her. "Is that lipstick on her cheek? Some twisted sex thing?" Young and too enthusiastic, I thought. Too young to remember the last time and too stupid to understand this isn't a game.

"That isn't lipstick rookie. It's blood. It's her blood and you won't find any of his DNA." The side of the tub was stained in thick dried blood. I had seen this before, only the empty face staring at me was different. It was another possibility that was snuffed out.

This was the part I had to look at. To examine and remember, even if it meant another image no man should want to see was going to be stuck inside my mind. Again, ghosts that would call out to me and linger inside my dreams. They screamed out that I must solve their murder. To avenge them.

The whole side of her face wasn't much more then torn muscle and bone. It was a bloody scene and I already knew that it would be determined that he'd carved up her face while she was still alive. I still couldn't imagine the agony that she must have felt as the sick bastard took his time removing the skin strip by strip. The skin would be found braided into some kind of dream catcher thing hanging above her bed.

"What the hell happened to her eye?" The boyish cop snapped as he pointed to the gouge where her eye once was. "Jesus Christ do you think that she was alive when he did it?"

"He cut it out while the poor thing was still alive." He didn't actually cut it out. He always tore out one eye. It was the most brutal and savage way to go. It took a stone hearted prick to look into the emptiness and not want to cry out. I wasn't immune to it. I was just the one that wouldn't let a possibility be forgotten so easily.

"So, Bruno why did Charlie call you?"

"Because I am the only one that came close to catching him. I am the one that had him in my grasp and let him slip away."

CHAPTER 02 – ASHLEY

It's been nine hours since I saw my Rosie. Nine long empty hours spent locked up in a six by nine holding cell wondering where she is. It's not the actual little confining space, but the unknown. Of course, I don't need to be close to her to feel her presence. She lives inside my heart like a brilliant mixture of reality and fantasy merging until I can almost feel her by my side. Wasting all these empty hours away from her has been a struggle, if I am being honest. Love is always a struggle. I love whole heartedly. It's a curse at best. You love someone with everything inside you yet, they can't love you back. Not properly at least. Rosie was beautiful inside and out, I saw it the first time we met. It was that very minute that I knew she was the one. She was a troubled soul calling out 'save me'. I knew I had to save her. Save her from herself. Maybe I needed her to save me too. Life is funny that way.

Rosie loves me in her own way. She is selfish and capricious by nature, so I think it confuses her. I guess the fact that so many other men want her, makes her see love in a twisted way. That's the problem with beautiful women like that. Too many men fill her head with ideas and it takes so much time and energy to fix it. To show her the error in her ways. She tells me to leave Friday night, but by Monday I know that she will be back. She needs me. We are meant to be together. It's not just a want, it's an absolute certainty. It's our certainty.

The problem is that when she is confused she forgets we are soul mates. She tells me to leave her life because I am an emotional vampire that drains the love from her heart. I love her, but she overacts and does things that she doesn't mean to do. Things like get a restraining order against me. She spent her $6 dollars and the cops told me I had to legally stay away. A whole damn 500 meters in any direction. How can I possibly be there for her if I am trapped 500 meters away from her? They expected a $6 piece of paper to keep me from claiming the love of my life.

That's what brought me here again. That is what got me locked up over night in the holding cells. A $6 piece of paper signed by some judge, who doesn't understand love. He expects it is supposed to stop me from watching over and protecting Rosie. Nothing should ever stop a man from protecting the one he loves even if she forgets sometimes just how much she loves him. Not a cop or new boyfriend and especially not a lousy $6 piece of paper.

A loud clinking echo bounced through the entire the room announcing Harold's entrance into the block. He always let his Billy club slide along the bars as he entered. This wasn't an intimidation tactic, he once told me, but his way giving those privileged souls locked up in here a chance to put their pants on. A lot of horny sickos get locked up on a Friday night. It's pathetic that I am in here so often that I know them by name. The cops I mean. Not just Harold, but all of them. There is Linda the flousy wearing so much make up that she resembles a clown, tight ass Norman who is so tense I am sure a half decent fart would kill him and of course Patty, the part time psychology student, who insists on trying to fix me like being in love is a disease and not a calling in life. Harold is the cool one though. Not so by the book either. He even sneaks in burgers and fries sometimes. Yes, Harold is good shit.

"What's up Harold," I asked as he came near. He was short and stocky, like me. As my mom used to say, 'a man needs to little extra to keep the cold out' and Harold had his fair share of extra.

"Damned if I know Lee. A murder or something big happened last night. Nobody ever tells me anything important, I might as well be one of those rent-a-cops you see at the mall. At least those guys get fresh hot coffee instead of the crap that they serve here."

"But then you would miss my charming personality."

Smiling Harold responded, "Oh for Christ sakes Lee you aren't that bad and definitely aren't as charming as you think."

"Oh really," I responded preparing for our usual round of verbal bitch slap. It's nice to be able to call a cop a pig or remind one that donut shops are for everybody without getting a shot to the mouth. "And what do you know about charm besides its a word in the dictionary?"

Laughing he added, "I don't know anything about charm or romance otherwise I wouldn't be asking you to write my wife love poems and shit." The idea that Harold was getting brownie points because of my romantic nature amused me. "You know Lee if you would put the energy into finding and winning another woman you, might actually find happiness. I mean I can't imagine waking up beside anybody else's happiness."

"You can't choose who you love Harold. It's like trying to change your sex or DNA. Besides if I wasn't here every Friday night, how else would your wife get turned on every Saturday morning?"

"There is surgery for the changing sex thing."

"You know what I mean by the changing your sex thing. I didn't choose to love Rosie, I was born to love her, just like you were born to love your wife."

Pointing at me he snapped, "Leave my wife out of this." I jumped back holding out my hands, but before I had a chance to say anything, Harold burst out laughing, "You should have seen the look on your face Lee. It was absolutely priceless."

Harold's smile dropped as he pulled the cuffs from the holster. "Lee, they want to talk to you in the interrogation room. I have no idea what you did or why the brass wants you brought up, but they do."

It wasn't exactly a shock that they wanted to talk to me. After all, I did snap Rosie's new guy right smack in the jaw. Had to make him see a real man doesn't slap up or belittle a woman. He slapped up my Rosie so I broke the assholes jaw. It's part of being in love. Nobody treats my baby worse than I do and I treat her like a treasure.

As I pushed my hands through the bars, he placed the cuffs around my wrists, they made a loud grinding clicking noise. Luckily Harold left them looser than most cops would have. Most just saw me as a monster and made sure the bracelets were extra tight. Opening the door, he asked, "What exactly did you do to suddenly capture so much more attention?"

As we walked out towards the metal doors and I started telling him my story. "Well last night started out magical."

Steering me towards the exit Harold laughed, "Why is it that all your stories start off with the night started off magical?"

"Because in my mind every night is going to be an absolutely magical night. Who the hell starts off thinking tonight I want a horrible night." Winking I added, "Here was the plan. I wrote the loveliest love song. I mean the kind that makes a woman's heart melt."

Still guiding me through the hallway he added, "Verbal panty remover."

"What?"

"You know what I mean. The kind of music that makes a woman want to sleep with you right there and then."

"Let me get this straight. You think a love song should be designed to get you laid and I am the one that they lock up?"

Slapping my shoulder, he laughed, "Well I married the one that wanted to take her pants off over a love song. You kind of...,"

It always came to this, one way or another. It's not love if the one you love says go away or if she gets distracted by another man. "I know to you I am a stalker. I am just another number in a cell."

Harold's eyes went dim as his head dropped, "I didn't mean it like that."

I waited for a minute or two as Harold tried to find his way out of it, after all I was his love connection. I was his incarcerated Cyrano de Bergerac. Hand cuffs and poetry. "Got you asshole," I chirped with a giant smile."

"Don't do that to me!"

Staring over at him, I asked, "Do I finish my story or not?"

"Yes of course. I live through you. My life is boring and the only excitement I get is hearing how you live your life."

"OK I had my guitarron. It's a giant Mexican guitar, just so you know." Harold tried to act like he knew what it was, but I could see he didn't. "Anyway, I am playing the sweetest love song ever. Singing 'when my heart thinks of love it's you it thinks about'. I was playing like I have never played before. A lovely simple love song I wrote just for Rosie."

"I honestly don't know how you can take a romantic gesture and end up here. Why spend so much time and energy chasing a woman that doesn't want to be caught?"

Harold was a nice wholesome guy, but he really knew nothing about love. He settled for the first woman that said she loved him rather than taking the time to find the one that he couldn't live without. Now I might have to work harder to gain Rosie's love, but she needed me. She needed to truly be loved.

The door opened and a short fat little cop I had never seen before was waiting for us. Not the usual friendly sort that was skulking through the cop shop. No, this guy had a flame in his glare. He was probably some little goody goody trying to save the world one convict at a time. Kind of like Butch my PO. He was always trying to save me with therapy and counseling.

Harold stopped at the door way, "Sergeant Lassitor, I was just bringing Lee to you."

Still glaring right through me, he snapped, "Oh yes I can see that. You two seem to be quite the chatter boxes. Some might even call you good friends."

"Sergeant I don't think we need to treat him like a

criminal." I wanted to laugh hearing the words leave his lips. Of course, I was a criminal, just not the dangerous kind in Harold's eyes.

"So you think mister Truelove's weekly reservation here is because he likes the accommodations?"

I blurted out, "This week it was a noise violation and assault."

The fat little prick snapped his fingers like a god, "That's enough out of you Mister Truelove."

Saluting I snapped, "Yes sir, Sergeant Lassitor, sir."

"Shut up convict," was all he said as he dragged me down the hallway. By the look of him, I was starting to think that maybe I was going to have some kind of man made accident. I had never had any before, but then again, I had never come under this guys radar before either. If they were going to play good cop bad cop, this little fellow wasn't the friendly one.

"So what exactly am I being interrogated about?" It seemed like a reasonable question considering the fact that I had quite a list of things that this stuffy little guy might want to talk to me about. Life isn't exactly going to plan right now, if you know what I mean. I never asked to fall in love though, I guess nobody asks for it. Not really. The dream or idea of love is that you will meet that one special person that will love you and make all your dreams come true. The reality of love is that you have to work at it every damn day just to keep her attention while she flirts and acts like she is a queen. It's the price you have to pay for love.

He just growled, "I am not interrogating you. We just have some questions for you." I was trying to decide if this guy was truly an asshole or if he was just having a bad day. You can never truly be sure with people, especially authority figures. In grade nine I was getting the snot kicked out of me by some seniors in our high school. You know, the popular pretty boy types that have nothing better to do then pick on skinny folks because they knew that they would always win. I wasn't the skinny fellow though. I wasn't the most popular guy, but I blended in. I was the funny guy that people liked and laughed at my jokes, but we weren't friends. No, my only friend was the skinny kid that the seniors abused. When you only have one real friend you defend them even if it means you are going to be rolling on the ground getting a group pounding. It wasn't so bad though. When you fight six guys at the same time even when you lose nobody wants to fight you. They call you unstable and unstable means scary.

That is the day I first met Slant. He was the scariest bastard that I had ever seen. A big man with a limp shoulder and some kind of twisting limp. He was always walking the halls looking like each step he took was going to cause him to fall right over. He was making a thudding sound as he walked in his faded gold dress coat. Rumor had it that he was in some kind of war injury. All I knew was that the whole time I was in school I never saw him smile or heard him laugh. Anyway, here I was covered in blood and when I finally open my eyes to see this towering authority figure standing over me like the grim reaper himself coming to collect my soul. I really don't know what I expected to come next, but Slant just stared down at me mumbling, "I don't care how it happens, but at least one Trulove will graduate with a diploma. You are the last one in your family so even if I have to teach you myself Mister Truelove you won't be expelled and you will graduate." It didn't take long for him to place a desk outside his office. It didn't make me respect authority figures any more, but it did teach me how make them want to help me rather than condemn me.

We were making our way down the narrow little hall and it seemed strange that everybody just stepped back and their faces were filled with empty stares as we passed. It was like they all though I was dangerous. Normally this would amuse the hell out me, but not today. There was something eerie about the silence. Maybe I was just imagining it or had been lucky enough to meet the rookies who seemed just a little more sophisticated and educated then you would expect from street cops, but now it seemed like the atmosphere had completely changed. I half expected someone to scream out, "dead man walking, dead man walking" like they do in the movies. The question really amounted too; was I knee deep in shit and about to drown or was my straight-faced jailor really this scary? No matter how you looked at it, I was going to have a long day.

We were making our way through the halls and with each step the darkness inside me seemed to grow. It was just like a haunted house. Not the real kind with ghosts, but the ones that are designed to scare the hell out of you and we call it fun. I was slowly creeping through the darkness unable to see anything. Feeling out, I could have sworn that I heard somebody breathing just in front of me. Inch by inch I made my way through the darkness and the only thing I could hear was someone screaming ahead of me. As my heart raced I kept thinking any minute now someone is going to jump out and scare the hell out me. Each step forward I thought its coming. Expect the worst because its coming. Of course, at the end, I stepped out of the darkness into the light and realized that no matter how I felt in the darkness, I would find the light. That was the second time I had ever seen Rosie. She was the one waiting for me just outside the blinding darkness. That is how I felt now. With each step I expected something to jump out me. The first time I ever felt this, I was so excited. The fear and the unknown were just an amazing feeling, but it wasn't so exciting now and I knew that Rosie wouldn't be standing at the edge of darkness shining like a beacon.

I honestly can't tell you what it is about her that makes her so irresistible. I can tell you that when she smiles her eyes light up and then I can't think of anybody else. She wasn't my only choice. The first time I saw her at the pizza place there were plenty of women to choose from. Most of them really looked like classy ladies too, but what can I say, the law of attraction demanded that I give my heart to her. Most laws I can break, but not this one. It's like a force of nature, trying to walk against the wind during a hurricane was almost impossible. I couldn't help, but wonder what was Rosie doing right now? Probably on the internet making Arthur those damn videos he demands from her. I would need to check that out when I got home. I would need to see what they did and hear what they were talking about. Rosie needed a guardian Angel watching over her and I was that Angel, only I had no halo or wings.

"Seriously what is so interesting about me that I am being marched to the interrogation room like I am a prize rooster at the county fair?" Sometimes you have to talk a little red neck so that the locals know what you are talking about and this little fucker was definitely red neck.

He snapped, "Just shut up and keep walking. Today the only rights you have is to answer every question that you are asked in as much detail as possible. There are always consequences to our actions. It's about time you learn that convict."

We turned the corner and I saw them waiting for me. Two flat foots just standing there. They looked tense and kept peeking through this little window then out through this glass window that separated the hallway from the reception office. They were bouncing from side to side and I am certain if I was close enough, I could easily hear their knuckles crack as they made fists. There was something in their eyes though. It was the same look that everyone of Rosie's college boys got just before they told me she was out of my league. Before they said that she was one thing that I could never capture. Of course, I could always find a way to change their minds. Usually it was a bloody message, but I always made my intension clear. This time though, I think it wasn't my intentions that counted, but the two giants that were standing at the end of the hall waiting for me.

CHAPTER 03 – BRUNO

A big part of my job is shifting through the dirty laundry of evidence trying to get a picture of who the victim really was. I don't mean the public face because the public face never matches the inner self. We all have many faces inside us. The inner child is the most well known, but there are so many more. There is that naughty side that most of us never let out. Looking inside, trying to see a person's soul can get complicated and messy. It's always the messy stuff that interests me, not because I enjoy it, but because it's the messy stuff I need to sift through to do my job.

I never liked examining a person's life or at least not the way I had to go through every detail of it. We all have our dirty little secrets and I am the lucky ass who gets to examine every little secret thoroughly and try to find every little dark thought that they ever had. Taking note of each one in my little black book. Some people only use computers, preferring to share information through spreadsheets and emails, but I am still old school. I like to record my thoughts and ideas as I find them and then review them as I go along. It works for me because you never know when your mind will find that one detail that can crack the case and having a little black book at your finger tips is valuable.

Living on a single hour's sleep and about a dozen cups of coffee wasn't anything new to me. Even before I was in homicide I would go for days on limited sleep trying to find the missing pieces of the puzzle. It wasn't just a game to me and not exactly a passion. Calling it a passion would indicate joy and entertainment and all those lost possibilities never brought joy to my life. No, this was just an addiction to know the truth. Of course, it used to be that a person's life was placed in a large folder or in some cases a thick book. It always seemed like that the bigger the folder the more life they had truly lived as you flipped through the pages of their life. I can still remember looking at my desk, as the pages of their lives were scattered all about, thinking "damn they must have lived a full life." That was all different now though. In the digital age where we call stranger's, friends on social media, upload and download naughty pictures and open our lives to complete strangers, there isn't a thick folder to proudly display our lives. I know that the files are just as big, if not bigger, than they used to be, but now a person's life is measured differently. Even the most famous killer gets only a dot in the database. You pop their name into a search engine and you will see about 419,000 results in 0.65 seconds but look them up on the computer and there isn't enough space used to fill a USB key. I popped in Rosie Macdonald and read about 7,750 results in 0.43 seconds. It was sad to think that in a day or so her name would bring up somewhere close to 100,000 hits. Her life was so small compared to her death and in the end, her life was even a smaller dot on the server's hard drives.

"I found our guy," Logan bellowed as he ran over and sat in the chair beside me. "Sure, as shit this is our guy and even better, he is already in a holding cell." Logan had a smirk on his face as he dropped the three printed sheets of paper onto my desk. "It's like he came to us gift wrapped. This guy has to be the prime suspect. He fits the profile to a tee," he said as he leaned forward tapping his hands together.

I had heard many versions of that profile, but I had my own theory about him. An older man about my age who was severely scarred on the one side of his face. He had an average education but considered himself smarter than the average person. He looked down upon what he considered immoral woman and in some kind of sick self-serving way actually thought he was helping the women he tortured and killed. A man of some kind of authority, like a teacher or a priest. I was looking at his rap sheet. Ashley Truelove was the perfect prime suspect to the suits, at least on paper, but not in my eyes. He was obsessed with the victim. I don't know if obsessed is a strong enough word, but I couldn't think of any other. He was brought in 27 times for breaking the restraining order she had placed on him. A violent offender shattering one boyfriends jaw and seriously beating another so bad that he was hospitalized and even had part of his ear bit off. He watched his mother die before his eyes, murdered, and was a loner. Serious shit followed this guy like he was a magnet that attracted violence and pain. A lot of pain. Currently on two years' probation, which means he should be locked in a cell by now, but he wasn't. That was our bad. Scanning through the pages he was almost perfect. He would easily fill the profile. Hard time keeping a job. Higher than average IQ. Yes, on paper he was born to be a killer except the age, 24 years old. He would have been nineteen when Callie was killed. Yes, there was the possibility that he did it, but the killer we were looking for was much older. Young men seem to get too excited about killing while older men are more patient. They take their time and plan each step out like it's a blue print. Based on Ashley's record, if he had killed anyone there would be a trail of evidence that led right to his door. No slapping the cuffs on him like they used to do in the 1920s when they would grab hold of the first vagrant they found and placed the blame on him because it was easier then actually chasing down the real guilty party.

I was still scanning the file as the words left Logan lips, "We can even pinpoint the trigger." Logan was the self-confident type. You know, two years out of university, dying to find the case that would make his career. I couldn't blame him and he wasn't the only one. There had been many Logan's throughout the years climbing their way through the ranks passing me by. Unlike some, I didn't mind that though. I could admit to myself that I was just too damn lazy to buck up and go to school at nights to further my career. I wasn't one of those guys that was waiting for retirement though. I just knew my skill set was in the crime scene. Finding the clues like some kind of Canadian Sherlocke Holmes.

"And what exactly was his trigger?" I asked thinking that I was about to be entertained by his fly by the seat of my pants police work.

Laughing he added, "This dude actually saw his mother murdered. I mean right in front of his eyes. If there was ever a trigger event, that is it." This little tid bit caught my interest. Not that I saw a tragedy as a reason to celebrate, but it did help put Mister Truelove's situation in the proper perspective. Unlike some of those people I work with, I don't believe that anyone is born a killer. I don't have a degree in psychology and never understood Freud, but I still think we are born innocent and life changes us. The reasons are always different, but there is always a reason. My mother didn't love me enough or sometimes too much, a father that couldn't see the light shining in his little girl or in Ashley's case, he witnessed his mother's murder. There was always a reason why things happened if you knew where to look. Logan was just too blind to search for the cause and follow that up with a solution. Too many people were sitting in prisons right now because nobody wanted to find the solution rather than just concentrate on the cause.

"The last page has all the details Bruno. You and Charlie will be truly interested in it."

"Why would we both be interested in Ashley's history?" When you are young everything is exciting and interesting. As we get older everything changes. Well for most people. Normally Charlie was immune to everything. Time had made him that way. One dead body had no more interest to him then another once the case was closed. Let the shrinks straighten out the twisted parts left behind, he used to say. We call it becoming unattached emotionally rather than letting the victims come alive in us because of a memory or even worse a fantasy. Take the idea of a lost possibility that your mind adds a personality to.

"Bruno, you and Charlie were the first ones on the scene. Jealous boyfriend threw hot oil in the victims face then stabbed her in the face. Must have been the bloodiest damn thing to see." I was too lost in the file to see the expression on his face, but there was a high pitched excited squeal to his voice. I was more interested in the case. The name Truelove didn't sound familiar and I always remembered names and faces. I was still scanning the file with the name Truelove still floating through my memory. It didn't sound familiar at all.

I was flipping through the pages when I came across the report. It wasn't the complete report but had highlighted passages. Under the name of the reporting officer was Charlie's signature. It was hard to miss since his handwriting was just squiggly lines that was worse than a doctor's. Under summary it said, "We were dispatched to 485 McEwen Avenue to the residence of Miss Jane Truelove at 23:45 PM because of reported domestic abuse. Evidence supports this as Miss Truelove had a bloody lip and swollen eyes. The suspect Daniel Walter, also residing at 485 McEwen Avenue, had scratches on his neck and face. Miss Truelove refused to press charges. We were able to calm the situation down and Mister Walter agreed to leave the residence for a cooling down period of twenty fours."

Under the heading of Amendment, it has written, "Upon returning to the residence of 485 McEwen Avenue, at 03:27 AM, we discovered the body of Miss Truelove. The eye witness Ashley Truelove reported that Mister Daniel Walter had returned to the residence intoxicated and proceeded to throw hot cooking oil at the victim, burning the left side of her face then proceeded to stab her. The victim was declared dead at the crime scene."

Reading the report was like a kick in the balls. Seriously this woman's death was on me. I was the one that decided to let her dead-beat boyfriend go free when I should have just arrested him then and there. Rookie mistake because I knew this guy was trouble. It was in his eyes and I saw it but didn't act on it. Half my job is gut instinct and I didn't follow it. Rookie fucking mistake. I should have pushed Jane to press charges, but I didn't. No, I let the bastard go and he came back killing the poor woman. I forgot the name, but not the woman or the circumstances of her death. You don't forget your mistakes especially the giant ones that steal away life's possibilities.

Logan stood up, "Listen, I think this kid is the guy and Charlie agrees. He has all the makings of a killer. Hell, he is the poster child for a serial killer and we got him. For once, we got the guy and it's a victory."

I was still looking at the highlighted sections sifting through the memories. When we arrived on the scene the kid was just sitting there in a pool of blood next to his mother's body. He was holding her in his arms crying out her name rocking back and forth. He kept caressing her hair whispering, "You can't leave me, I need you. You can't leave me all alone, I am not strong enough." He kept looking at his bloodied mother and softly touching the right side of her face as he rocked. I always thought that he chose the right side because the left was disfigured and he wanted to remember his mother's beauty the way it was rather then what it had become.

Back then, he was a kid. Looking at his mug shot he hadn't changed that much in the last decade. It still seemed strange to me that I couldn't remember him considering his mother's image was still living inside me like a ghost that would never go away.

Charlie asked him his name. I remember he just kept rocking holding his dead mother in his arms whispering, "Don't leave me. Don't leave me." It was such a sad sight to see. Finally, he looked up and said, "My name is Lee." His next question shocked both of us. "Are you going to arrest me?"

Charlie had compassion back then. He had seen a lot less

horrors then and none had actually touched his life. He still thought that we could save the victims and the assailants both. We both did. I remember him kneeling down over the boy's body, reaching out, touching his cheek and asking, "Why do you think we will arrest you?"

Teary eyed, the boy mumbled through his bloody teeth, "Because I couldn't save her. I tried, but I couldn't save her from him." It was a heart-breaking scene to see. A boy thinking, he should be a man and seeing his youth as a failure.

Charlie just patted the boy's cheek whispering, "You didn't fail her son. The man that killed her did and we will get him." I remember struggling to hold back the tears thinking that he didn't fail her, I did. I was the reason that she was lying there on the floor covered in her own blood.

Lee looked up, "Someday you will have to arrest me." There was definitely deep hate inside the kid's eyes. Not just pain but loathing and I understood it. It would be revealed later that Walter had been abusing mother and son for too long with numerous calls from neighbors and friends. Countless times Jane refused to press charges so the cycle continued. Young Lee was just too young to defend his mother, but the scars on his body showed that he had tried desperately too.

Charlie's face went straight as he asked, "And why will I arrest you?"

The boy was writing a "W" on the floor in a streak of blood as he whispered, "Because when I grow up, I am going to kill Walter. I am going to burn his face and cut out his eyes just like he did to my mother." Looking up there was still innocence in his eyes even if there none left in his words. "Wait and you will see."

Logan waved his hands in front of my eyes, "Hello. Earth to Bruno. Did you even hear a word I was saying?" as he pointed to a piece of paper on the desk. I stared down at the folder on my desk with a picture of Rosie's dead body fastened to it with a paper clip. "Here death was brutal. I mean horror story brutal and we have her killer locked away so let's break him and make sure that this never happens again."

The autopsy results came back faster than usual, but this was personal to Charlie and he would have forced the coroner to drop everything else and jump on this case. I don't know how many favors he had to cash in, but there must have been a lot of them to get Rosie on the table this fast. Of course, I didn't think it was going to give me any information that I didn't already know, but I would review the findings. You never know what little tidbit might open an unseen avenue to catching the killer. This wasn't just a case of making the bad guy pay or of stopping him from killing again. No this was a case of catching the one that got away. The only one that escaped my grasp.

I grabbed the folder and tried not to think of the bloody image on the front, but I couldn't. It was another example of a lost possibility and stolen beauty. He didn't just take her life but made her last minutes on this earth a living hell. Opening the folder there were the usual autopsy details. Scanning the file, I jumped straight to the important details or at least the important ones to me. Under the opinions section at the bottom of the page. Manner of death was listed as homicide which was obvious. Under remarks. Presence of the pre-mortem ligature marks on wrists and mutilation of face suggests that suicide in this case is highly improbable. The blood trace resembling a kiss only contained the victim's DNA. No other trace detected. Essex detectives were notified of this finding immediately upon conclusion of examination.

CHAPTER 04 – ASHLEY

I was just sitting there endlessly waiting, shackled to the table. There was this giant round clock with arms that was right in front of me. It was one of those ones that has a second hand constantly moving round and round. No matter how hard I tried, I couldn't help, but stare at it. Nothing like watching time fly at a turtle's pace. Nothing like the feeling that fifteen minutes is an hour and if TV was right, I would be here for an hour at least before Sergeant tight ass came in to beat a confession out of me. Good luck with that, because without knowing the crime, I aint saying one damn word. Still, it seemed like way too much attention just because I slapped up Arthur. If there was ever a guy that needed to be slapped up, it was Arthur. Not only did he manage to grab hold of Rosie's heart, but he treated her like a dollar store whore. If Rosie couldn't stand up for herself, I would. As long as I had a heart beat I would defend her. I beat the guy before him something bad and even put him in the hospital. Nobody yanked me into a room for that. They just asked why I did it and I told them.

I don't know why, but I expected to see one of the mirrors that are really a window and have people standing on the other side analyzing me. I knew how to test it. You just put your finger against it and if there is no gap between your finger tip and the glass, it's a real mirror, but being shackled to a table I couldn't test. I am certain though that it's a real mirror. It was just a small room with off white walls, cheap speckled tiles and a small black camera in the corner. Well at least I was important enough to watch. I guess that actually wouldn't be a good thing. After all, this was my first time being in an integration room and I had this idea that soon enough my PO was going to be marching in telling me that I was going back to county. I am not afraid of going back to prison, just of being away from Rosie. Rosie needs me even if she isn't in tune with her emotions. Ironic isn't it? Most relationships it's the woman complaining that the man isn't in tune and for us, it's the exact opposite. That is the hell of it. The longing I feel to see her when we are apart. Wondering if she's happy, crying and safe? I worry about her too much these days. Since they slapped that restraining order on me, they placed an invisible fence between us. It just means that I need to be more creative. That I need to love her from a far so to speak.

I was tapping my thumbs on the table top trying to amuse myself and kill the boredom. I was starting to find my rhythm and since I had nothing better to do, thought that I might as well write Rosie a love song. I just hoped that the song stayed in my heart until I could write it down on paper. That's when the door opened and Harold's beak like nose slowly peered around the door. I can honestly say that I was so glad to see it was Harold and not that cold Sergeant. That dude had the personality of a wall and looked like he was anal probed by aliens and liked it a little too much if you know what I mean.

"Hi Lee," was all Harold managed to mutter as he stiffly walked towards the little chair on the other side of the table. My ass was still asleep and ached because of the smooth hard plastic chair, but I noticed Harold's chair looked rather comfortable. Lucky bastard.

Normally I would lean forward and bellow out a smart ass verbal bitch slap to him, but he looked like he was about to throw up or cry. This was getting serious. "Hey Harold. What's going on?"

He was puckering his lips as he croaked out, "I don't know

how to ask this Lee, but I have to ask it." Harold was like a book if you just knew how to read between the lines. He was being forced to act like a cop and it scared the hell out of him.

Still tapping on the table top, I blurted out, "Just come out and say it Harold. It's not like I have anything to hide." Well nothing too terrible at least.

Harold was about to say something when the door opened and in came sergeant anal probe tapping a rolled piece of paper against the palm of his hand. He took slow measured steps trying to add to the good cop bad cop affect and just leaned back against the wall crossing his arms casually. "Oh, don't mind me. I am just here to observe." Harold just stared down at the table like he was about to burst out crying. The sergeant was still tapping the paper against his hand as he looked at Harold, "Go ahead and talk to your friend."

I almost laughed as the word "Friend" left his lips. I liked Harold, but we weren't friends. I didn't have friends. I was likable and most people enjoyed my jokes and witty personality, but they weren't friends. They were just people I met in this journey I call my life. Friends added obligations to your life and I didn't need that kind of pressure. Who really has time for get togethers, lunches and worst of all moving days? Not me. I didn't want friendships.

"Lee, I have to ask you a few questions and you aren't going to like it." Harold's hands were trembling as he placed them on the table. Running his finger nails on the table top he added, "I have to ask these questions because it's my job."

Reaching my hands forward, I couldn't believe how fast Harold yanked his back. It was like I was a leper or something like that. I slowly moved my hand back and suddenly the whole room seemed so much smaller. Not intimate smaller, but buried alive. Leaning back, I added, "OK Harold I will stay back here, so ask me whatever you need to ask."

"Thanks," was all Harold managed to blurt out before looking over at the short authority figure who appeared impatient as hell. Guess he wanted to go home to a cold beer and true crime TV rather than be part of it. "Whose blood was on your hands when they brought you in last night?"

It was a relief to hear this was about that punk ass boy friend of Rosie's. I did pound his face hard last night, but it was more for show then actually meant to harm him. He needed to know his place in the world, especially Rosie's world. I guess more assault charges were coming my way. "I would have to say it's that asshole Arthur's since I drove him in the face."

"Are you sure it's his? We are doing DNA analysis on the blood from your hands right now, so are you positive that we will find the blood came from him?"

This was a side of Harold that I had never seen before. Trembling hands and all wide eyed. "Who else's blood would it be? Beyond Arthur I only like beating on skate boarders and didn't see any of them last night."

A slight grin filled Harold's face, but faded just as fast as he glanced over at Sargent anal probe. "Have you hit or hurt a woman before Lee? I mean either reported or unreported. Have you ever physically hurt a woman?"

"What kind of question is that? Anybody that says I hit a woman is a lying bastard," I screamed as I tried to stand up which made Harold jump back. Such a damn insulting question. What kind of man did he think I was? "Just tell me the name of the bastard who said that and give me ten minutes alone with him." I wasn't a good guy that was one thing I knew already, but I wasn't a monster. Weak men hurt women and life had made sure that I couldn't be weak anymore. It was damn insulting that Harold of all people was asking this damn question, even if it was forced.

Harold's hands came between us as he said, "Calm down Lee. I want to help you through this, but right now you aren't helping yourself. Right now, you are adding doubts."

Still struggling with the cuffs, I snapped, "What doubts?"

"Lee, have you ever physically hurt or abused a woman? In your memory, have you ever hit a woman? Maybe someone five years ago, or even last night? Is there a name that comes to mind?"

No, I had never hurt a woman, but I was flipping through the images in my mind. I hadn't loved a lot of women. I wasn't like most people that way. Most of the women I had loved moved away never to be seen again, no matter how hard I looked and I searched far and wide to find them. The first girl I ever loved was in grade nine, her name was Traci with an "I". Oh, how I loved her, but she was stuck on Billy who treated her like a party game. You know the kind of guy who thinks just because he sees something on a video he has to do it? The day he called her a little sex toy I broke his jaw and never saw her again. She moved to Peterborough. I looked for her, but she seemed to fall off the face of the earth. I often wondered if Traci ever got to play her flute in front of the world. She loved music and spent so much time practicing that it was like an obsession. I often think of her and wish that I could see her again.

Next there was Angelle. Met her at the local college. It was some kind of gender class. Woman's equal rights or something like that except that it seemed more like a man hater class. The kind of thing where modern women still hold grudges about the way men historically treated woman. Still don't know how they can blame us modern men for things that happened a hundred years ago, but those bras burning women do. I never understood her though. She was the kind that really believed women deserve the same as men, maybe even more. Of course, she was easily confused. There was this guy named Barry who signed up just to get laid. Poor bastard had no way of knowing the day he slapped her was going to be the last day he had all his teeth. I enjoyed watching him desperately trying to pick his teeth off the ground as I put the boots to him. He had the dentist try and put them back in.

Then there was Rosie. She was the one though. She is the one my heart has been searching for my whole life. I never really understood her either. I know that she loves me even if she can't admit it. Even if she refuses to let herself believe that she was lovable. "Nope none at all. I am rather selective in the women I love. Just because I don't wear a wedding ring doesn't mean I can't remember their names. There's only been three."

Harold seemed way to nervous about these questions. Maybe he saw me as a friend or maybe it was his boss standing there examining us both with those cold hate filled eyes. Either way, I think that Harold was going to need to book a day off after our little talk here. He might wear a badge, but I really think that he is too sensitive for this part of the job. Way too fragile. Guy should probably have been a boy scouts' leader instead of a cop, but he'd probably get lost in the forest.

"Lee they can test the blood from last night and right now there is a team of analysts examining your whole life. Are they going to find anything?"

I screamed out, "I don't talk about the past Harold. it's not important and nobody's business, but my own." My mother used to say the past is like a nightmare. It only exists when you sleep and you choose to either let it chase you in the day light or push it aside. I chose to push it aside. To know it exists, but not let it guide my days.

"Just calm down Lee, it's just part of the murder investigation. We always thoroughly examine every suspect and right now you are the prime one."

I snapped, "I am what?" The cuffs were digging into my skin, but I was too pissed off to care or feel it. I was being railroaded and they thought Harold was going to be able to spoon feed a confession out of me like I was so stupid I was going to be out smarted by an over paid security guard. The nerve of these assholes. "Listen up Harold. Whatever crime you boys in blue need to solve or want a prime scape goat for, it's not me. I don't just kill without a hell of a good reason."

The Sargent's hands slammed against the table. "So, you admit that you have killed before!" His whole body trembled as he leaned over so close I could feel his breath hitting my face. "Who exactly did you kill? Was it an innocent little college girl?"

My temper was getting a head me and that was going to cost me. "It was a figure of speech, that's all." God, damn it, I fell right into their trap hook, line and sinker. A slip of the tongue is all these guys need to screw you over. Learned that way back in Bloodvien juvenile facility. One small slip up will screw you for life.

"So, tell us who did you kill you Ashley? A young college girl? Say five years ago? We have finger prints from an unknown assailant. When I run those prints against yours what will I find?" My heart was pounding as he moved in closer and whispered, "We always thought you were a brilliant killer, but now I think that you were just lucky. Lucky enough to kill a helpless college girl and get away with it for five years, but guess what? Your luck ran out today."

"What luck? I didn't kill any college whore five years ago. I am a lot of things, but I am not a killer!" Of course, they would never believe me. They wanted to close an unsolved murder and I was the one lucky prick that they were going to pin in on.

"That wasn't a whore. It was a 20-old girl named Callie. She wasn't a nameless victim." Slamming his hands on either side of my restraints, he bellowed, " She was taking biochemical engineering and was in the top 5% of her class. Do you realize how great of a future she was going to have?"

"I never even met the bitch, so how the hell do I know how great of a future she might have had?" I shouldn't have said anything derogatory about this unknown woman, but it was too late the words were already out there.

I heard the loud whack long before the pain hit me as the Sergeant's hand slammed against my face. "She wasn't a bitch, she was my daughter and you killed her, you bastard." The crazy bastard was bitch slapping me like he was a school yard bully. "I know you did it you little prick. She was slaughtered just like your mother was killed when you were a kid. Did we arrest the wrong man that day? Did we?" My eyes were tearing up and blood was flowing from my lips as he man handled me.

He forced the image into my mind. He shouldn't have made the memory come alive again. He was pulling the fragments of my past piece by piece like a clown pulling scarves from his sleeves. I was gasping for air trying to kill the image, but I couldn't. The image of my mother just lying there staring up at me. The side of her was mangled from the cooking oil that Walter had thrown at her. My mother was beautiful. She was like a playboy bunny, all hips and tits. That's what everybody used to say. All hips and tits. Walter stole that from her. The skin on the side of her face was peeling like cracking paint on a wall. Little shreds of burnt skin just rolled off her cheeks.

I was running my fingers through her hair like I did after a bad day at work or one of Walters benders. Ever since I was a small child, throughout all the boyfriends that hit her and hurt her, I could always calm her with just a touch of my hand. That was the gift I brought to her horrible life. She felt loved when I ran my fingers along her ears and through her hair. I couldn't even see the beauty in her eyes. He stole that too. I just wanted to look into her beautiful eyes one more time, but all that was stolen now.

He kept screaming, "Why did you have to kill her?" He was crying and screaming out, "She was such a sweet girl and you killed her." I was trying to scream out that I didn't kill her. That I didn't even know anyone named Callie, but how the hell are you supposed to scream out with somebody's hand clamped around your neck? There was so much pressure that I could feel my eyes throbbing and it seemed like they were about to pop out. Still he kept screaming, only his words started to become muffled until I could have sworn that I was going to die right there and then. Slowly, I was starting to feel like I was drowning and no matter how hard I fought, I couldn't catch a breath. My strength was starting to fade. The world was growing blurry, but there was nothing I could do about it. This was the first time in so long that I had felt fear burning inside me.

CHAPTER 05 – BROWN

Most people live their whole lives in blissful ignorance. They like it better that way. It's easier to just get by then to reach out and take the life they were meant to have. My old man always called it grabbing the bull by the horns even though it's more like kicking the doubters in the balls. That's exactly what you need to do, kick those who say that you can't do it hard enough and they'll never say it again. Yes, I know that the psychiatrists of the world would analyze them and find that their parents are to blame or that its some kind of chemical imbalance or some other horse shit like that, but I don't believe it. 90% of the world are either too stupid to stand up and scream, "give me respect" or are just too weak to fight it and accept it. I used to be one of those people. I used to be so weak that all I did was follow the crowd like sheep being herded to the butcher. I was too weak to scream that I want more from life or reach out and grab it.

If I was stronger, I might have been a five-star general by now. It's a regret that is for sure. When I needed courage to say "No mom" my courage failed me. I was 18 then. When you are 18, you need to have a strong role model to guide you. All I had was a broken father who was so pussy whipped by my mother that he stopped living and was content just existing. I said screw that, I want to live life, not become a victim of it.

Victims are weak and Mister Brown here isn't weak, at least not anymore. I should have joined the army back then. I had everything filled out and was ready to go. I didn't want to fight in a war because only an idiot wants that, but the army offered education and a secure career. There is always a need for security in life, especially in this day and age when your neighbors can be enemies and strangers might be your best friend. Anyhow, I was there hearing some lieutenant tell me about the world of possibilities and I was excited. Not the kind of excitement that fades away when your back is turned, but the kind of excitement that makes you open your eyes ten minutes before the alarm goes off because you don't want to miss a single minute of life. It was like every dream I ever had was being explained to me and this guy was the leader. Hell, he was so big his shadow could have weighed more than me back then. I was just about to sign my name on the paper work when my mother comes charging in ready for an all-out war if need be to stop me from chasing my future. She even went so far as to say that I could never be a hero. That I was meant to stay on the farm where the work was hard, but no brain power was required. Even that lieutenant laughed as she dragged my ass out of the place. That's my last memory of him and the freedom I craved. My mother made it so I would never the hero I wanted to be, only a broken boy being pulled away from a real future.

I see it happening all around me. People beaten down like dogs and they just take it. I try and help them see their value, but there is only so much I can do. It's frustrating, but it's my calling. Everybody needs one true calling in life. A writer is meant to write, a singer to sing and a priest to pray. Mine is to make those that can't see the light inside themselves see it and then watch it shine. There are many of them out there. Too many in fact and I am sure even if I lived to be a thousand, I wouldn't be able to put a dent in the number. Now I never openly tell the world around me what I do because if everybody knows, it takes something away from it. It makes it less special.

Today was an especially frustrating day. I was scanning through the police reports waiting for them to find it, but they were too blind to notice. That is the problem with most cops these days. They depend on their profiles and technology more than actually pounding the pavement and chasing down the evidence. Lazy police work is killing our country, but I can't do everything for them. I can't save the whole world, but I try and push those little tidbits that they need to them. The problem is that they don't always see what's right in front of their face.

They had the poor misunderstood bastard Lee in the interview room for over an hour now. I know Charlie was going to try and break him and pin his daughter's death on him. Charlie was too emotionally involved to see straight. He wasn't searching for justice. He wanted closure. I can understand that, but I don't think he truly understood his little girl. Daddy's are blind to the flaws of their only children. If he wasn't so close to the crime, he might just see that the man they had selected was a defender not an abuser. If they looked close enough and examined his rap sheet they would easily come to the same conclusion I did. He was a stalker that is for sure. I wouldn't be surprised if he had a room dedicated to those he stalked complete with an alter and candles, but he was too much in love with those he stalked to be dangerous. Besides he wrote these women love songs and the only way that they could hear them was if he was up close and personal. Besides that, I don't think he even spoke to them. Maybe the odd email or letter, but he was always at a distance. That's what you need to look at. Motive and actions.

That's the problem with being too close to things. You miss the motive and the history. A man like Lee can't kill the woman he is stalking. It just isn't good for him. He probably doesn't even see it, but from talking to Rosie I see it and even told her as much. Lee loves her from afar. She brings out the romantic in him and gives his life meaning. That's why I never interfered with him even though she asked me to many times. Lee was my unknowing partner in building her up even if Rosie couldn't see it herself. He wrote her love songs and only saw the best in her even though there were an arms length of flaws in her life choices. The only time he ever got violent around her was when he was defending her or when somebody tried to take her away from him. I don't think even he realizes that his dear dead Rosie resembles his long dead mother. Seeing her die scared him and the fact he couldn't save is mommy makes him vicious when it comes to defending Rosie. Both real and imagined dangers. I bet if he wasn't locked up last night she would still be alive or they would both be dead. It's probably a good thing he was locked up because I would have missed him and I want to keep an eye on his future. He could even help me find those broken souls that need my help. I was hoping that Bruno would look at that and find what I left for him, but he is just a little slow if you know what I mean.

At some point, they will start to examine Rosie's life and to solve this they must. It's her desire to be loved more than anything else that got her killed. Behind every action, we take in life, is a reason. Whether it's stealing diamonds, going to Africa and dedicating our lives to the church or never saying no to anything our partner asks us to do. If you don't take the time to see the why and only look at the actions, you miss the important stuff. It's the why that solves most crimes. Of course, it's not my job to solve murders so I don't, but I always know the why.

Bruno's desk was at the end of the make shift hallway. Head high cubical walls formed a maze through the offices in the back. This is where all the hard work is supposed to be done or at least in theory. Since they didn't notice my first attempt to help them find the best fit for the crime, I decided to use a more direct approach. Not do all the work for them because everything must be earned or the victory isn't a true win, but enough to make Bruno look in a different direction. Sometimes you need to point even the best blood hound in the right direction.

If you look at Arthur Andersen's file on the outside, you will probably see an average everyday Joe. Plays darts on Wednesday nights and works a 9 to 5 job. Very average, but if you know where to look, you will find a man who takes the dark fantasies most people have and forces them into reality. Rosie wasn't proud of the things that she did, but she hinted and eventually I found it. If you search long and hard enough there isn't a dirty secret safe out there in the world-wide web. He was too proud of it. I mean the abuse and humiliation that he put women through. He wasn't the first man to do this to her, but he was the last. Every race ends and hers ended, but at least she was saved from abuse and in her death, her inner beauty was restored. See if you understand the why, you can always solve everything.

The first time I realized that Rosie wasn't so pretty on the inside was watching a video that Arthur had posted. Pretty women respect themselves and Rosie didn't respect herself. If you look at her personal online presence you will find prerecorded video's and erotic pictures. You know the kind desperate people post to capture attention and build interest. Of course, I heard her cry for help. She was willing to trade everything to feel loved and I heard her whispering, "help me love myself." That is where she failed me. She was hearing what I said, but not listening. I hate when they don't listen. I offer to save them from themselves and the just can't follow the plan.

I dropped the page on Bruno's desk. Those dark little secrets that nobody searches for. Those naughty events that bring more doubt into your mind. Arthur had never been charged with anything, but he should have been. He never seduced a woman but intimated her like a puppet. He knew the words to say and how to say them. The problem was that he offered them everything and used their hidden secrets and desires to control them. He wasn't controlling anyone now. He was guilty and if Bruno opened his eyes, he was certainly going to be able to connect the dots.

CHAPTER 06 – BRUNO

Logan was passing by my desk and jokingly snorted, "Did you get in on the pool?"

Looking up from my paper work I asked, "What pool?" There was always a pool of some kind going on from sporting events to re-offenders. I am in the lottery pool, but that's it. To me pools are a lot like gambling and I work too hard to just throw away my money like that plus I am a softy. I prefer to think people can change. That a zebra can change its stripes and become a giant white stallion.

"When the stalker will crack. Most people say that Charlie will have him confessing by the end of the day, but I am thinking it's more likely tonight he will beat it out of him." Logan smashed his fist into his palm, "The real question is will Charlie stop when the little fellow confesses."

Logan was trying to joke, but it wasn't funny. I jumped up, "What the hell? Charlie has him in the interrogation room?" beating a confession out of him was going to be more than just a figure of speech and despite his arms length of crimes, Ashley Truelove wasn't our guy. He needed long term therapy and probably so many drugs that it would knock out a horse, but he wasn't guilty of this crime. Only this one.

Logan shrugged and laughed, "Well he is the boss or at least mine, so what am I supposed to do? Scream out don't use whatever force is necessary to get this prick?"

I was running through the man-made tunnel of cubical walls that lead to the main hallway leading to the interrogation rooms. The politically correct term is interview room thanks to the bleeding hearts. I am not complaining about it because I know very well our job is to protect the guilty as well as the innocent, but it was definitely an interrogation room right now. Charlie was about to end this kid as well as his career if I didn't jump in and stop him. Plus, I am almost certain that it was going to fuck up my whole case. There is nothing worse than a lit firecracker that hasn't exploded. Deep down you want to reach out and check, but the fear of it exploding in your hand always makes you pull your hand back. That was Charlie. A god damn firecracker that hadn't quite boomed yet.

Looking back, Logan was just standing there looking stupid like the ten bucks he had on the pool was more important than stopping Charlie. I screamed back, "Get your ass up here and help me." He immediately started running after me, but there wasn't any enthusiasm in his step if you know what I mean.

Turning the corner, I saw a small group of people gathering around the interrogation room door yet not one of them had the brain power to step in and stop the show. I expected better from them even if I already knew that they were just like every other person who can't turn away from the site of an accident even if the thought makes their stomach turn. It's times like this when you start to realize that those late-night burgers and gallons of coffee steal away your strength or at least it did mine. Gasping for air, I hit the door driving it inward feeling the whole wall shake as the metal hit it. I charged in half tripping over a uniform lying on the floor curled up in the fetal position. Generally, I would stop and take care of him first thing. It's the code that we take care of our own, but right now stopping Charlie was bigger and stopping him from killing an innocent man was more important.

A loud thudding noise echoed all around as Charlie wailed on the Mister Truelove and by the looks of it, we were about to have our first law suit. To my knowledge there had never been any kind of law suit or investigation against our department, but this time Charlie had taken it too far. We would be lucky if the kid had any teeth left after this.

I reached out to grab Charlie from behind in my foolish attempt to stop him. As his massive fist came back preparing to strike, I slipped my arm under his trying to place enough force to stop him. It's strange when you realize that a pot-bellied man in his fifties has iron hard biceps. Yes, five years of rage, twenty years of police work and five in the paratroopers left Charlie one tough SOB. He jerked forward dragging me with him, which was damn impressive considering I weighed 220 lbs. slipping my arm under his other one I tried to force my hands together.

"You killed my baby," Charlie screamed in near madness. "You slaughtered my little girl like she was a lamb at the slaughter house."

I was pushing my hands together trying to lock my fingers so that I could apply all my force. That was great in theory, but theory was easier then actually doing it. It always was. Clenching my teeth together I snapped, "Charlie let it go. He can't be the one. Too young and too stupid."

He was trying to force my grip to break. The sweat was making my fingers slide apart. "Just walk away," Charlie muttered. "Just walk away."

As Charlie twisted and turned trying to break free, I felt the strength draining from my arms. It had been sometime since my strength had been measured and right now I didn't feel so tall. "I can't let you screw your whole career Charlie."

Charlie was struggling to break free with everything he had in him. Being this close to the man he thought killed his daughter was his breaking point. He never mourned her loss, so for that past five years he'd been growing colder and colder as the hate festered inside him. To most of the people here, he was just another hard ass old school beat cop who got lucky and climbed the ladder, but a few of us knew better. For a few of us, we saw the truth. We witnessed the changes as he went from one of the most caring men you would ever meet to one of the coldest bastards on the streets. We were partners for so long though that I was lucky enough to share in most of the sacred family moments that a man can share and after awhile his family was almost like my own. There was a time when Charlie would give you the shirt off his back, literally. I had witnessed that too, but that version of him was long gone.

My arms were trembling as I fought to keep my fingers locked while trying to drag him away. My training and experience weren't going to be as useful with Charlie as they were on the streets because you never truly worried about hurting the thug who was trying to hurt you, but a friend and fellow officer, you worry about hurting even if he is being an absolute ass. I was using all my force to lift upward while yanking back as I tried to force Charlie out of arms length from the bound victim, but it was slow going. Too slow and by the looks of Ashley Truelove if I had been a few minutes slower there would be a different set of murder charges being laid.

Charlie managed to twist his whole body and lift his legs driving us both backwards from the force as his feet connected with the table. The back of my head snapped against the hard tile covered cement floor and my neck and shoulders tingled forcing me to lose my grip. Charlie seemed to roll up landing on his feet while I was still laying there trying to catch my breath, almost blinded by the reeling pain. Like a good little soldier, Charlie was back up ready to charge and I knew that I couldn't let him do it. I was about to kick the feet out from under him when he stopped. Of course, it could still go either way since Charlie's mind wasn't where it was supposed to be and anything could happen. He just stood there then looked at me and over to the uniform sitting on the floor with a bloodied nose. Charlie was silent and just covered his mouth preferring to stare down at the floor then actually looking me in the eyes. Part of me wanted to scream out that he should be ashamed the dumb ass, but I honestly think he was going to be harder on himself then I ever would be.

Slowly, I climbed to my feet and Logan was just standing

there still looking stupid. A team player wouldn't have just stood there. No, he would have at least attempted to restrain Charlie. I pointed, "Get Charlie out of here while I try and do some damage control." Damage control was another politically correct way of saying I was going to try and calm things down enough so that the department wasn't sued and Charlie didn't find his ass inside a cell too. I watched Logan pull the broken Charlie out the interview room and slowly close the door.

Ashley looked pale and a little flushed, but surprisingly, even with a swollen eye and bloody nose, he grinned. I had seen that grin before, but usually it was on court day when some sorry son of a bitch who should have gotten jail time walked away with probation. It was always a struggle not to hunt the bastards down, but it wasn't my job to judge them and pass sentencing, only to find the evidence and let justice prevail. That was the legal system though.

"I didn't kill his daughter," Ashley muttered. "I am not that type of monster."

Grabbing a chair, I flipped it around and sat down. "Oh, and what kind of monster are you exactly?"

Tapping his fingers on the table he just paused. "The kind that can't let go. Call me an optimist if you want, but that is what I truly am."

"So, I guess you are just a misunderstood romantic. A soft heart on a quest for love." Usually I would try to follow our standard interrogation methods, but I figured the first go didn't work, so why would it now?

Still tapping his thumbs on the table, he just looked at me before grinning again. "I like you. You seem to be asking the right questions that lead to me trusting you with the hopes of a slip up or some kind of confession. Don't worry I am not going to take it personal, but I know nothing about your friend's daughter." Raising his eyebrows, he smiled, "True romantics like me we don't forget faces or names."

"You mean a stalker, don't you?" He didn't seem like the beat around the bush kind.

"I don't see myself as a stalker. Those guys hide in the

shadows and eventually become dangerous. I have never hurt a woman in my life. Not unintentionally or intentionally."

Like most creepy little bastards, he was self confident and twisted things to suit his idea of how it should be, not how it was. My father used to call it seeing the world through rose colored glasses. I always thought that he just wanted to see his false hope as sunshine because it allowed him to think he had a bright rich life. It was a good thing I took off those bullshit glasses and left as soon as I was old enough. Give me the cold hard truth to false hope any day. A man can be broken by the truth and bounce back from it quite easily. False hope doesn't help you grow, it just lets you linger, waiting.

"I didn't kill anyone last night or five years ago. I am just a normal everyday guy trying to find love in a loveless world. I don't care how you see me and I am certain that one of these days Rosie will admit what I already know." His face wasn't filled false hope or any lie that I could see. This crazy little bastard actually believed that she loved him. It made him dangerous because even if he didn't kill her, which I was a certain in my mind the minute he got out of here he would have his own list of suspects and that would mean that somebody was going to get hurt.

"So, tell me about Rosie."

He smiled. It was not just a smile, but true happiness that glowed. "What can you say about your soul mate really? Have you ever found a soul mate? Not just one special love, but your one love? Your only love?"

It's a scary thing when you realize that a psychopath has the heart of a poet. I am not sure if I should be jealous or not because the closest thing I have ever come to love was the booking officer Maria at the Christmas party five years ago, and just like Christmas, it only lasted one day and seemed like a lot of work to open a disappointing present. Career cops like me generally don't keep girl friends long enough to build love. We might find a little lust, but never love. Tapping my hands together, I responded, "No I can't say I ever found a soul mate."

Slapping the table Ashley muttered, "That's why you will never understand me. I see love at the very foundation and like a house, I build it brick by brick."

"Brick by brick?"

"Yes. Love and happiness isn't just a destination that you arrive at. It's a complete journey. Just think about what me and Rosie will tell our kids."

"You have already planned your family?" I raised my eyebrows in surprise. I knew he was obsessed with the girl, but never figured he had a whole life planned out.

Ashley blurted out, "Hell yes I have. Not anything specific, but the general idea. Rosie likes horses, so I will buy a little farm with a forest in the back."

He reminded me of Callie when she was in high school. Always telling me about her planned dream life with mister wonderful, even if she hadn't met him yet. She always said that she wanted a little cabin like house by a small river with a golden retriever. Dreams like that were a luxury of the young, even if most of them would never come true. "So why a forest?"

"Kids need trees to climb and shit like that."

"So, what did Rosie think of these grand plans?"

"She doesn't know. No matter how hard you plan these things, first you have to get the person to admit they love you. You see I know she does. I can see it in her eyes. It's like a silent whisper that never fades. So, it's my job to send flowers, write love songs, poetry and shit like that. Once she realizes that, then I tell her the plan, but make her think it's her idea. That is the secret. Not that I am trying to trick her or anything like that. I am just opening her eyes to the millions of possibilities life has to offer."

All the possibilities in life was probably one of the saddest statements that I ever heard. Rosie had no possibilities. Every possibility that she might have had, died with her last night. That statement alone was enough to convince me that Ashley didn't kill her. He was still seeing the wedding in his head.

Leaning forward I asked, "What can you tell me about

Rosie's boyfriend?"

Ashley sighed and his eyes narrowed. "Do you want to know the truth? What I really think?"

There was definitely rage in his eyes. If I was investigating her boyfriend's murder, Lee would certainly be my guy. "Yes, I really want to know what you think of him and his character."

His fists clenched. "He isn't like me."

"Okay let's start there. How isn't he like you?"

"He acts like a king. He doesn't earn love, he rents it. They say money can't buy love, but king Arthur proves you can rent it."

I hadn't had time to truly look at Rosie's life. Between going over the crime scene with a fine-tooth comb and all the paper work, I hadn't taken the time yet to meet the real Rosie. "So, was Rosie for sale?"

He jumped up and the chains that bound him clanged as they went tense. His eyes were throbbing as he screamed, "You call my Rosie a whore again and I will kill you." Those chains were still tensing as his whole body shook, "This isn't a threat because you look like you can't be intimidated, so let's get this straight here and now. I will kill you if you insult her again. She isn't an evil or cheap woman. She is just a little confused."

"I didn't mean to tarnish your memory of her. Tell me about her boyfriend and how you see him? Not how the world sees him, but how do you see him?"

"He isn't exactly a stand-up guy." Something was floating inside his head. Maybe it was a memory or a desire I don't really know, but his body tensed as he whispered, "He didn't treat her right. Didn't treat her like a princess."

This was getting interesting. Ashley had a view that most people wouldn't have seen. Maybe a little bias, but definitely he saw more than most of us would have. "So how did he treat her?"

Tapping the table with his finger he mumbled, "Let's just say if that bastard dies, you have a good reason to yank my ass in here."

I had no doubts that he would kill him without a second

thought or that he saw reason to hate him. "So, do you think this Arthur would hurt Rosie? Physically I mean?" I needed more information. It was a unique situation to have a witness who not only knew everything about the victim so intimately, but also those who surrounded her. It's the first time I ever thought of a stalker as important.

His whole jaw clenched as he muttered "No, he did once, but he won't do it again. He won't dare hurt my Rosie again." The hate inside him was burning like fire, "I made sure of that." It was like something clicked inside him. He glared at me, "Who's blood do they think was on my hands?" His breathing started to become more rapid as he started yanking on the chains, "Did something happen to my Rosie?" He was making fists and pulling on his chains, screaming, "Did that rich bastard hurt my Rosie? If he did, I will be serving time and he will be going to the hospital because I am going to teach him fifty new kinds of hurt."

CHAPTER 07 – ASHLEY

They just wouldn't tell me what had happened and not knowing was so much scarier than anything they could tell me. My hands were trembling and for the first time it wasn't fear, it was the panic setting in. Fear a man can grab hold of and control, but panic was different. Panic wasn't something you could break. It was like being in a dark room and there is no sunlight. Some might say panic leads to fear, but panic is like dynamite inside you. Fear is always on the outside. I was back in the darkness again slowly forcing myself to crawl forward even though I was completely blind. I was trapped by the unknown and that unknown was always just around each corner, waiting. It was there and I never knew when it was coming to jump out at me. "Tell me what happened to Rosie? Just tell me," I screamed as my hands pounded against the table. "Damn well tell me now or I will kill you!" The tall wide cop in the brown suit wasn't exactly emotionless, but there was something in his eyes. If I didn't know better, I would say that it was curiosity. He was tapping his fingertips together as if he was just waiting for me to tire of screaming. If that was it, he'd be sitting here a long time because I never tired of screaming. Slamming my hands on the table I bellowed, "Answer my damn question!"

He had faster reflexes then I thought he had. As my hands

pounded downward, he reached out and caught them. In a low whisper, he said, "Calm yourself."

I don't know why, but all I could say was, "What the hell?"

Still holding my hands down with lots of force he whispered, "Calm down and I will tell you what you want to know, but there are consequences to your questions."

I knew a lot about consequences. My whole life was filled with them. Everybody thinks that we must accept the consequences for our actions, but most of my life I was forced to accept the consequences for others actions. The consequences of Walter killing my mother wasn't because of my actions. The consequences of being beaten by her drunk boyfriends wasn't because of my actions. So many god damn consequences. Looking back now, I could handle the results even though my whole body trembled on the inside. Something was building inside me. Something new or maybe something old that I hadn't felt for too long. "Just tell me."

He took a deep breath and slowly loosened his grip on my hands and leaned back in his chair. "OK let's talk like old friends."

"I don't have friends."

Laughing he said, "Neither do I." I don't know why, but I believed him. He shared the same look that I have when I see Rosie. I guess we all have our own bitch we chase. His just happens to start with spilled blood and ends in the court room. Law and order is the whore he sees as an angel just like my Rosie.

"OK old friend tell me what happened to Rosie "

His eyes twitched as he shuffled in his chair which was never a good sign. He cleared his throat and finally whispered, "Have you ever heard the term 'the kiss of death'?"

Everybody wants to be a gangster. Deep down inside their souls I mean. Priests, school teachers and even the middle aged bald cop sitting in front of me, they all dream of being bad boys. It's because of how TV and books romanticize it. You know the gangster life style. The money, power and idea of it is so inviting. That's what most people think of when they hear of terms like' the kiss of death'. Me, I think of something slightly different. "Isn't that related to Judas? He kissed Jesus or something like that to identify him to the Romans."

"Really? I wasn't aware of that. No, I am talking about a little-known killer that haunts our city every few years."

It seems like he wasn't accusing me, but you can never tell with cops. Usually they are good shits, but you cannot be too careful. "Here I thought I was the biggest monster you guys were after."

Shaking his head, he muttered, "No not me. I have been preparing to meet him again for the past few years. Waiting for him to strike."

What kind of cop waits for a killer to strike? I mean why not just hunt him down and stop the killing rather than wait for the headline to catch him? "What does this have to do with me or Rosie?"

His hands forcefully clamped over mine as he whispered, "Because he killed Rosie and Charlie's daughter, plus the whole department thinks he's you."

The world ended for me right there and then. To this guy Rosie was just a headline in the morning paper, but she was more to me. I wanted to scream out, but I couldn't. I went numb. Not just physically, but emotionally. I loved Rosie with everything that I had inside me. Not just empty words whispered in the heat of passion, but a lifelong love. Most people live their whole lives searching for love and claiming that they found it over and over. That's what I call everyday love. Then there's me. I fall in love and it becomes an addiction. It's all part of my personality. They literally say I have an addictive personality. Everything I do is extremes. Part of managing it is understanding and accepting it. I choose my addictions. I like to call it choosing what controls me. My love for Rosie controls me. It's like the need to live. I once saw my uncle accidentally park a car on a ground hog's tail. The damn thing chewed off its own tail trying to get away. That's how I felt. I would rather have faced any horrors then hear that my darling Rosie died.

"Are you OK?" He asked, but I still could answer. I was screaming and cursing on the inside, but nothing left my lips except for a few growls and grunts. "Ashley, are you OK?"

The idea that I would never see Rosie's smile again bit into my heart like a shark feeding on my emotions like it was flesh. I could feel it inside me. The devastation that she was gone. That I couldn't search for her like others I had loved. She hadn't just moved to another city. No, that spark that I loved so much had been snuffed out and it would never shine again. The darkness was returning and without her it would not just give way to sunshine because the sunshine she brought to my life was gone.

The giant bellowed, "Ashley are you going to be alright?" as he reached out towards me. "I know that it's a lot to take in."

I didn't know how to answer. What do you say when the meaning of your life is taken away? It wasn't just a lot to take in. Everything stolen and you can't just replace it. Nothing would make it alright because Rosie was the best part of my life even if the love was one sided. It was genuine and true. I snapped, "Don't call me Ashley!" I muttered. "My name is Lee." Most people think that having a girl's name makes you tough and those sorry bastards where it like a badge of honor. Those assholes would be wrong. It's the collection of drunken fucks that the mother who gave you a girl's name brought home that makes you tough. Every one of them beat me saying, "This is to toughen you up boy. Being raised by a woman and treated like one means you need a few good smacks." That generally means bruises and broken bones. Rosie was the only one who called me Ashley and never made it sound like a weak name.

Placing his hands on the table, the big man said, "Sorry. I will call you Lee from now on." He just sat there as if waiting for my approval. "So, Lee the way I see it is this way, you followed Rosie, for what? Eight hours a day?" He was close, but not too far off. I worked eight hours a day slept three or four and dedicated the rest to Rosie. Not just following her but protecting her and worshiping. Most people only see the creepy dude hiding in the bushes always watching the poor helpless girl and I am sure that in many cases they are right, but not me. I am not the savage predator. I am the defender who watches and protects.

"So how can I help you?" Before I can tell a guy to go to hell you at least have an idea of what he wants, besides I need to know what he knows if I am going to hunt down and kill the guy that did this. That is the only goal I have and one thing I know how to do. Dedicate myself to one goal. It's all I think about, like an addiction. My new addiction is killing the guy who killed my baby. My Rosie.

"The man that killed Rosie only comes out once every five years. We call it his cooling down period." It was obvious that this guy had been thinking about the killer a lot. Too much in fact. Of course, now I was going to be thinking of him a lot too. Too much in fact and when I finally killed him, his face would be etched in my mind forever. Just like my Rosie. "This man would probably have suddenly showed up in her life. He would have been charming and friendly. Not the type that stands out of the crowd, but he would watch her. Probably not somebody that she would call a friend, but she would enjoy talking to him."

"You just described half the damn school." It was obvious that this guy didn't have anything on the killer. They were grasping at straws, but just maybe he could help me narrow down the list. I was still certain it was Arthur, but time would tell. Kill one or two or three just to be sure. Somebody would pay. Somebody had to pay.

"This guy wouldn't be a student. No, he would need to be in his late forties or early fifties. Has there been anybody like that who suddenly popped up in her life?"

It seemed to me that he was describing a lot of people who passed by her, stared at her and wanted her. There are numerous dirty old men in the world. Most of them though only get to see my Rosie on the Internet. They watch her online. I have skills that allow me to watch her too only I don't pay and I know things. The truth is, Rosie made thirty or so videos and had her friends chat with men. Nobody ever realizes that they are being scammed. Flipping through the faces one by one I went through the list. There were many faces that a beautiful young woman comes across in her day, but none that came to mind. "I still think it's dear old Arthur."

"The obvious choice isn't always the right choice. You are actually the obvious choice." Tapping his hands together he smiled. "We aren't looking for mister obvious. We are looking for mister not so obvious. You don't have to answer right this minute. Just take your time and think about it. I can use your help narrowing down who did it."

Take your time and think about it he said. There was quite a list of day to day people. Not just older men, but young ones too. Most though, I would have noticed and the type that he described I would have seen for sure. Rosie had a thing for older men. I hate older charming men. Especially the intelligent type. No, the guy that I was looking for was going to be virtual. Of course, he must have met her, but he was online. Traceable if you know exactly where to look. There were many. Too many, but I would find him. I had to find him.

"What are you thinking about?" he asked with a giant smile on his face. "It seems to me that a face came to mind."

No, it wasn't a face that came to mind. No image that you could track down or that I would able to find looking through mug shots. I needed to follow screen names and IP addresses. That was my skill set. I have been working with pcs before it was Windows. Back then it was a visual interface that ran on top of dos. This is the modern world where most people find comfort online. No, the guy I wanted couldn't have been just random. "No, I think it has to be Arthur." There were three men that came to mind. Three men that acted like friends but wanted more. Three screen names. Of course, there were more and I would have to go through them one by one.

"I will investigate him of course. The boyfriends are always a prime suspect, but I need you to think about every person that she came in contact with. Don't rush through it. Just take your time and think of names and faces. Scars or tattoos."

The door opened and a baby-faced cops head popped in, "Hey Bruno you almost done here? We are running out of real estate and we just brought in another one.

Bruno didn't look happy. It was like we were 2/3 of the way towards finishing the race and suddenly found a flat. "Are you sure this can't wait?"

"Bruno this guy came in voluntarily and only has an hour, so yes, we need the room. You can talk to this piece of shit any time you want." It was a polite way of saying that in the cops eyes the other guy was a law-abiding citizen where I was just another crook that got caught.

"OK let's finish this later if that is OK with you."

Well he was being polite and all, but it didn't really matter if I said yes or no. At least if I was in here it didn't. "Hey I got nothing, but time." A few minutes later I was being escorted from the interview room to my holding cell. Two screen names came to mind and haunted me. Fabrice and Mister Brown. Those were their screen names. All I needed to do was track the virtual name until it leads to a real one.

Bruno asked, "What are you thinking about? Seems like you have a name bouncing around your head."

I had much more than a name in mind. The face that I hated was walking towards me smiling like it was just an average day. Smiling like he had not a worry in the world. My body started the shiver as he came closer. It was like every horror that I ever faced was coming back to life inside me. Every little piece of pain that I ever encountered was slowly burning me alive. He was just five steps away and that's when I decided to kill him. Right there and then I decided he was the one that hurt my Rosie.

CHAPTER 08 – BROWN

Some experts will tell you that investigating a crime is 50/50; 50% skill and 50% luck, but I think most of the so-called experts spend too much time looking at graphs and spreadsheets. In my experience, it's all skill and determination. The skill to know which clues lead down the proper avenue and the determination to keep running when common sense tells you its hopeless. Bruno was like a bloodhound that caught a scent. Pure determination. Now he has skill, I can't deny that. He spends all his free time chasing down the monsters of this world. He understands that the real monsters look like normal men. They dress like us, sound like us and blend in with the normal everyday people. He has his flaws also, such as too much empathy and he builds personal attachments to the poor souls that were victimized by the creatures he hunts. The problem wasn't if he was a good cop or not, but whether or not he would able to see the trail I left behind for him. That's the only thing that mattered to me. Could he open his eyes enough to follow those bread crumbs I had so tactfully laid out before him?

I felt like I was trying to share a sunset with someone that would never see its beauty. No matter how hard I try to describe the vibrant oranges, purples and yellows, unless you have seen those bright colors with your own eyes you would never truly understand it. No matter how long I spent attempting to share the vision they would never understand it. Luckily though there was always Logan. Bruno was the obvious choice to hunt down Arthur, but Logan was the one who I could easily lead in the direction I wanted. The one I could control like a puppet. Men who only see the possibilities that benefit them are easily lead astray. History is full of ambitious men that choose their wants over everything else.

I needed Logan to help me bring Arthur under the radar. There was always a small chance that they would bypass him and spend too much time chasing Ashley or even worse, discover my connection. I didn't want to be in the lime light and I didn't want to see Ashley railroaded either. No, I needed to open Logan's eyes to my version of the truth with the hopes that Bruno would catch the scent I wanted him to follow.

I decided the best way to start the whole process going was an anonymous phone call and luckily, I was in one of the few places left in the city that still had a pay phone. Cops always got anonymous tips. Hell, we even offered rewards if a tip led to an arrest. I was walking down the stairs towards the lobby trying to think of what I should say. Logan wasn't at his desk, but I knew his cell number. I walked down the short hallway towards the pay phones. There were two of them and luckily most people didn't know they existed, let alone used them. I walked over and picked up the receiver and heard the familiar hum. I dropped in my two quarters while covering the receiver with my handkerchief. He picked up on the first ring, "Logan here."

"Hello detective. Are you investigating the murder of the young woman last night? The horrible one that was on the news?" The trick was to sound like an average Joe while feeding his ego. Men like him always wanted to feel important. It was necessary to make him feel like he was getting the case breaking tip. You know, the one piece that connects the dots and breaks the case.

He beamed, "Yes I am one of the investigating officers."

"Oh, not the lead investigator. Should I call somebody

else?" Yes, he needed to feel important, but he also had to earn it. That was the trick. He need to feel that the tip was important so it made him important.

"No, you don't have to call anyone else. I am the one that follows up all the important leads, big or small. All of them."

"Oh, that's good. Very good. I have a friend; her name is Melissa."

"Did she know the victim?"

"No not really, but she has a common connection to her." When you are setting a trap you always must use the proper bait. It's like fishing. The guy with the freshest worms catches the most fish.

"What's your friend's connection to the victim?"

"The victim, what's her name, Rosie contacted my friend three days ago, Not just her, but many of her husband's friends. Too many of them. She even contacted me." That was the secret to planting doubt. Give him something that he really wants but make him work for it. You hand let him know that you are spoon feeding him.

"Did she threaten you or your friend?"

"No, god no. She brought a lot of pain to my friend's life, but she didn't threaten her. No, she did something worse and I think that it might have led to her death. That what she did is the very reason that my friend's husband became mad with fury."

"Who is your friend's husband and what did Rosie do to him? What did she do that would make you think that he killed her?"

Now it was time to add the bait. He was just about the bite down on the hook, then he was mine. "Oh, maybe I am just being a gossip. You know taking something out of context and blowing it out of proportion."

"Nothing is too small and it's my job to investigate and determine what's real and what's not. You can trust me to look at every detail with an open mind. It's what I do daily."

"OK. Well that young woman that was murdered? She shamed him. She contacted not just his wife and family, but all their friends."

"Who is this friend's husband and what exactly did she send?"

"She sent messages and links. Asked questions and shared too much. She embarrassed him. He isn't handling it very well. He wrote her saying that he would make her pay for the stress that she brought to his life."

"He actually said he would kill her?" Now Logan was asking the proper questions.

"He sent her a message stating that he would make her life a living hell if she ever contacted his family again."

"And what did she do then?"

"She emails a link to a few unwelcome sites. You know the kind of thing you don't want the world to know about. A man can be driven to do the most horrible things when he feels like he has nothing to lose. That's what she did. She stole the respect of everybody from him."

"So, what did he actually say?" he muttered in anticipation.

"He said that he would show the world just how ugly she truly was. Just how selfish she was and that he would ruin her."

"Ruin is not kill."

"Check her email. You will see what I mean. Talk to those that know him best. You will hear that he is consumed with rage and that he can be violent. He might not have ever been charged with anything, but I heard he was investigated. I heard that he was abusive." I hung up the receiver and started walking towards the interview room. He would consider things immediately. Luckily, I was aware that the computer geeks were already going through her computer. They would examine all the bits and bytes and eventually find the emails I sent. Yes, planting evidence isn't respected, but it works. Of course, Arthur would deny doing it, but he couldn't prove his innocence and I was designing his guilt like an artist paints a portrait.

I made my up the stairs and found Logan exactly where I expected I would. He was talking to the guys in IT. Sometimes all you needed to do was plant the seed and just sit back and watch. It was always a good thing to see simple minded men thinking that they were geniuses when truly they were just pawns in the game of life. I was a chess master making a pawn feel like a king. It's the strategy that counts. I liked watching my pawns following the path that I had set out for them.

"Looks like Logan caught a break. If you aren't careful you might be taking orders from him one day." It was Randolph from booking, he was marching by with a handful of papers. "That damn kid is always catching the breaks."

"Well he likes to chase down every lead. It's part of being the new guy. You run faster trying to get noticed." It was a polite way of saying the kiss ass was trying to get as much attention as possible. Some people, like Bruno, are career cops while guys like Logan see it as a stepping stone. Probably has his sights on politics or something like that.

"Damn right he is. Seems like he has his nose right in the middle of everything. If he was looking to get noticed, it's working."

It was true Logan had a bright future in front of him and with my guidance it was going to get a lot brighter. "Old dogs like us just don't have the energy to keep up." I discovered long ago that using words like "US" and "WE" make common folk feel included. It makes them feel like they belong and to most people it's all they need to see you in the proper light. I needed to seem like I belong even though I had probably forgotten more than most people would ever know.

"Oh, don't act like he can't keep up. I see him here at ungodly hours reviewing files and taking notes. It's like you and he are fixtures."

"That's not ambition, it's just an old dog trying to keep up."

Logan was still looking through the thick stack of papers that IT had given him. That's exactly what I wanted him to do. Look at the emails and start to build a case against Arthur.

"I got the break that we've been looking for," Logan said as he passed by. I am not sure if he was talking to me or announcing it to the whole precinct. "The boyfriend wasn't just a boyfriend, but her sugar daddy. Bet he didn't think that everything we do online is out there forever."

"What did he do?"

"Let's just say they were a lot more than just friends."

"What were they then?"

Laughing he added, "Oh you must read through the history and see the pics."

There was the little IT guy walking behind him with an even thicker handful of papers. He went from desk to desk dropping stacks of papers on each. Written in the folders were three names of interest. Arthur, Fabrice and Brown. I had obviously missed something. I thought that I had deleted everything that had my name on it. Carefully I went through her system only leaving what I wanted them to find, but I had missed something.

"What's Brown?"

The little man from IT responded, "it's the damnedest thing. Her system had a tracker on it. Tracked her chats, social media, web cam, emails and everything. Somebody tried deleting a butt load of data, but the tracker app had it all cached. Those were the three people's messages that were deleted. So far, we've only been able to restore 22% of the data, but in time we will have it all."

Shit! "How does that work? I have heard of keystroke trackers, but systems?"

"Well it's the same principle except this application captures everything. It's not something most people could get. This appears to be some proprietary software. I will still need to do further research, but I do have an IP address."

This was something that I hadn't expected. I wasn't supposed to be involved in the actual case let alone be a suspect. I should be impressed by Ashley Truelove. Few people can get one over on me and here he had somehow managed to not only track my time with Rosie, but he managed to bring me into the public eye. Yes, I think I found that one man that I can shape into what I want him to be. To be just like me.

Logan looked back, "It seems that Arthur Andersen is

more of a monster then anybody imagined. You need to read this to believe it. Hard to believe he just marched in saying my life is an open book when the book is borderline erotica and BDSM. I can't wait to read the rest. It's just like being able to look into a person's mind and yank out their darkest fantasies."

CHAPTER 09 – ASHLEY

Time is a strange phenomenon. It's either something that you have too much of or not enough. If you really think of it, there are only two states, either it goes by too fast or too slowly. Right now, it's going by too slow. Trapped in my little cell all I have are my thoughts and regrets. Regrets are like ghosts that haunt you in life. They are always there. You can see them, but they always seem just out of reach. Rosie was gone and there was nothing that I could do to bring her back. Most normal men who love a woman would be able to remember the smell of her perfume or the touch of her body, but all I truly have had been the fantasy of it. Not exactly what it was like, but what I wanted it to feel like. The idea of her would linger even if I could never touch her cheeks or taste the passion in her lips.

Soon they would let me out and I would go back home. I had never done that before. I mean literally I always checked on Rosie every time I was around, but now Rosie was gone and home was the only place I could think of to go. I only had one real friend, Denis, but he would be busy doing something. He was a work friend. You know the kind that you talk and laugh with at work, but that's it. No let's go out for a few beers after work or come on over and watch the game on Sunday afternoon. Just see you on Monday night when we were both working again. Usually I liked it that way, but today I needed a friend. Today I needed Rosie, but Rosie wasn't there anymore.

Harold was slowly trotting towards me. The thudding sound he made when he came in gave it away. It was the first time I wasn't happy to see him. Not that we were friends, but I felt normal trading insults. Guys like me don't get to do these little normal things. Sharing everyday little things like verbally bitch slapping other men for fun.

"Lee, we have to talk." His hands trembled with good reason to be. He had betrayed me and I don't take betrayal well. I don't forgive or forget easily.

"What do we have to talk about? How I killed Rosie?"

"I never thought that you did kill or hurt her, but that asshole Charlie made me do it. He didn't give me a choice." That made sense. Harold was always more like the obedient solider then the rebel type. He had a nervous personality and always seemed to fear losing his job if he opened his mouth. Jobs are a dime a dozen though. I have had so many of them that the list of where I haven't worked is smaller then the list of where I have.

We always have a choice though. We just need the courage to make them. Even I have choices. I could have chosen not to love Rosie. My life would have had little or no meaning and there was a great void in my life, but I had a choice. Of course, telling Harold how I felt about it wouldn't do any good. I might need him someday and it's better he keeps his guilt thinking he owed me rather than defending it and hating me. "It's OK Harold I don't hold anything against you."

Dropping his head, he mumbled, "I don't know if it matters, but I don't think you are the prime suspect anymore. It seems that there is a lot of evidence that points to Arthur. He uttered death threats and apparently, she had made sure a lot of people knew about them."

That wasn't a secret to me. I read the emails and saw the pictures that Rosie shared with the world. It was desperation I think that forced her to lash out like that. She fell in love with a dream and an idea that in her eyes was slipping away so she fought the only way she knew how trying to keep it. There was nothing about Arthur that I didn't already know. His address, the secret room that he rented just three blocks from Rosie's place and even their arrangement. I didn't like or understand the arrangement, but I knew it was there. Hell, if it weren't for a little Mittal schnauzer, he never would have met my darling and she would probably be alive. That's how they met. Rosie did dog grooming part time on the side. Of course, until recently I thought I had beaten him so hard that he would never dare lay a hand on her again. A world of hurt was in his future. Sometime the pains in life won't leave and Arthur's pain was just starting.

Harold ran his shaky fingers through his hair almost yanking it out. "Lee, do you know anything that might help us get this bastard? I really want to get him for what he did to the poor girl and Charlie's daughter. Is there anything you can tell me about him that will lead to his arrest?"

They never told me what exactly happened to Rosie. I didn't want to know. My imagination would provide me everything I needed to find reason to punish him. It would fuel my hate enough to let me do unthinkable things. It wasn't really a matter of guilt or innocence, but me making sure that anyone who might be guilty gets punished. There were names already bouncing in my mind and the list was always getting bigger. When you only have a general idea of who did the crime, you punish everybody to make sure the right person gets what's coming to him. "You won't find enough to arrest him, but he will get what's coming to him." I couldn't help but think about Rosie. Was she terrified in those last moments? Did she feel all alone and helpless? Did she even think of me as her life flashed before her eyes? I would never know the answers to those questions, but she would be avenged. She would have her justice even if I had to trade everything to give it to her.

"Lee stop talking like that. If something happens to him, you will be in the spotlight again." He was waiting for a response and when none came he continued, "Arthur is right on the hot seat, but he has made many enemies here. Not just you, but others and when you talk like that it makes you look guilty if anything happens to him. You don't want that kind of attention. I am telling you as a friend. Work with us, not against us and we will get this bastard."

It made sense to step away and let the cops do what they do. If Canada had the death penalty I think I could do it. Step away that is, but we don't have it. No instead he gets a cell and free cable TV. No, I couldn't just step away. "I will try and help, but that bastard Arthur deserves to die. He deserves to get what's coming his way."

Harold seemed too calm as those words left my lips. I guess he decided that he had saved two lives right now. Mine and Arthur's, even if Arthur's life span was now reduced to hours and minutes not years and months. Placing his hand on top of mine, he said, "Good."

The door opened and Harold handed me a business card. "If you need to talk, call this number."

I don't know why, but I expected It to be his card. You know the kind of thing where the cop gives the witness a card and says call me day or night, but it wasn't his card. The name on it was Bruno Norcross. "Why would I call him?"

"Because he is the lead detective, he actually believes you are 100% innocent and is probably the only guy that wants to catch the actual killer as much as you do."

"Why because he thinks the guy killed a cop's daughter too?"

"Rumor has it that this guy is the only one that ever got away from him. That Bruno had him in his sights, but for some reason couldn't take the kill shot. It has haunted him year after year they say. So, he is the one that you need to call. The only one that wants to hear what you have to say."

"And you?" I really don't know why I asked since obviously, he was just following through the motions that somebody else had told him to follow. He was a yes man after all.

"I want to help, but I am not on this case. I am not even

supposed to know anything about it. I just hear things."

So basically, Harold was a rent a cop with a gun. It makes you wonder if the reason they say crime pays is because there are too many Harold's and not enough Charlie's. I hated to admit it, but if Charlie wasn't trying to pound my ass until I confessed, I would be cheering for him. A little police brutality can go a long way. "Don't worry about it Harold. There isn't anything wrong with just getting by."

I don't know what was going through Harold's mind after that. He was quiet though. I think he had seen himself as a real cop until today. Maybe it was true, maybe not but either way Harold was pondering his life. The is the way it was the whole way through processing. It was that way right up until they handed me back my stuff. There was this awkward silence with everyone though. That questioning look of did he do it or is he innocent? I was used to the sick bastard stares. You know the one where everyone thinks I should be locked up in a mental hospital and not allowed to walk the streets, but I had never had the 'is he a killer' look.

I stepped out into the street and opened my phone. A little gray heart marked the last location where Rosie's phone checked in. It was right here at the police station. Probably in evidence or at some cop's desk. The program was my own design. I always called it my stalker app. There are similar apps out there, but mine is customized. I could turn on her camera, where she was, her photos and videos. Mine was the perfect stalker app. When you are chasing perfection, you need to truly think outside the box.

"I am not completely satisfied that you are innocent," a voice bellowed from behind me. "Usually it's the most obvious one who is the guilty bastard you want, but there is always the other guy Arthur."

Laughing I blurted out, "You could just kill us both and be sure you got the right guy. That's exactly what I am thinking." Grabbing my shoulder, he pushed me along towards the little alley just around the corner from the doors. Generally, I would try and bitch slap him until he collapsed to the ground under my feet, but I had this feeling that he'd drop my ass right out from under me before I had a chance to get a single punch in.

"Let's have a little talk in a more private surrounding."

"You mean some place where nobody can see the police brutality unfold." He'd already slapped me around once so I think he wouldn't have any issues doing in again.

"I lost my temper. I am not an animal and if you aren't involved in any of the murders, you will be alive and well."

The words might be saying 'I am sorry', but that hate filled look was telling another story. Hearing him accusing me of being involved in Rosie's death was enough to start the burning inside me. Enough to force me to remember the other tragedy in my life. Those memories were a tool. That was where I went when I needed to feel pain because that pain was still strong like a gasoline fire and right now I needed to feel the flames. The image of my mother just lying there lifeless on the floor started to flow again. Her beautiful had been burned away. I remember staring into her delicate face and desperately trying not to let that image be the last one of her I would remember. It was though. I don't know how it happened, but Rosie's face replaced my mothers and the fire inside me grew stronger. It was like that sudden whoosh when tissue paper first catches fire.

"Your whore isn't the important murder, she is just connected to the one that is important."

That's when I lost it. I spun around screaming, "Rosie isn't a whore," and my fist shot out at him. It was like hitting a wall only this wall smiled as my fist connected with his chest.

His arm immediately sprung up slapping me right across the face. It burned as his open hand snapped against my flesh again. I put everything I had into it and drove my fist into his ribs. I am not sure if they cracked or not, but the way his face curled and screamed out in pain made me think so. I like to call that silent pain because no matter how tough a guy might be, when you snap a rib it hurts like hell. His hand came down hard against the top of my head and it sent me to my knees. My whole head felt like a spider web of mini earthquakes that was shattering the bone as my legs started to wobble. "You little prick. I was giving you a chance to clear your name and help me get the real killer and you pull this shit." It took me a few seconds to realize that he had snapped me on top of the head with the handle of is revolver. The king of cheap shots. I could feel the warm blood running off the top of my head from where he struck me. The thought occurred to me that if he didn't kill me today, I might just have to kill him on principal. "I can beat what I need out of you right here and now," he muttered. "Nobody would really know."

I drove my fist upward with all my might again, this time I was certain that it connected with his balls, but the blood flowing over my eyes made it hard to see. Of course, the fact that he dropped to his knees and the fact that he was wheezing made me think that I had hit a sensitive part. Blindly I just swung my fists through the air feeling them connect with his face. "I didn't kill Rosie or your daughter and I can tell you this, I don't have anything else to lose so killing you won't bother me one bit." He seemed dazed and I am sure if someone snapped me in the balls, I would also be stunned. Either way I was throwing fists left and right trying to keep this tough fuck from getting off another shot.

A loud click filled my ears as a voice snorted, "Assaulting an officer of the law is a crime in this country." The cold barrel was pressed against the back of my neck, "Now place your hands on the back of your head nice and slow."

This day was getting worse by the minute and it seemed to me that I just might not survive the day let alone avenge my lost loves murder. "And a cop beating my ass is just over looked." I snorted.

The cuffs clicked around my wrists as he muttered, "I didn't see any police brutality, I only saw a known violent offender attacking a respected member of the law enforcement community after an interview." He placed a knee right in the middle of my back yanking on the cuffs almost forcing girlish screams to explode from my lips. "Charlie, you OK? This the guy that killed your little girl?"

Sergeant anal muttered, "That's exactly what I am going to beat out of him." A series of punches smashed into my stomach driving all the air from lungs and making my whole-body tremble. My body wanted to fold over yet I was being torn backwards by the guy behind me. "I am fine. He took a cheap shot and knocked me in the balls. Damn punk ass can't take a punch and took a short cut." A long series of punches followed, then I fell to the pavement and just laid there in a pool of spit and blood.

"Do you want to bust him?"

"No, he will be better use outside a cell. I think if he didn't kill her, he saw who did." A foot smashed into my face as he screamed, "And I want him to tell me who it was. Arthur or somebody else, this guy saw him and he is going to give him to me."

As the cuffs were taken off he knelt down whispering, "This can go down two ways. Either you prove that it was Arthur or somebody else or I am going to blame you. Do you want to be the one that I blame for killing my little girl?" I couldn't respond. My body was weak and felt broken so the best I could do was wheeze. "I will be looking you up again. Don't disappoint me because you really don't want every man with a badge thinking that you killed one of our own. Do you?" They both put the boots to me. Again, and again they pounded on me like I was a drum and they wanted to make sure they didn't miss a beat. "We will see you later Ashley. You better have something to give or today will seem like a fond memory. There were worse things than death. Let's just let you think about that. You are the artistic type, so be creative." That was all he said as they laughed leaving me laying on the dirty pavement.

CHAPTER 10 – BRUNO

Arthur was sitting in the interrogation room for a little over two hours now. Most people think that the interrogation is hardest on the suspects, but I always find the waiting to be unbearable. Maybe it's adrenaline or just the fact sometimes you just want to break him before he decided to call a lawyer and they tell him to shut up. Silence might make him look guilty, but in the eyes of the law it's not enough. In the eyes of the law it's never enough. That damn silence I mean. We did the usual steps, turning up the heat and just letting his imagination take over, then we waited. I hate waiting.

Logan muttered, "Are we going to start anytime soon? I truly don't think Arthur will wait all day," as he fidgeted around. "Besides unlike some people, I actually have a social life and don't want to waste my whole night here with you."

"We don't need him to wait all day. We just need him get nervous. Really nervous." It was true the more nervous we could make a man the easier it was to break them. In a few rare cases when they were innocent of one crime they ended up confessing to another. Those cases were very rare and I had this feeling Arthur was about to tell us more than even he knew. He was in the right age group to be our guy. A hell of a lot closer than the Ashley kid.

Logan sat in the chair beside me, "Well I am getting really

nervous."

Of course, he was getting nervous. Every case, in his eyes, was the big one that was going to make his career. Every snot nosed rookie that came through these doors was like that. It wasn't a bad thing because most worked hard, but Logan was different than most. He had all the makings of a great cop but was also lazy and loved to jump to conclusions when he should be examining the evidence. They can't teach experience in school. That needs to be learned over time. I guess it was time to give the kid experience. "Do you remember the questions that I told you we needed to go through?"

"Yes, I got it all firmly planted in my mind." He paused for a minute, "Do you think I am ready for this? Look at the mess that Harold did with the Ashley kid."

It wasn't Harold that screwed up that interview. It was sloppiness on my part and stupidity on Charlie's part. He broke protocol in so many ways that we would be attending seminars on professional conduct, police protocol and a shit load of other programs that would probably never end. Charlie was escorted out of the building and placed on suspension for two weeks. Suspensions were not that common, but not unheard of. Being escorted out of the building, now that was something new even to me. "Harold didn't screw up the interview that was all Charlie."

Holding his hands up Logan leaned in, "Hey I thought you and Charlie went way back. You know partners, friends and shit like that."

It was time to school the kid. Maybe it was time to drop the TV stereotype of taking care of our own rather than enforcing the law. Not that I am not loyal to my brothers in arms, but there are lines that you just don't cross and stupidity is one of them. "We are friends. We have been friends for a very long time."

"And you protect him because of it, right?"

"I have been protecting him for a long time now. Charlie loses his temper and Bruno sorts the crap out. The day he got promoted over me was the happiest day of my life. So, ask yourself why I would be so happy that my friend got the top spot and I was left behind with the rookies like you?" This probably was the first-time Logan ever saw me as more than a beat cop bumped up to homicide. It might even be the first time that I ever admitted the top spot was where I wanted to be when I first signed up. Nobody gets a badge and thinks yes this is all I want.

After some thought, with a confused look on his face, Logan blurted out, "We all thought that you just liked homicide."

Rolling my eyes, I muttered, "Hell yes that is the dream. Work harder and longer hours for less. I am living the dream."

Smiling Logan asked, "Then why? Why would you be happy that you were bypassed and he got it?"

Pulling my badge out, I slid it across the desk and said, "Because I love that badge. To be a good cop the integrity of that badge must always come first."

"So, you think Charlie is a bad cop!"

"You ever say that again and I will bust your chops kid. Charlie is not a bad man or cop. He just grew blind with heart break and rage and forgot what carrying that little piece of metal means."

"So basically, you got tired of babysitting him?"

"Not exactly. I might get tired of babysitting you, but me and Charlie got history."

Logan leaned back crossed his arms and whispered, "So I guess I am going to be schooled."

"Better you learn it now than in front of a review board." It must have been the first-time Logan really thought of the consequences that Charlie was going to face for man handling the kid. The first time that it occurred to him that none of us were above the law. Not even Charlie.

"Ok professor Norcross, I am all ears."

All ears weren't just a figure of speech with Logan. He looked like his head hadn't grown big enough to support those puppies and a strong enough wind would turn him into a glider. "So, listen. I am going to give you a little history lesson about why we have protocol." Logan looked cocky enough leaning back in his chair, but I think he was listening. "How many innocent men do you think have been railroaded into prison because of bad confessions? I mean historically."

"I really don't know, but when they pop up from time to time, it is embarrassing for all cops. It's just bad press."

"That it is. In the 1920's right up to the 1950s it might not have been publicized, but shit like that happened. Most times the cops involved thought that they had their man and used any means necessary. If they were guilty, we always thought so be it, but when they were innocent, my god when they were innocent. Kid goes to Bloodvien prison with a lifetime sentence and suddenly a decade later the real killer confesses and we realize that we ruined the kid's life. That is where protocol comes in. Charlie probably could have beat a confession out of the Truelove kid, but that doesn't mean he is the guilty party. It's bad enough when we follow the evidence and it leads to convicting an innocent man, let alone using brutality to get it."

Logan had that this 'I am so smart' look on his face as he chirped, "Do you really think Ashley Truelove being locked away from the general public is a bad thing? Really?"

"Are you a judge or a cop?"

His lip puckered as he pouted, "Yes I know our job is only to enforce the law and investigate the crimes not to judge innocence or guilt. That is the judges job."

I slapped my hands on my knee, "Yes that is it exactly, but there is one thing that everybody seems to miss in cases like this. If Charlie beats a false confession out of Ashley Truelove, he not only locks up the wrong guy, but the case dies. It gets marked as solved and five years later the guilty bastard that did the crime does it all over again. Another father loses a daughter, everybody lowers their head and says well the guy confessed. Why would you confess to a crime that you didn't commit? That also leads to lawyers questioning other cases that had solid evidence because of one bad confession. It just locks up the gears of justice. Plus, it screws the public image."

"Yes, I get that."

"Plus, there is one thing nobody thinks about."

Logan seemed intently interested now. "What's that?"

"Public faith in the police force. Let me give you an example, ok?" Logan nodded and waited. "Say a cop shoots and kills an innocent man by accident. It's a horrible thing, but accidents happen. If it's a rare event the public screams about it, then they slowly forgive and forget it. It sounds horrible and it is, but its life. Now say we have one hundred hot heads who accidentally on purpose shoot an innocent man thinking that they are guilty because of their past or they think that law doesn't work or even worse, they just want their own justice. The general public starts to remember and never forgives. That is why we have protocol and why I was happy that Charlie was given a desk rather than a squad car."

"Intense," was the only word he muttered as he leaned back further in his chair. "I never realized how much one pissed off Sergeant could screw things up."

Not wanting to leave the impression that Charlie was an absolute monster, I added, "We all have the potential to screw things up if we forget the value of the badge."

"Bruno, have you killed anyone? I mean shot an innocent person while going after a suspect?"

Everybody wonders about their first kill. What will they feel like afterwards? Will there be a face that haunts them endlessly or will it end their career? It happens. Suddenly you can't sleep at night or when you do there is a face staring back at you in your dreams or you tremble with the mere thought of carrying a gun. I don't know the numbers exactly, people are people. Some do it and it never seems to affect them and others, it breaks them like a dried twig. I guess it's just human nature. "Luckily I have never had to kill anyone on the job. I once had to shoot a dude in the leg, but that's it."

"Charlie?"

"Listen we don't talk about that. It isn't something that anyone should discuss." It was an unspoken code. The only person you talk about on the job killings with was your shrink.

He was the only one and we never discussed such things openly. Charlie never mentioned what happened in that alley. Not really. He had his version of the truth and we backed him up 100%, but it was always just his version of the truth. He said it looked like the kid had a gun and he defended himself. I always wondered why he didn't aim for the shoulder, but I wasn't there. I didn't feel the fear or the excitement.

I opened my desk drawer and pulled out my little gun safe. It was one of those small little ones with the six-digit push button locks. I opened it and took my gun out of the holster. Slowly I removed the clip and unchambered the extra shell then placed it into the case. I didn't have a spare stashed away like you see on TV. I didn't really see the point of a second since generally if the first failed me, in my eyes, I was already unconscious, screwed beyond hope or dead. That is just theory though since I have never actually lost my gun.

Logan bellowed, "You actually lock yours up when you go into the interrogation room?"

Rookie statement. I really didn't know how else to put it. If you don't bring it, they can't take it from you and use it. It was protocol and thanks to a biker named Kevin Tracy I met in my rookie year, it's a lesson I would never forget. It only takes a second for a desperate man who thinks he has nothing to lose to change the world forever. "If I don't bring it nobody can take it."

"I am not a complete idiot. I don't bring my gun into the room. I just slip it into my top desk drawer or locker."

"You are an idiot. Lock it up." The way he upholstered his gun and slowly unchambered the bullets then dropped it into the case reminded me of a child that just got caught stealing cookies, but he needed to learn this lesson. At least it was better from me then from experience. Learning to much from experience can ruin a career. His has a promising career.

"Don't forget to grab a bottle of water," I said. "We need him to see you as the friendly face of the law and it all starts by him thinking you are trying to comfort him from any discomfort. Don't forget to apologize for the delay and blame me. Make sure he sees me as the tyrant and you as his savior."

Logan smiled, "I am a rookie here in homicide, but I have done my fair share of interviews. When I am done, he will think that he just had his first bromance."

I watched Logan head over to the interview room with the folders that we had of paper work that I had selected. There was a lot of stuff on Rosie's hard drive. The IT geek said that it would take at least two days to scower through all the emails, chats and pics, not to mention her social media profiles. As he put it, her online sex life would make a porn star blush and something told me I should believe him. I guessed that he knew a lot about porn. No girlfriend or life, just the internet and all the temptations that come with it. The true question though wasn't really the kind of pictures she posted or what naughty comments she might say or share. The real question was why she did it and how exactly it related to her death.

I made my way into the interview room three minutes or so behind Logan. He had a friendly face and could quickly build a rapport with Arthur. They both seemed to be trust fund kids or at least both came from one of those gated type communities designed to keep white trash out. I was the white trash type so it was best to let them have their little bonding time. I stood in front of the door and watched them through the little window. By the way they were casually talking they were definitely becoming quick friends just like I wanted.

Opening the door, I heard Arthur's high-pitched bellow, "That Ashley guy is an absolute menace. Did you see the way that he came at me when I was being lead here? He is the craziest bastard I have ever met and I would not be surprised if he killed Rosie. His obsession with her knew no bounds."

Logan was sitting in the chair across from him, "I looked over his file and we understand what you mean. He was picked up countless times for harassing her. What do mean no bounds? Did he ever actually threaten Miss O'Donnell either verbally or through other means?"

Arthur looked pretty banged up with a swollen eye and bruises along the side of his face. I expected that's because

Ashley had given him a small beating the night before and of course he would see only the monster that stalked her. I do think though that Ashley's mommy issues would have seen him fight and protect her if he hadn't been locked up here when it happened. She might even be alive and the monster I have been chasing might have ended up in the morgue instead.

"What do I mean no bounds?" Pointing to his face he snapped, "Look at my face. Do normal people just walk up and sucker punch you when you are on a date?" It was at this point that he saw me for the first time and his rage simmered. That was the good thing about being the bad cop. He was looking to Logan for support. A friend in his time of need.

Logan was playing his part like he deserved a Gemini Award. "Yes, I remember it took four of us to control him and we still struggled."

Slamming his hand down, "That's it exactly. Four trained cops could barely contain him." Pointing at his face he snapped, "I was luckily this was all I got last night. He just attacked for no reason."

His fingers were twitching and he refused to look at me. Nervous Nelly I thought and we were just getting started. Logan added, "So did he ever threaten Miss O'Donnell to your knowledge?"

"Who knows what goes through a maniac's mind? Did he threaten her? I don't know, but obviously he could do it. Look at what he did to me. I did nothing to provoke this. "

Logan immediately chirped, "Yes I can see. It must be painful."

Arthur blurted out, "The bastard broke my nose so you can bet your ass it hurts. I am thinking of suing his ass. It's going to cost me a small fortune in dentist bills before I am done. That is what I am going to do as soon as we are done. Call my damn lawyer."

"Did anyone else happen to threaten Miss O'Donnell to your knowledge?"

Shrugging Arthur stuttered out, "I am sure many people threatened her. You know a woman like that doesn't make friends."

That comment was the one I had been waiting for. The one that we all knew the pompous ass would throw out there and it was Logan's cue to turn the tables. My role was to be just the bystander and Logan's was to become the watch dog. "What exactly do you mean a woman like that?"

Running his hand across his mouth he faintly muttered, "Well you know the type, the kind that thinks she can fuck her way into marriage and happiness."

Slamming his hand on the table, Logan's whole face went cold as he yelled, "I don't think I heard you correctly. Did you say fuck her way into marriage?"

Arthur snapped back hanging his head low. "Yes, that is exactly what I said. Look at her life? Posts erotic pictures and video's here and there. She gets off on what strange men say about her body. The more they say, the more erotic the pictures are. I couldn't have been the only one." Rubbing his chin, he muttered, "Besides I am not violent like that Ashley character and she had this guy that she used to run to for advice. Every god damn time I did something wrong she would run to her Mister Brown like a bitch."

That name Brown popped up again. The computer geeks were still going through her system and online life taking special interest in him. So far, the only picture we found was of some green smiling avatar thing, but the computer geeks were certain that in one way or another this green picture resembled what Mister Brown looked like. It was something to do with it being a custom made little picture and human nature. You know shit like that. One of them even joked that he could be my twin if I had a brother. Either way, our guys were on that like flies to shit. Our guys would track the bastard down.

Logan took out a piece of paper and slid it across the table stating, "Can you read that to me?" Wide eyed Arthur's lips quivered as he slammed his fist on the table again, "Should I read it to you?" Logan asked looking innocent.

Holding his hands up he muttered, "Now you have to understand the context of that message." Trying to move back he added, "We were struggling then, but we fixed things."

"I think the context is pretty obvious." Pulling the paper towards himself Logan pointed to a highlighted section, "If you ever contact my wife and friends again, I will destroy you." Pulling out another page of paper, "And here we have a collection of emails that you sent her forwarded to your wife, your mother and various other family members." Leaning forward he whispered, "And how did that make you feel? How can you destroy her?"

"I didn't mean kill her. I am not a violent man."

Pulling yet another sheet of paper from the folder Logan added, "You mean nothing that you have been convicted of. It seems that you were investigated twice for abusing your girlfriends."

"Accused, not convicted. There is a giant difference and that was over twenty years ago. We all made mistakes when we were in our teens."

Staring straight at me, Logan asked, "I never hit a woman in my teens. My parents raised me to be a man. How about you Bruno? Have you ever hit a woman?"

I was surprised that he brought me into it. I was supposed to just observe, but I figured I would run with it. "No, I have never hit a woman. Not even on the ass and I am pretty sure that if you look, there is a video of him beating her. She is tied up and begging him to stop."

Flipping through the pages Logan stopped, "Yes that looks rather violent to me."

"Oh, come on. It was foreplay."

His idea of foreplay wasn't anything I had ever seen. It was a man living out all the fantasies and fetishes that he had seen only in porn and online video clips. It wasn't really a bad thing since fantasies are only the first step to reality. Yet, some fantasies should never leave your head. Something's aren't meant to be reality.

"So, is this video the reason Ashley smashed in your face? Did her cries of pain turn you on? Has your wife seen just how twisted her husband is?"

Arthur stood up and snapped, "This interview is over! I came to clear my name and help solve her murder, not have my name dragged through the gutter. If you have any more questions you can contact my lawyer." We watched him storm out of the room and almost run through the little hallway. There wasn't really anything we could do since we had no grounds to hold him on other than circumstantial evidence and a really bad feeling.

Logan watched him run away and looked over at me, "And things were just getting interesting. I am not sure if he did it, but I am damn sure that he has something to hide." He was right about that. Most of us do, but something told me Arthur Andersen's secrets were a lot more interesting than mine.

CHAPTER 11 – BROWN

Arthur reacted better than even I expected. He might as well have pasted a sign on his forehead stating 'I am guilty' and that is exactly what I needed. He would call his high-priced lawyer and they would try and tie things up in the courts for as long as possible, but it was inevitable. His family and professional life were scared beyond repair if not completely ruined. Now he was going to end up at Bloodvien prison or at least go broke trying to stay out of it. Either way, I helped karma balance the books. That was the thing about karma, I believe it follows us through life, but it's a slow process and sometimes you need to influence the time frame. The outcome is a constant, but why wait decades when a few emails planted here and a few pictures left there can speed things up.

Bruno might be a problem though. There was a twinkle of interest in his eyes when it came to my name. As soon as Arthur stormed away he went right to his desk and called the Brainiac's in IT to grab everything they could about me. I went from just a passing interest to his new obsession. He bypassed Lee going straight to me and Arthur. Luckily, I had already prepared for this. I was untraceable and basically untouchable. Bruno would find tidbits about me, but he would never find me again. I wasn't happy about him finding my name in amongst the evidence, but there were safe guards in place.

You always needed safe guards, especially when you had a bloodhound on your ass.

I wanted to sneak away and look into the crime scene. Not actually enter it but see who was still there and what they were doing. I enjoy watching them examine every little piece trying to fit the evidence together. Most of the guys involved were trained by me. You know what they say, teach them everything they know, but not everything you know. I just had one last thing to do before I went. I needed to clean up a couple of things just to make sure Bruno couldn't catch my scent. I was meant to observe the investigation not become part of it and definitely not a prime suspect in it.

I opened my desk drawer and removed the small tablet and spare cell phone from it. I used both to communicate with Rosie. You can't imagine the number of hours I wasted trying to talk her up when all the time she just ignored my advice and experience. She was the most frustrating creature I had ever met. Until I met Rosie I thought Callie was the most childish woman in the world with her temper tantrums and overly emotional pity parties, but Rosie was far worse. I said to let it go and move on yet, she still chased down his family. I really thought that Ashley was going to try and kill Arthur, which was exciting because if he had, I would have gotten a chance to see my future protégé in action. An opportunity to see Ashley hunt down a true waste of life like Arthur. Yes, that would have been very interesting, but that boy spends too much time on the wrong side of the bars. There is only so much I can do to save him. If it weren't for me, he would already be behind bars for the long haul.

There is one great thing about having a badge. It's the evidence locker. Anything you can think of comes in, gets processed, used at trial and conveniently filed away to be forgotten. Nobody ever grabs the high-ticket items like Rolex's or diamond rings because those will always be missed. The number crunchers look for those when they inventory shit, but the small things are never missed. In my case, it's a drug dealers cell phone that keeps getting paid month after month even though he is doing a dime in Bloodvien and a little seven-inch tablet. My communication to the outside world and neither lead back to me. Carefully I cleaned the tablet then the phone. I then skillfully slipped them into a bag. This is the interesting part. Wipe away my prints and then if need be, let them be found by the bloodhound chasing you. Blood hounds like Bruno can be misled if you change the scent. They get confused and follow blindly.

I made my way to the locker room. This time of day its always empty so it was easy for me to leave a little gift for Charlie, plus he was predictable. The man started out with this locker on his very first day when he was just writing tickets and giving drug seminars at the local high school and refused to change it. I know Charlie better than most. I know his life inside and out and that includes his combination. Hell, he figures nobody would ever steal from him, plus he doesn't have anything valuable inside unless you consider used gym clothes and a copy of "The Adventures of Tom Sawyer" valuable. I slipped the tablet onto the top shelf and slowly closed the door. That blood hound would eventually stumble across it if he managed to catch my scent. He would sniff around until he came across it then he would ponder its meaning. There is nothing I like more than watching a blood hound trying to decide if he should howl or not.

I was making my way out of the station fairly confident that if plan A failed plan B would be a slam dunk. I had a plan C, but it was blood and brutal and I hated getting my hands dirty unless there was no other option. I preferred saving people through skill and persuasion. So far, I had an 80% success rate which isn't that bad when you consider I am rebuilding broken souls. It's a challenge and I might not have the sheer numbers that the church has, but I am sure my success rate of converts would make any priest envious.

I was cutting through the alley towards the back of the restaurant that sat behind the station when I heard something. I had a little apartment above the Wong's. Really close to work and nobody really ever bothers me. I can still catch the Wi-Fi and who really looks for anybody around a cop shop? It's a crappy little one bedroom and all you can smell is fried chicken, but it's convenient. One of my neighbors, who obviously didn't know what I did for a living, actually had a Canada wide warrant for arrest. He lived there for almost five years and even said good morning to the boys in blue every day. If it weren't for the fact he was dating one of my broken souls, I never would have called on him. That's how I discovered Logan. My first call lead to his first real arrest. His is like a legacy. His daddy and granddaddy both carried a badge. I truly think that I am the reason he high jumped through the ranks rather then slowly climbed the ladder. It helps him and gives me an ally even if he doesn't know that he joined team Brown.

I was half way through the alley when I heard a high-pitched whistle and an even louder grunt. Scanning the alley, I found a body lying there beside the dumpster. Obviously, he didn't crawl there by his own means since he was stashed out of sight. This probably wasn't the place that you'd expect a mugging to go down since we are right beside the station, but now that I think about it, it's the perfect place to run into criminal types. They are even driven to the front door and told to go away. This alley is on the way and there's a bank, church and investment firm close by. The perfect victims and most have cash to spare. Whoever actually worries about a crime happening right beside the cop shop? Well I did that's why I have my apartment close to here.

I walked over and saw slow movement from the body on the ground. Damn this guy had his ass handed to him. I mean there isn't a pool of blood around him, but a whole damn lake. Had to be some kind of mafia thing. You know don't testify or we will really hurt you next time. Perhaps a pay up or else we take out yours knees if we gotta come back. I must admit, I am not one to turn to violence first unless there isn't any other way, but I like seeing the end results. It's a testament to just how tough the human body is and just how animalistic men can be. The after affects always stand out.

I took out my little pocket flash light and looked him over. There was so much blood that I barely recognized him. It was that Ashley kid and he was worked over something well. Here was a prime example of police brutality. Couldn't have been Bruno or Logan because they were upstairs with Arthur. Well I assumed at that time, but they hung out for an hour discussing the case. That leaves Arthur, but I am fairly certain that I would be seeing his sorry ass laying here if he encountered Ashley. Quite the mystery.

He looked up, "So are you here to finish what your Sargent friend Charlie started?" I couldn't help, but smile looking at him. Defiant right the end. That boy could survive many things that would break most normal men. "Get that light out of my eyes."

Moving the light over to the side I said, "Ah poor Ashley had his ass handed to him and all he did was love a girl ... A little too much." The poor kid really took a beaten, but I had to admire his spunk. Most kids would be lying there crying like a little girl with a scraped knee, but the kid was already staggering to get to his feet.

"Fuck you and your friend."

Defiant I liked but being rude was uncalled for. That would be something I would need to break him of as time went on. He didn't realize it yet, but he was going to assist me and eventually replace me in my quest. He had potential and the rest I could teach him. "He isn't my friend really. If you want though, I could go up and call him to come back down. I am sure that he'd love to talk some more." Charlie wasn't a good cop. Maybe a decade ago, but those days were long behind him. He sure as hell worked the kid over. I am sure that if I didn't redirect Charlie's rage he would end up making the kid eat through a straw.

"Yes, go up and tell your friend to come back down so we can finish our conversation. Only this time tell him to leave his friend behind. I have a lot I want to tell him."

Yes, I am sure the kid would fight on to the very end and given the proper circumstances, the kid might beat him, but I am certain Charlie would kill him and not have a second thought about it. That wasn't part of my plans for either of them. No, I couldn't let them face off or my planning was all for nothing. Besides Ashley wouldn't be of any use if he was locked back in a cell or even worse, six feet under. I couldn't let him get distracted. At least not yet. "Let me take care of Charlie and don't forget Rosie. I need you to keep catching her killer firmly in your mind."

"Yes, that's it. I know how it works. You boys take care of your own."

Yes, most times we took care of our own. If it weren't for Bruno, Charlie would have seen the inside of cell years ago. Bruno was like a linebacker, always protecting him, but his protection was about to stop. "No, I am not protecting Charlie. I have a murderer to catch."

Looking up he muttered, "And just like the rest, you think I can lead you right to him."

"Yes," that was all I needed to say. Of course, Ashley had no idea that nobody needed him to lead the way to solve this case because I had already left crumbs guiding them. "If you love her, you will leave Charlie to me."

"Fuck you. I loved her more than you will ever know." I had no doubts about that, but I needed him to follow the path I designed, not the one he wanted to follow.

"Then man up and prove it." It was the words 'man up' that caught his attention. Challenge a man's love for a woman then his manhood and he will defy you on principal.

He was staggering to his feet mumbling, "Just get out of my way and I will take them all out."

"I can't do that. I can't exactly enforce the law if I let you break it." It sounded realistic. Ashley needed to be motivated. He was too important to my cause right now. He was part of my plan B.

"You are such a saint," he snapped sarcastically. "Someday there will be a statue of you in the town square for birds to shit on."

"Yes, probably or maybe even a made for TV movie. You

know eventually I am going to be famous. I will be studied and examined by the best."

Ashley smiled, "Yes me too. The name of the movie will be, 'The boy that loved too much'."

I hate it when people steal my comments. It's like stealing your identity. "So, do I call 911?"

"Screw you. They ask too many questions. It's not like they will believe me over one of your boys in blue."

That was obvious, plus with Charlie's position and Ashley's record, he would not stand a chance. Also, I had no intentions of calling anyone. I just needed to distract him enough to strike. "OK let me take you home. It will be safer that way."

"I would rather crawl all the way home," he said as he tried to pull himself up to his feet. I waited until he was almost all the way up when I drilled him right in the face. He fell back and just laid there. There is one thing about good old brass knuckles. It only takes one well-placed punch. The only issue now was stashing him in the shadows until I could drive over and fetch him. I could not let anyone find my protégé or else I might lose him.

Twenty minutes later Ashley was laying in the back seat as I smuggled his broken body through the city. The city of Windsor has these unique lanes that run behind the houses. It's not exactly a road, but you can sneak along the back of the houses unnoticed. That's my thing. I am always there in plain sight, but blend in enough that nobody really notices me. I pulled in along the back by Ashley's apartment. It wasn't anything unique for the area. Big brick houses divided into small one-bedroom closets they call apartments. Of course, like everything about him, his apartment was chosen because of his obsession with Rosie. He had the third floor and a window that looked straight towards Rosie's apartment. You had to respect the guy's dedication. Most people don't truly understand that if you can redirect obsession elsewhere to something more positive you can make something special.

Ashley was a damn lot heavier than he looked or maybe I should have spent more time at the gym rather than sweet talking broken souls. It's the price I pay for having a kind heart. That's life though. We all pay a price no matter how great the cause. Anyway, I had him over my shoulder struggling to climb the narrow metal stairs that lead up to his place. It was typical of student housing. I guess nobody ever thought that these steps would be used to carry a body. Usually it's cases of beer and pizza. Gasping for air, the idea of just grabbing him by the feet all the way up crossed my mind, but I think the kid had enough of a pounding today. Besides I think being the type of guy he was, his mother must have dropped him on his head a lot as a child. I probably shouldn't risk dragging his ass up and allowing his head to snap along each step as I went. Easier on me, but he'd wouldn't be a lot of use to me if he couldn't spell his name afterwards. I finally made to the door and almost dropped him over the side. It probably wouldn't have killed him, but I am certain that he would have broken something that was important.

I opened the door and it was like stepping into a trailer park. Faded paneling on the walls and wood framed windows that didn't close properly. Ugly brown carpet rolled along the floor with an ugly old couch that doubled as a bed. The smallest damn place I had ever seen. I thought my place was a dump, but his made mine look giant. I dropped him on the couch and looked around the place. There wasn't really a lot of places to stash anything and I needed to find a good place. I searched the room looking for the perfect place. After going through the whole place, I finally decided on the fridge. It's not the best place, but how often do we look behind the fridge unless we are looking for something that we know had to be on top of it? I took the drug dealers cell out of my bag and slipped it behind the fridge. It was all part of my plan B. Ashley was the one I wanted for my protégé, but we weren't friends. If things got desperate, he would have to be sacrificed.

Right in front of the window stood a wooden chair and a telescope. Not one of those $100-dollar ones you pick at the chain stores, but the high-end ones that star gazers and stalkers get. You know where the picture is so clear you can see a pimple one a woman's nose. Damn this kid took love seriously. I looked through it towards Rosie's apartment. There was Arthur's Volvo parked along the side, out of view. Yes, I am sure there was something incriminating that he didn't want found. That wasn't exactly part of my plan A but was a welcome surprise.

The wall was covered with pictures. It was like an alter to the goddess Rosie. Image after image plastered on the wall. Even I had to admit that Rosie was a beautiful woman with a body to die for. I wouldn't be the one to die for her, but I had a list. I would never put Ashley on my list, but I know he'd force himself on it regardless. He needed to be on such a list. In the corner, I found pictures of Arthur and a few unknown individuals. He was trusted by Rosie, like I was, otherwise he would have known that there was nothing in her eyes. No if he only knew the truth. Rosie was searching for marriage. For family. She hadn't grown up in a happy home so she desperately tried to find it. Her identity as a woman was so twisted that she was certain saying yes to anything would keep a man. That's how Arthur got her. He offered her a dream even if he never intended to give it to her.

There was something that never occurred to me. Right there in the corner was a picture of me standing next to my car. Luckily in the printed picture you could not see my face clearly, but the boys in the lab would be able to blow it up. The boys would surely be able to identify me. A man in my position couldn't afford to be identified. Obviously, Ashley hadn't blown the picture up or he would have attached it to me. This was not part of my plan. I had to ponder this. I didn't want to kill Ashley, but I couldn't afford to be brought deeper into the case.

I went to the make shift kitchen finding a white plastic garbage can. Generally, I preferred metal ones, but I was straying from the plan. I walked over to the wall yanking off everything. I know this was going to make Ashley bat shit crazy, but it had to be done. It was the food chain and Brown was always at the top. When the wall was, empty I went through his cupboards endlessly searching for something flammable. Finally, I came across a can of barbecue fluid. Why the hell a guy that doesn't have a barbecue needs barbecue fluid is beyond me, but I needed it. The little desk that sat at the other window had two laptops sitting on top. I grabbed both and headed towards the door. It was time for me to make my escape.

I pulled a disposable cell phone from my pocket and dialed Logan's cell. He answered in a slow murmur, "Logan here."

"There is someone breaking into your crime scene right now."

"What?"

I stated, "I just saw Arthur what's his name breaking into that murdered girl's apartment." Hanging up the phone I slipped it into my pocket. I poured the fluid into the can and dropped a match into it. The flames exploded and jumped up. Ashley's obsession and evidence against me vanished in a few seconds. My plan was safe and everything would proceed as I wanted.

I dropped the laptops into the backseat of the car and jumped into it. As I drove through the back lane I stopped and waited with the lights turned off. It only took five minutes for Arthur to be escorted out of the building. Arthur was now pushing himself into my plan and he didn't even realize it.

CHAPTER 12 – BRUNO

I just laid there listening to the hum of traffic passing by through the open window. The collection of images from over a decade of death had haunted my dreams again last night. This time was worse than any of the others. Every new grizzly image blended into those that already call to me until they become one. If being haunted by the dead faces of strangers isn't enough, there are the shivers and shakes that come with them. A cop with shaky hands is like a pilot that is afraid to fly or a song writer that can't sing. It is something that you just don't talk about. I reached over grabbing my bottle of water and took a sip. Some turn to self-medication, but I find the harder stuff gives the dead voices and the images a louder voice and become too hard to handle without letting them speak more.

"Bruno," a voice broke through the silence causing my heart to explode in my chest. My first thought was to run to the locked box, but it was across the room and out of reach. Everybody thinks that cops sleep with a gun under their pillow, that does happen on TV and I assume in a few rare cases, but in my experience, sleep and guns don't mix. If they did, you would hear a lot more bad headlines in the newspaper and there would be a lot more widows. "We need to talk."

Sitting in the chair across from the bed was a figure. I

couldn't see his face, but I didn't need to. It was Charlie. Taking a deep breath, I waited until my pulse slowed before answering. "How long have you been there just watching me sleep?" The idea of him watching me sleep was creepy as hell especially in his current state of mind.

Charlie just sat there motionless. "How long have you been yelling out the names of the victims from the crimes that we couldn't solve? You were calling out their names for a while now." Even in the darkness I could tell that his head dropped as he said, "You called out to Callie, you told her to run. I don't dream of her anymore like I used to."

"Something's you just can't forget." It's a fact of life. Most people get their happy memories. Their first kiss or the first time they get to slide their hand under a young woman's bra. I don't get those anymore. I only see lost possibilities. "How long have you been watching me sleep? Its creepy as hell."

Charlie whispered, "Not that long. They brought Arthur in last night, but nobody will tell me anything."

"I know. They called and I told them to let him sit there overnight. " They called about 1 AM, but I was damn exhausted. It seemed lately that I could never get enough sleep no matter how hard I tried. I couldn't understand it because I was the guy who could grab four hours of solid shut eye and maybe steal a nap in the afternoon and I was ready to go. Mind you, I was running out of steam and those days seemed to just suddenly vanish. "You do realize you could have called or rang the doorbell?"

"I thought it was best that nobody see me come in. Do you think this Arthur guy killed Callie?"

That was the question that had haunted Charlie for too long now. Who killed daddy's little girl? Callie was another victim who died a horrible death. She wasn't just murdered but tortured in her last hours. It wasn't quite the same as with Rosie though. No, her death was more personal. She knew her killer much like Rosie because she had let him into her room. They didn't have sexual intercourse, but the way he went about it was very intimate. Too intimate if you ask me. He went about the same ritual but didn't leave her naked body in the tub to be just found by anyone. He covered her up with a shower curtain. That was the first time we found a bloody kiss on a victim's cheek. Of course, that also asked another important question, was this his first murder or did he change his ritual?

Now that it was happening again, Charlie was compelled to finish this. To kill the man that killed his only daughter. One way or another, if Arthur was proven guilty he would never see the inside of a cell. Charlie was beyond looking for legal justice. He was after revenge and no matter how I tried to look it, I understood it. Watching Callie grow up from a pigtailed little girl that used to ask me to join her and her daddy playing princess to a woman who called me asking for my help so that daddy wouldn't find out she was caught drinking under age made me partial.

Obviously, they weren't letting him back in the station so I was his only connection to the case. Give him nothing and he was going to assume the worst which, in his present state, would amount to murder. Give him too much and he would kill someone. He was certainly screwing me on this one. "Arthur suits the profile a lot better than the Lee kid, but I am still on the fence."

"Bruno, you can't drag your feet on this one. You owe me and I need this."

That is the problem with favors. Everybody says don't worry about it until they decide that they want to collect. Charlie has been collecting on my favor for so long now that at times I wish that he had just let me die. "What do you want me to do? Do I just tell you what you want to hear or actually solve the crime?"

Charlie stood up and walked to the window but stayed silent. I hadn't noticed before that he has his .45 in his hand. He took it from a kid a long time ago and never turned it in. Back then he always gave a warning and second chance. He truly believed that changing the world started when you educated and uplifted rather than terrorize and intimidate.

Seeing that gun in his hand reminded me just how much he had changed. "Bruno, I need this. I have already lost everything and I just want justice."

"Your justice or mine?"

"It doesn't matter Bruno. I simply want to kill the man that tortured my baby. Call it revenge, justice or anything you want to. Just decide beyond a shadow of a doubt if Ashley Truelove or Arthur Andersen did it and walk away. That is all you have to do, walk away and never look back."

I was trying to decide which was worse, the monster I was chasing or the one that was standing in front of me now. "Do you think I could just give you the name and turn my back on justice?"

Waving his hands around he muttered, "I saved your ass and you owe me. You owe me big time."

"Put that gun down. The last thing I want is to be a news line. Besides if you shot me, I would be missed."

Charlie snorted, "By who?" with a small grin on his face. For a split moment, he resembled the younger kinder Charlie that I used to know.

"Well I would."

Charlie burst out laughing, "Yes I bet you would and the world would cry because it could no longer enjoy your sparking personality and charm." It was nice to see Charlie being Charlie again. I know that people change, but sometimes you just need a little hope. Hope that the person you once knew and loved like family still exists when all logic says that they are gone.

"Take some personal time and let me do my job. It's way too early to properly say who is guilty and who just has really bad luck."

Charlie's face went numb. "You owe me Bruno. If you can't tell me who killed my little girl so I can get satisfaction, I will be forced to take them both out whether they are guilty or not. I wouldn't shed a tear for either of them. A stalker and a pervert won't be missed. " I watched him walk away wondering if it was a threat or a statement. I guess it really didn't matter since Charlie drew a line in the sand and we both seemed to be on a different side of it.

I stood there thinking about Kevin Tracy. A two-bit biker wanted for armed robbery and drug trafficking. Most people think it's a legend and when I tell the story I forget to tell them who the rookie was because it makes me feel better. Like most people, I don't like to brag about my flaws and failures, only my victories. When your failures amount to the bad guy getting off, or even worse, somebody dying, you stop counting them. You don't talk about them and you certainly try not to think about them.

Kevin Tracy was guilty. We had enough evidence to convict him, but I was wet under the ears. I wanted a confession to speed up the process. It was just a rookie's ambition and a fool's pride that guided me. I saw a chance to stand out and took it. The problem is that he saw a chance and took it too.

I remember looking at him sitting in the little metal chair smirking at me as he muttered, "You got nothing on me." Trying to be the bad cop I slammed my fist on the table demanding he spill, but I knew that he wouldn't. He was a career criminal so a short prison sentence meant nothing to him. As a reputable member of a local biker gang called the "Dark Wings" it was a requirement to say nothing and serve your time. You had to do a dime in Bloodvien before they even looked at you.

I tried to rough him up by slapping him around like I always imagined it to be. You know the good cop bad cop game, only I was alone and there weren't any good cops. That's when he snagged my gun from the holster and shot me in the shoulder. He had the gun on me preparing to shoot again and I knew that would be the end. The next thing I remember Kevin Tracy is lying on the floor beside me and Charlie was there, gun in hand.

It was still early when I left the house and headed to the station with Charlie and Rosie on my mind. Generally, you get a feel for people and logically you can break things down until they make sense. It's not the direction you want, but there is always a logical direction that the evidence and details lead you, but this time wasn't so easy. Arthur Andersen fit the profile and was an all-around sick fucker, but was he a killer? There was enough evidence to make him a prime suspect. More than enough to make me examine his life minute by minute, but I think Charlie wouldn't be patient enough to wait. Then there was this mysterious Mister Brown. He seemed to be a ghost. Just a name floating through the internet. Of course, I was well aware that people do that. They can't handle the real world where they see themselves as ordinary so they become someone else. Young men become older and wiser and old men become younger and wilder, while in some cases they even become women. It made me miss the good old days that was for sure.

I turned into the parking lot at the station and slowly made my way towards the doors. Usually I was excited about the process of interviewing suspects. It was like chess even though I never had the patience for the game. Everybody I had ever met, but one man had a tell and it was just a matter of twisting words and meanings until they slipped. Everybody slipped at some point. I wanted to get everything done and over as soon as possible. This time I would do the interview myself because there were going to be hard questions that had to be asked. Logan had five years in a patrol car but was still too new in homicide to successfully do the next step.

I went straight to my desk and grabbed my gun case. I was just setting my gun into it when Logan plopped down in chair beside my desk. "Don't bother, there won't be any interview today."

Pulling my gun back out I muttered, "Lawyered up?"

Logan leaned in, "Yes and he is somebody who knows somebody, plus he wasn't actually in the apartment just heading down to the storage locker." Shrugging he added, "Who knew the apartment was his?"

"So, we had to let him go."

Logan muttered, "Yep and now every interview will have his lawyer present."

That always made things just a little complicated. You can't use the same type of techniques with a lawyer present because they know the process as good as we do and always tell their client not to answer. A good lawyer is better than being innocent if you think about it really. A really good lawyer has been known to take serious jail time and turn it into probation like its magic.

Logan asked, "So what are we going to do now?"

"Haunt the little prick like a ghost."

"Ok so I guess we are pounding the pavement." He stood up and was walking away when he stopped. "Speaking of ghosts go see IT. They said that they found something scary and interesting about your ghosts IP."

"Which ghost?"

"The one that is haunting you I guess." I watched him walk away then immediately called the geeks in IT.

CHAPTER 13 – ASHLEY

When I was eight one of my mother's boyfriends caught, me stealing money from the change jar. The way he bellowed, "You little thief, I will teach you to steal from me," still terrifies me even to this day. The memory of him clamping onto my neck still haunts my dreams, both awake and asleep. He was such a brutish man and the fear made me wet myself which, just made him even more angry. He was a part time biker and a full-time construction worker who hated life and blamed the bitches bratty kid. I hated him then and if he hadn't ended up in Bloodvien, I am positive that I would be locked up and he would be in the ground. His name was Sebastian and he only knew one way to teach anybody anything and it always hurt.

The day he caught me stealing those five silver quarters, he took the strap off the wall and screamed, "Hold your hands out boy." My hands trembled, but the fear of making him angrier forced me to do it. After all the times I saw my poor mother man handled by him, I was too scared not to. He forced me to keep a steady hand even though the fear inside me said to run away. He brought the three-inch-wide strip of conveyor belt as hard as he could across my hand, but his aim was off and it twisted. I still remember the snap it made followed by the flowing blood. Shock might have killed the pain almost immediately, but the blood was still there. Even decades later the scars had begun to fade, but in my mind the blood is still there. Somethings you just can't just forget. It lives inside you long after the pain fades away. That's the memory I see when I think of poor Rosie. The scar can fade with time, but the blood is always there.

They say that you can build a tolerance for pain. That over time your nerve endings degrade and you can endure it easier. I don't believe that because I have been beaten all my life yet, laying here my whole-body burns. Each breath is like being stabbed and even the smallest task like blinking causes my whole head to pound. Those cops sure worked me over last night. To serve and protect my ass. It's more like ground and pound because they sure as hell didn't protect me. I have never liked cops, that's no secret, but now I have a few more names to add to my hit list. First, I avenge Rosie because she deserves justice, but then I chase them down. The great thing about being on the bottom is you don't need to worry about falling down or in my case stumbling.

"You ruined my life," a loud voice squeezed. I tried to open my eyes to see who was there, but my vision was blurred. It's the after affect of a good ass kicking. "Not only did you kill my plans for the future, but you actually ruined my life. You helped destroy me." I looked up trying to force my vision, but all I saw was a large outline of a man. "My life was planned. I had everything arranged and I would have had everything I wanted, but you just couldn't leave it alone could you?"

You know that inner voice that pulls out all the sarcastic stupid things that most people never say. I got one too only it spits things right out that generally get me in trouble. I blurted out, "I am a stalker so it's kind of what I do."

He screamed, "Shut up and listen. You are going to write a confession stating that you murdered Rosie. You are going to make sure the world knows that you are the monster."

My body was stiff and ached as I tried to force my body up as I responded, "There is no way in hell that I am confessing to that. I would rather have my finger nails yanked out."

He started pacing across the floor, "Oh you will. You must

admit that you did it. You have nothing to lose, but I will lose everything." He was standing over me screaming, "Don't you get it? You stole everything from me."

I was running my hands across my eyes trying to break away the pieces of caked on blood. It felt like sandpaper being ripped across my skin, but it had to be done. Usually twenty minutes in a hot shower would clear it all away, but I really don't think I was going to get the time. "I am going to be taking a lot more from you." There was no bullshitting this. I am going to kill him, the real question is was it going to be today, tomorrow or another day? The problem right now was I certainly had broken ribs and god only knows what else was broken inside me.

"Not if I kill you first," was all he said as he walked towards the other side of the room. I was still trying to pry the caked-on blood out of my eyes and kept thinking, 'thank your inner voice, you just gave him an idea'. He came to beat a confession out of me and now he is looking for ways to kill me.

As I fought to get the last pieces of grit from my eyes, I heard clanking coming at me from the other side of room. Luckily my vision was starting to clear even if my body was betraying me right now. It was the constant wheezing that scared me. All past injuries never lasted longer then a day or so, but the way my lungs felt scared me. Fluid in the lungs was a bad thing.

He placed a pen in my hand and dropped paper beside me stating, "Write what I say word for word." Pacing he stated, "I killed Rosie O'Donnell on Friday November 25. It was a crime of passion. Since I couldn't have her, I decided nobody could have her. Ashley Truelove." My god it would be the worst confession note ever, but there was no way I was going to write it. I wouldn't hurt Rosie, ever. Nothing in the world could have made me hurt her, let alone kill her. Even if I wasn't innocent for once admitting to it would let the real killer go free. No, they might call me a sicko and a killer, but never would I ever admit to hurting Rosie. Looking at the blank paper he screamed. "Write it!" Grabbing my hand, he smashed it onto the paper sending waves of pain shooting up my arms right into my chest. Guiding my hand, he screamed, "I, Ashley Truelove, killed Rosie." I was still struggling to stop my hand, but the pain was unbearable. He screamed, "Write the damn words," as he tried applying more pressure.

It's at our times of weakness that we truly wish we were at our strongest. Well I do at least. When I am hung over I promise to never drink again, when I lose a fight, I started telling myself that I will never be that cocky again and when I saw Rosie crying for the first time, I told myself I would never scare her again. It's always the same. Right now, I was trying to fight through the pain screaming through my body, wishing I was strong enough to fight him off. It was the first time that I ever thought of my darling Rosie struggling with all her might but being helpless. He was screaming at me with such hatred, "Sign the damn paper," as he slapped me across the face. My face was tingling and my eyes were throbbing the more he slapped me. The image of Rosie being beaten and tortured was growing inside me and I couldn't push it out.

He was still trying to force my hand to write what he wanted me to and my trembling hands were about to fail me. Through his clenched teeth, he screamed, "Just sign it you little prick. My life is worth more then yours and I am not going to prison over a two-bit whore."

I screamed, "She wasn't a whore," and yanked my hand free. Maybe it was rage or instinct, but somehow, I managed to drive the pen into his shoulder throwing him to the floor. "I told you that I would kill you," I screamed as I forced myself up onto my shaky legs. I was still struggling to breathe and he looked so pathetic just lying there crying. I wanted to start kicking him in the ribs, but considering how shaky my legs were, I think kicking him would have made me fall over.

He whined, "Don't kill me," as he curled up into a ball. "Just don't hurt me." Just looking at him made me want to laugh. Prison was going to be hard time for him. Really hard time if you know what I mean.

"It's too late for don't hurt me," I said. "The minute you

came after me it was too late for that." It happened so quickly that before I knew what was happening something smashed into the back of my head driving me into the floor. The last thing I remember seeing is faded blue pants and scuffed up black shoes.

In less than a twenty-four-hour period, I had been cold clocked twice, both times waking up thinking of Rosie. In a world where love is just a word easily transferred, from one smile to another when it should be timeless like the oceans, Rosie was my deepest sea. The scariest part was the idea that I would wake up feeling like I was drowning for the rest of my life. It took some time for me to get up to my feet, but when I finally made it Arthur was no where to be found. The only sign that he ever existed was a blood stain in the rug, a broken pen and a blood-stained knife. Taking a deep breath, I looked around wishing I knew exactly how much blood a person needs to lose before they bleed to death.

A knock at the door caught my attention. "Lee it's Harold."

CHAPTER 14 – BROWN

They acted like drones. The Bloodhound Bruno and his side kick Logan went from person to person asking the same questions and receiving the same answers. Rosie's online life wasn't the same as her everyday, real world life. That was the first thing I taught her. It was a hard lesson for her to learn. Maybe even the hardest lesson she would ever learn. People judge based on what they think they see. It doesn't matter if they only see bare shoulders and a head shot, they are imagining her naked tits and ass in every one that she posts. It's not always what you show, but what people imagine when it's out of focus. She assumed erotic, but she was looking cheap. The next lesson was that those sick, rude men asking to see her tits were attracted by those same pictures. It wasn't fair that men assumed that she was that kind of woman, but life isn't always fair, now is it? Of course, she never really got it. Too focused on being the bride rather than the prize. Bruno would see that at some point. He might even understand her need for belonging and approval if he looked deep enough.

Rosie was a complicated, yet she was a confused young woman to say the least. The online world and that portion of her life was soulless yet filled with such passion. Every part of it was sexual in one way or another. She saw it like an author sees his character's personalities. Purely fiction but needed to pull people into the tale that is being woven. Rosie saw the pictures and false sexual confessions to attract a mate, a lover, a partner and protector even if it led to her being used and treated like a toy by men like Arthur. She hated giving away control of her life and body to men like him yet she did it over and always expected different results. Foolish girl.

As expected, after talking to a couple of middle aged male professors, Bruno pulled out his little black book and wrote a few details that he wanted to either remember or research. Both men had characteristics that fit the profile of the type of man he was looking for. That Bloodhound would never stop searching for the man he so desperately wanted to find. You know the usual crap, middle aged male, highly intelligent, a loner and so on. They even said he sees the woman's outer beauty as insulting because of some tragic childhood event that occurred with his mother or an aunt. I am still not sure if I believe in these profilers. In my experience, seasoned cops are just as accurate. Maybe a clinical psychologist would be a bit more accurate but that was neither here nor there. For this type of case, I doubt there is a profile that would fully fit regardless. On rape cases these profilers seem to do alright, but rapists aren't as crafty as a skilled killer with a purpose. Bruno already knows that he is chasing a skilled killer. It's the purpose that confuses him.

I watched them enter the crime scene one last time. In a case like this, a cop car was parked outside twenty-four hours a day until forensics decided it was clean. Today was the day that they would walk away leaving a vacant apartment that suddenly wasn't considered prime real-estate anymore, even though it was a mere ten minutes away from the university. Murder has that effect on a place. Suddenly everyone is convinced the home is over shadowed by bad juju, a fear that is embedded in anyone who considers to live there, other than a select few who enjoy that sort of thing. It was dangerous for me to be here since Ashley could be watching the place, but I needed to see them leave. I always watched them start the investigation and walk away defeated. When you start a journey, you must see the end and that is exactly what I was doing, seeing the end.

We lingered inside the crime scene for sometime after everybody left. Logan and Bruno were probably trying to reenact it or something dramatic like that. You know try and see it visually or something like that. There had to be a few details about the crime, or Rosie, that Bruno couldn't let go of, yet couldn't decide if it was important. That Bruno is old school. It's the details that becomes evidence and the evidence solves the crimes. Thanks to Ashley, he has more evidence than I would like, but not enough to connect all the dots. He couldn't make a line out of the evidence yet. No, his dots are the ones I left behind and lead exactly where I want them to go.

Finally, they left the building, jumped into separate cars and Logan slowly drove away towards the river front. Anybody that knew Bruno at all would have realized that he was pondering the case. He would spend hours letting everything muster in his mind. It's the hound in him.

Life is always full of little unexpected moments. Some good and some bad, but they are always there. Today's unexpected moment was good old' Charlie. He didn't even wait for Bruno and Logan to go three car lengths before he slipped into traffic and followed them. He was smart enough to use a rental car though. A white little KIA that blends in is what he drove rather than his red pickup that stands out, but he didn't wait long enough before pulling out and following them. Too much emotion. Hate seems to have blinded the years of experience that he had collected being a cop. Hate does that to you. That is why I don't give in to it. Love and hate can ruin even the best plan and I always have a plan.

If Bruno didn't step up his game soon I was going to have to use plan B. Charlie was determined and that might become an issue. I knew Charlie was going to be passionate about this case, but common sense said he would leave it to Bruno. Not just because Charlie couldn't separate emotion from it, but because Bruno, the bloodhound, had the skill set to get the job done. Where as Charlie was now a desk jockey and too many years pushing paper have dulled his skills. There would be no challenge in it if Charlie was in charge. Of course, Charlie was now a wild card, unpredictable at best and he was interfering with my plan A. I hated having to drop down to my fall back plan, but since I had to, Charlie was certainly going to have a starring role in it. It wasn't personal, just survival and I am the one who must survive this game if I was going to save the next broken soul.

Once Logan left, I watched Bruno sitting in the car making notes and decided to make my way up to Rosie's apartment even if the idea that Ashley's prying eyes might be watching was fresh in my mind. I hoped that the distraction I left for him was enough to keep him busy. At least busy enough to let me do my ritual. Every man needs his ritual. I needed mine. I walked around to the back of the building and punched in the code to open the back door. Rosie had given it to me some time back along with detailed instructions where to find the spare key. The poor girl had a fear of being alone. She always said she feared the dark, but what she meant was being alone in the dark. She once told me that people die in the dark when there is nobody there to protect them. That is when she told me where she hid the spare key.

I went to locker 181 and jiggled the door. I heard the key slip down and bounce onto the floor. I knelt down and slipped my fingers underneath feeling the paper against my finger tips. pulling the paper back, the key slid out under the door. More creative than one of those fake rocks that's for sure. As I made my way up towards the side door, as to not get spotted by the camera's, it occurred to me that this little key was the reason Arthur came last night. Maybe there was something here that he didn't want the bloodhound to find. Obviously not in the apartment, but inside storage locker 181. Maybe the bloodhound was slipping, but then again, until now I didn't think of it either. Another unexpected surprise, I thought. I didn't have time to investigate now because a man needs his ritual and it wasn't part of my plan, but I would throw a bone to the little pup Logan. Help him run up the ladder kind of thing.

I made my way through the doors to the small steep stairs that lead to her little room. These old houses were like run down apartments really. Small rooms and a shared bathroom. The great thing Rosie's room mates was the fact that they were all in engineering and spent too much time at school. Counting the bicycles was always a sure way to tell who was here and who wasn't. I walked through the little hallway and slipped into her room. It wasn't as tidy as I remembered, but with a team sifting through every miniscule piece of her life, it was expected. The forensic team isn't known for their house keeping skills. I walked over to the bed and just sat there looking around the room. Rosie was free of all her miseries and now I just needed to say good bye. It was part of the process like a last kiss or hug before a soldier goes off to war.

I walked over to her desk and there was a scattered collection of pictures laying on the desk. It might be the digital age, but I liked pictures. I mean physical pictures that you can touch and feel in your hands. There was one here that was made just for me. It wasn't sexy or erotic though. Only a dirty old man wants those types of pictures and Brown isn't a dirty old man. No, this picture was one that was taken along the river this summer. Rosie was wearing just plain everyday clothes with those thick dollar store sun glasses. I needed it for closure. I slid the pictures around, but it wasn't there. It was very disappointing because it I knew it was there in a little plastic frame. Rosie called me her father figure and said every father needs a picture of their favorite kid. I was going to miss her. I skimmed the pictures again and decided on one of her when she was about sixteen. She looked sweet and innocent then. I placed the picture in my pocket and headed for the door. Slipping a chained small cross from my pocket I gently placed it onto the door knob and whispered, "Rest in peace child. You are now beautiful on the inside and out."

In most cases after the crime scene has been cleared the mourning family comes and removes all the personal possessions and keep sakes. It's human nature to grab hold of something that reminds us of a special moment or time and treasure it, but Rosie didn't have anyone to do this except me and maybe the kid. She died the same way she lived. Alone, crying for love and protection. Tomorrow or the next day everything she owned would be thrown into boxes and probably be given to good will. Pieces of her life would be integrated into a stranger, but her memory will fade. It had never occurred to me really until now just how much she needed to be free from this existence.

Later tonight I would call Logan and point out the storage locker. I bet there is something Arthur was dreading them finding stashed inside. Something that might just push the bloodhound into believing plan A. I would then sit back and wait for it. Even I like to be surprised every now and then by unexpected events.

CHAPTER 15 – BRUNO

I sat on the bench watching the ships passing by letting everything roll around my head. I missed the days when murder cases were just open and shut. You know, drug crazed spouse stabs drug crazed spouse and its an open and shut case. The geeks in IT told me that the Brown ghost chatted with Rosie every night. Unlike all the other guys that she spoke with who flirted with her or demanded ungodly things, this guy seemed gentle and educated. Almost fatherly. They reviewed around a year's worth of texts and chats and with the exception of Rosie's panic moments when she cried out to him, it was almost like they were family. At least it seems like she saw him that way. Maybe he was just acting like that hoping his sweet fatherly mannerism would slowly seduce her. Impossible to tell unless I can actually yank his ass into the interrogation room and right now that seemed unlikely.

The scariest part was the IP address he used. The geeks in IT said the emails came from the guest WIFI at the station. Not sure how they can pinpoint that detail, but it had great meaning. Scary as hell because it meant that he was one of us, I am sure, since he was on it everyday. The same time everyday. How was that even possible? How could he use the computers at work and nobody notice? I mean I can blend into most environments unnoticed if I wanted to, like I am just another old guy drinking coffee or reading a book, but the police station of all places? Of course, there was that felon that lived in the restaurant out back for years with a warrant on him, but that was close by, not inside. That was troubling at best. Right now, we were going through surveillance and employee records, trying to determine if it was one of our own. The idea that I probably walked by a killer everyday and didn't even realize it was terrifying. The media frenzy alone would be a nightmare, not to mention the horrors that would come with internal affairs. Plus, there was always the career aftermath. We take care of our own, so even thinking about it, would end my career, let alone investigate it.

I never took the time to truly place a value on my career. It's not like just having a job. With a job you trade hours of your life for a price and if it ends, you find a new location to sell your time. A career is more like an investment. You don't just sell your time. You invest your time in a future with the dream that at the end of your journey you made a difference in the world. It's not just for a pension or a gold watch, but a part of you that means something. If I followed the evidence I would be selling my career. Was justice enough? I always thought that nothing meant more then justice, but now I questioned it. I hated the idea of an innocent man being locked away, or even worse murdered, for a crime that they didn't commit, but if I investigated one of my own it would be career suicide. What was an old war dog like me supposed to do? Perhaps retire and spend my days fishing off the shore like the other retirees I know.

Flipping through my little black book I reviewed my notes regarding Ashley Truelove. He was broken and twisted that is for sure, but this wasn't his crime. His true crime was loving a woman too much. You can call him a stalker and argue that Rosie could never love him back, but in his eyes, he loved her dearly. In many ways he is just as big a victim as Rosie was. He was reaching out for help. For family and that feeling of belonging. Of course, he was reaching out in the wrong fashion, but he needed help, not a prison cell. Of course, he wasn't a friend or family to me. He is just a monster that I helped to build. I wasn't the one that started his journey into madness or the one that pushed him to it, but I was there somewhere in the middle. I still failed him in a giant way and added another stain on society.

Then of course there was Arthur. Up until today, he was my prime suspect. He wasn't rich but had enough cash to support and impress most women. He wasn't handsome, but in the few emails I came across, he seemed sweet. He was like a poet that way. Most of it was probably bullshit, but it sounded sweet and genuine. With a few well thought out words he could make any woman feel special. Of course, his wife might not like the idea and we still had to interview her since she had motive, that was for sure, but why would she kill Callie? Callie didn't know Arthur, that is something I am sure of. Plus, she didn't fit the profile, and the murder did not match that done by a woman. The murder was too brutal to be a woman if you believe the profilers who see women as gentler in their crimes. I didn't like Arthur at all, abusive and disrespectful to the women in his life. Not much of a man or human being. He reminded me of one of those oil companies that you hear about that push their pipeline through sacred Indian land. They make all these claims, but at the end of the day its just because they want to do it. Not really a need, but a selfish disrespectful want. Was my career worth more then an innocent man's life even if he was a despicable piece of shit?

I was lost in these thoughts trying to decide who I really was when Charlie's voice bellowed, "I would ask if you found the guilty party, but that look on your face says everything."

Looking up, his face was filled with an evil smile and those cold piercing eyes were staring me down. "Don't look so thrilled. This case gets more and more complicated by the minute."

Sitting beside me, he clasped his hands together, "It doesn't seem so complicated to me. You give me a name," then made a gun with his hand, "Boom. We skip the trial and save the tax payers $113000 a year." That was the cost to feed and house a prisoner for one year. I had always known that the numbers were high but placing a value on a life as a reason to murder wasn't right. I guess we all make our excuses to rationalize the things we do in life. Charlie was no different. I guess I wasn't that different either.

I couldn't help but wonder if the man I trusted with my life for so long was still in there. Had rage and agony choked out the spark of sunshine that made him like a brother? Was there even a trace of the man, who I used to admire and envy, left? The question that lingered inside me wasn't really why he demanded it, but why I felt like I owed it? A name was all he wanted and I was still trying to convince myself that giving up Arthur was not the worst thing in the world. Arthur wasn't the kind of guy who added value to the world in general or those around him. "It's never that simple." It was the reality of it. Do I tell him that one of the men he worked with and laughed with was the man that stole his daughter?

"Bruno, I know I am putting you in a tight spot, but what would you do if you were in my shoes? Day after day I am haunted by the vision of seeing the lifeless body of my little girl staring back at me." Putting me in a tight place was a mild way of putting it. Twisting my nuts in a vice was a more accurate way of phrasing it and wondering why I wasn't thanking him for the extra twist at the end. It was the first time I saw anything close to a human reaction escape him in recent days. A small stream of tears fell from his cheeks as he whimpered, "You know me. I need this."

Taking a deep breath, I truly wished I could give him a name. The proper name to help him end his misery, but I was torn inside. On one hand, I owed him my life literally yet, the price he was demanding of me was against everything I believed in. The code I swore to live and die by. The case wasn't cut and dry. The obvious suspects weren't always the real culprits. There were too many surprises and unknowns right now. I kept finding maybe's and those little pieces kept leading this case in unexpected directions that I needed time to review and follow. "It's not that simple Charlie. I am a cop.

The best and worst days of my life have been spent doing just that. Being a cop. Most of yours have been too."

"No, my happiest times were spent watching my little girl and she had an amazing future ahead of her. Do you hear me? She was going to be anything that she wanted to be in life."

Callie was one of those amazing possibilities that I truly wanted to watch grow up. Maybe it was the emotional attachment a childless man makes with the closest thing he ever had to a daughter, but I still miss her and still see a world of endless possibilities that was ripped away when she died. "She only became the shining light in your life after she died. Right up until that day, she was your daughter and I know that you loved her, but don't bullshit me. She came second to the job like everything else in your life. You are a like all of us. The job was your life."

"Bullshit you," he snapped. "Don't you dare tell me that I didn't love my daughter. You were there to witness how close our family was."

"Charlie I am not saying that you weren't a wonderful father or even that she wasn't a good daughter. I am saying that she never lived up to your expectations until after she was dead then she surpassed them all."

"Just give me the name," he snapped, "Then your debt to me is paid in full." Slapping me on the back, "One name and you are free of me."

"Free of you? Charlie one name will ruin your career and send you to Bloodvien." Pointing out the obvious consequences, I muttered in disbelief, "One name and everything you have worked to protect your whole life and to build, is gone. It means everything that you have lived for your whole life is a lie."

"Just let me worry about what I lived for. It was all about family and now I have no family or career." I was staring at a friend with the soul of a stranger. A man that looks and sounds like a friend I once knew suddenly was as strange as the killer I sought for so long but couldn't find anymore. Death changes a man. Not just the man that kills another but seeing it and especially those that are affected by it.

He was braver then me, I had to admit that, but it didn't make him smarter then me. He was going to spend the rest of his life looking over his shoulder fearing whose out there. How long did he really think he would survive in a jungle filled with animals that he helped put there? My grandfather once told me that the day a man looks in the mirror and hates the man staring back at him, he isn't a man anymore, but a shadow of one. Giving him a name would make me a shadow. "I don't have a name to give you and even if I did, what you are asking for isn't justice."

He pulled out that .45 he treasured so much and just stared. "You will give me a name or I will just take things into my own hands and you don't want that Bruno. You can't save me and you can't fix any of this or who I have become. Just give me the name Bruno."

"What you are saying is that if I am not with you, I am against you?"

Sliding the gun back into his holster he muttered, "No Bruno I am not going to touch you. If you can't point out the one that killed my little girl, I will kill both of them."

"And if they are both innocent?" It was an obvious question, but an even greater moral thought came to mind. "Don't tell me what you plan to do. I don't want to be involved or know and I am still a cop. I must stop you even if it costs me my best friend."

Shrugging he muttered, "If they are both innocent, let god tell me." He was walking away, headed towards the river when he looked back muttering, "You can decide if the guilty one dies or if they both die."

CHAPTER 16 – ASHLEY

The panic that hit me was worse than any beating that I had ever received. I mean the sheer shock of having a cop pounding on my front with a giant blood stain right in the center of my living room was reason enough to feel that way. My whole body tensed up and my heart felt like it was exploding inside my chest. I felt like I was going to collapse as the breathing increased and the streams of pain shot down my body. The door rattled again as Harold bellowed, "Lee are you in there?"

What the hell do you say when you are knee deep in blood and there is a cop at your front door? You lie like a son of a bitch. "Give me a minute while I throw some pants on." I was lost searching for something to throw over the blood stain, but there wasn't anything I could find that would look natural enough to cover it up. My little hole in the wall wasn't exactly the kind of place that you would use throw carpets. It was the kind of place that was too hot all summer and too cold all winter. If it weren't for the view of Rosie's place, I couldn't have handled it.

I ran to the kitchen looking for something to wash away the blood, but I don't think even the dish soap with all the grease fighting action in the world was going to help me now. I sometimes wonder if I was like a barbarian or something like that in another life. You know, the Buddhists talk about being reborn a grass hopper or ant in the next life so you can't just stomp on them, like everything else in life. I think in my past life I must have killed kids or tortured nuns because so far in this life, I am paying all my dues from all the past ones. What the hell was I going to do? I was searching my apartment for some way to cover the stains, but there wasn't anything no matter how many circles I turned. You never actually realize just how much your life sucks until you are in a tight spot and have no idea what you are going to do about it.

I went to the door and said, "Harold can you come back later? It's not a good time." It makes you wonder if there ever was a good time to have a cop at your door, even the ones like Harold. He wasn't exactly the stop or I will shoot type, he was more the accountant type if you ask me. I bet somewhere deep down he is one of the people pleaser types and his mom and dad made him join the force. To think that people say I have mommy issues. I bet even his wife looks like his mom.

From the other side of the door he muttered, "Lee we need to talk. It's important."

"Harold, can't you just tell me the next time I am locked up?" The awkward silence came after that. Sometimes the meaning of the words doesn't matter. It's just the words and the emotions that they bring out of you. In Harold's eyes I was just a stalker pulled in for singing love songs to a lost love that I could not let go of and in many ways, he was right. It only took one date for me to fall in love, one smile and a few laughs. If you were to ask Rosie, when she was alive, she would have said that it was only coffee and that we never dated, but it was a date. A simple coffee doesn't steal your heart and ruin your life, but one date can have a powerful affect on you.

"Lee open the door so we can talk. Your whole life depends on it. I mean your whole life."

Right now, my whole life wasn't looking so good. Opening the door wasn't going to mean Harold would save my ass and then we would skip off into the sunset becoming best friends and all that shit. No, opening the door would mean Harold would try and slap cuffs on me which wouldn't go well for him or me depending on how screwed I was from my injuries. Besides I think Harold doesn't have the stomach for it. You know, Harold walks in and sees the pool of blood, then faints. With my luck, when he fainted, his gun would go off and he'd end up shooting himself. You know two murder charges against me, not one.

"I don't think there is going to be a next time. Lee I can't be seen here and you have to listen to what I have to say. Before you ask, I can't just scream it through the door."

I opened the door just a crack and peered out at Harold. He was shifting from side to side and looked like he was going to burst in through the door. He had a swollen lip and a black eye, but other than that he didn't look that bad really considering yesterday he was getting bitch slapped by his boss. Harold's jaw dropped, "Jesus Christ! You look like your face was used for a baseball."

"Yes, well I ran into your boss last night and a few of his friends. They decided that they wanted to have a little talk." Harold's face dropped as the words 'little talk" left my lips. He was just a glorified security guard so I guess, the closest he has ever come to a real beating was either in bed or watching Friday night wrestling. All fake and unable to prepare you for the real world.

Leaning against the door, he whispered, "I have heard rumors that the sergeant might try something, but this wasn't anything like I imagined."

"I hate those kinds of rumors actually." Harold seemed to have more to say and was beating around the bush. Small talk might be good when your ass is being walked out of a holding cell, but not when you keep waking up and finding yourself sinking deeper and deeper into a pit.

"What kind of rumors?" Harold asked staring down at his feet.

"The kind that gets you black eyes and cracked ribs." I tried to act like my charming carefree self, but when your arms are trembling and every breath feels like a thousand paper cuts at the same time, it's not exactly an easy task. The next thing was to get Harold as far away from my place as possible just in case Arthur turned up dead. The last thing I wanted was a dead body and his blood laid out in the living room. I was being framed like one of those paint by number pictures that you put in a two-dollar plastic frame.

"I think that you should call Bruno. He isn't like Charlie. He believes in the law and that the badge he wears means something."

Of course, he is. Every cop chooses a criminal over one of their own. You see it on TV all the time where all the good cops scream out, 'don't abuse the bad boy'. Real life, just like in the movies, was the good cops stand up for the bad cops. They might look all shiny in the sunlight, but no matter how squeaky clean they look, the minute they get you in a dark alley, they sucker punch you right in the face. "No, I think I have had enough little talks with cops."

I went to close the door, but Harold slipped his foot in there to stop it. "Lee look in the mirror. Do you really think that the Sergeant is going to stop?" Harold might be a total pussy, but he seemed concerned. Who knows? Maybe I had made a real friend. You know those guys that lend you a hand when you fall, not punch you in the face again while laughing. I always thought that having a true and tried friend was something that I would like to try, but never actually experienced that before. I always thought that the closest I would come to true friendship was going to be Rosie. I always wanted to say that I married my best friend. Seeing Harold and being in my current situation, made me think friendship was over rated.

"I will be fine Harold. I can take care of myself." I wasn't fine and I knew it, but what do you do when there is nobody to trust? Everything I ever cared about was stolen from me and having a street thug cop hunting me would not stop as long as he thought that I was his guy. You can't just run away and hide. Evil always follows you. Its what evil does.

"Lee there is something you should know." I waited for

him to tell me, but he kept looking towards the ground scanning the yard. "This morning Arthur's lawyer called asking why we were holding him. We set him free, but now the powers that be, think he might have skipped town."

Finally, some good news, I thought. At least with him on the run, I drop down to suspect number two. "So, that's good news for me."

"If he is on the run and not floating somewhere in the Detroit river. Just be careful okay? I think that the Sergeant is out for blood on this one. For your sake, I know it would be best if Arthur turned up dead and with the way the Sarge has been acting, it would take it all off you, but just watch yourself."

It was finally coming together. The sergeant knocks me on my ass, then kills Arthur in my house. I am not sure where he took the body, but with all the blood, there isn't a jury out there that would think I was innocent. "So, what happens next?"

"Officially I wasn't here, but right now we are looking for Arthur. If he happens to turn up dead, there will be two people that will be investigated, you and the Sergeant. The Sergeant has friends on the force. Lots of them. You only have me and Bruno so just watch your ass, okay?" Handing me a business card he said, "In case you lost the first one. Call Bruno, he is as straight as they come." I watched him walk away realizing just how screwed I was. That cop killed Arthur and now I am going to be so screwed, like a whore on payday. I watched Harold jump into his little gray Honda and slip away realizing that I was two heart beats from dying in a 6 x 9 cell.

I turned and found a couple of bloody foot prints running from the living room towards the door. In my panic, when Harold knocked on the door, I had somehow missed them completely. I placed my foot beside one and luckily for me, they were way too big to be mine. Yet, that didn't mean that they weren't Arthur's or that evil god damn cop. It just meant that I didn't run out of my crappy little one bed room with blood on my feet. The real problem though was the old hardwood floors. They rose and fell like a river with wide cracks between each board. Everything got stuck between them and you can never get it out. Of course, there was the giant stain in the middle of my living room.

I ran to my desk by the window to do a search on how to remove blood, but my laptops were gone. Turning I realized that even the walls were bare. Every picture and detail about Rosie was ripped away leaving only small shredded pieces of paper hanging on the few remaining thumb tacks. Besides that, all that was left of my shrine was small little holes in the wall. It was like they stole the happiest times from my life, leaving faded patched squares behind where my dreams and memories once stood. I just stood there trembling in disbelief. It was all gone. Everything was like Rosie never existed and was meant to be forgotten, but you don't just forget the one you love. You can't just ignore the emptiness.

I stepped closer to the wall and just ran my hands across it. I couldn't feel her presence anymore. I had always felt like she was standing right in front me, calling to me when I stood this close to her. They didn't just steal her life from me, now they stole the memories I had collected. The question wasn't why they stole this part of my life, but who stole it? The cops, the killer or Arthur. Whoever it was that knocked me on my ass last night should have killed me because I was going to find them and kill them. I don't really know how long I stood there brooding only that I was lost.

After a while I walked over and looked out my window. How many nights had I spent here staring towards Rosie's place wishing I could be there holding her, rather then loving her from a far? It always seemed so poetic that the man who loved her the most was the one she couldn't let in. Few people realized that a woman like Rosie was just looking for love but couldn't give in to the emotion. She didn't think that she was worthy of love, so in her eyes, sex was the only way that she could find it and keep it. I never saw her like that. I saw her as the woman who could make me want to be a better man with just a blink of an eye and a smile. I never saw her as a toy to play with. I saw her as a prize to be cherished and protected.

I watched the blue sedan with the words "Police" running along the side street. It was one of those new stylish cop cars that have the writing that is meant to blend in with the color of the car. Of course, for seasoned guys like me, just seeing the hub caps is enough to point out who's driving it. I watched two figures get out of the car and head towards the building. The smaller one, I hadn't seen before, but the large older one was that Bruno that Harold seem to love so much. I wondered if he was really as good as Harold thought he was. He seemed to be lost and desperate to find a clue. He was like a red neck Sherlock Holmes without the charm or intelligence. From this angle though he looked familiar. I can't exactly say what it was about him or where I saw him, but I had seen him before. Not just in the cop shop either, but from a distance, high above the world. Even that troubled me. Seeing him from my window gave me an eerie feeling.

Staring down at the oval shaped red spot on the floor, it occurred to me that I have never tried to remove blood from anything. Generally anything that was covered in blood was either soaked right away or thrown away. I can't remember the number of shirts I tossed after a fight, but there were way too many. One of my mother's better boy friends was a bouncer from one of the clubs she worked at. A giant man with bulging biceps and a thin mustache named Terry. He didn't drink or smoke and went to the gym everyday. He was a part time wrestler and body builder. I always expected to see him on TV like the heroes from my childhood, but I never did. He was the only one that never beat her and I truly believe that if she wasn't trapped with a snot nosed little brat, he would have stayed and my mother might still be alive. On a few rare mornings, though, I would wake up and find his t-shirts soaking in the bathroom sink. He used to say that bleach would shorten the life, but cola would do the job. He even showed me how cola could remove rust from an old nail. Of course, he followed that up by telling me that my body was a temple and drinking the wrong drinks and eating the wrong foods was like disrespecting it.

I went to the fridge and found a bottle of cola. It had sat in my fridge for a long time. It was free with the last pizza I bought and I never drank it. Grabbing it, I went towards the blood spot. I opened it and slowly began to pour it onto the spot hoping that it would make it disappear like magic. I wasn't dumb enough to think the cops wouldn't be able to find any evidence, since they always do. Maybe if I was lucky, nobody would come charging in, searching for evidence in Arthur's disappearance or, perhaps, murder. With any luck, they are the ones that stole my laptops and shrine pictures so they might not come back. It made sense that while I was locked up some fast-moving cop would grab some kind of warrant and steal my stuff. Of course, they would find a lot of interesting stuff on my systems and I am sure I broke a couple dozen laws that they would charge me for, but not murder. Nothing on my systems would indicate that I would ever hurt my darling Rosie. I couldn't, not even if my very life depended on it. I stared down at the carpet and decided that I needed more cola. I needed to get as much as I could to remove the blood. I know some might think that bleach is the way to go, but it stains the color and makes your house smell like a hospital. That is what makes the cops suspicious.

CHAPTER 17 – BRUNO

The whole way from the river front back to the crime scene, something was bothering me, like an itch that I couldn't scratch. I didn't like this uneasy feeling that grabbed hold of me and wouldn't let go like a cold December chill. I liked Logan. He came from good stock and was ambitious as hell, but he just seemed way too lucky. I mean it was like every major crime that has happened since he got here pushed his career up another rung in the ladder of success. I have seen my fair share of lucky breaks in a case and even fell into a few case breaking clues, but the criminals seem to be throwing them at him as if screaming for Logan to catch them. He received another anonymous call pointing out a storage shed that nobody realized existed. Was it possible that Logan was being steered into something that just happened to further his career or was it something more? Something a little more sinister. Could he be involved with or know the killer? I can't really say that he seemed like the killer type, but then again, I don't think any of them are, but recent events have made me question that. It was making me question a lot of things. Not just Logan, but Charlie too.

As we made our way to the back of the building, I kept thinking of this mysterious Mister Brown. He had to be a cop, but not just any cop, he had to be adaptable is the best way I can put it. Mister Brown adapted to Rosie's needs and wants. Within the first few messages, he read her and adapted to become what she wanted and then slowly he adapted to what she needed. How many cops had taken counseling courses that the department offered? How many of us had interrogation training? It made sense now that I think of it. If you remove the emotion from Rosie's interaction with him, it was just a lighter version of an interrogation. It had all four stages; Formation, preparation, interaction and completion. That in itself was scary enough, but Brown was intelligent, not just intelligent, but crafty. Few men at the station had that, at least not like Brown. Looking back at Logan, he had to be connected. He was adaptable and he had minored in psychology or something like that. He was a ladies' man and seemed to be the only one who could benefit from solving such a high-profile crime. It just occurred to me that he was just starting his career around the time Callie died.

"The caller said there was a storage locker at the back," Logan said as he trotted towards the back of the building. "Said that Arthur wouldn't want us to find what was in it."

"What exactly did he say was in it?" The problem with anonymous calls was that you never know the source or the integrity of the evidence. Generally, I never gave it much thought, but with everything pointing to one of our own I was starting to question things. Planting evidence isn't unheard of. I was going to need to be a little skeptical about what we found.

"He didn't, he just said that we would find something interesting in it. The fact that Arthur was caught trying to get to it the day after the murder makes it even more interesting." Smiling, Logan was almost skipping towards the locker. "I have a feeling that this will break the case."

Was it a feeling or did he know the contents of the locker would break the case? I decided just to go with the flow and watch things unfold. Certainly, Logan was now on my watch list, but I couldn't do or say anything unless I had proof. Innocent until proven guilty. I was starting to wonder if there was any real innocent party. "Don't get too excited. Most anonymous leads don't lead anywhere.

"I still think whatever we find will be the case breaker. I just have the feeling it's going to be a good day for the good guys for a change."

Who were the good guys? Up until now, I thought anyone who carried a badge was the good guys. We were the ones who risked our lives to save strangers. The ones you could come to when you had problems and even the guys who you could talk to when you were scared. The good guys in blue. Now I was starting to think that one of us wasn't so good and it seemed to me I was following behind him. Logan turned the corner and screamed, "Shit!" I pulled my gun and ran ready for anything. As I turned the corner Logan was just standing there staring at this little door that was creaking in the wind. His gun wasn't out and he seemed more frustrated than scared, so I lowered mine and walked towards him. "Somebody has already been here," he snapped.

The door wasn't broken, just open so at least we could safely assume that it wasn't robbed. The lock was dropped on the ground right in front of the door. Logan stepped closer and slowly opened the door wider pointing to the door frame. "There's a bloody palm print. Looks like whoever did this cut his hand on something." Scanning the door frame a little closer, he muttered, "Damned if I know what it was though. I can't see anything sharp enough that could have done it." Sticking his head into the opening he muttered, "Son of a bitch there is a pair of handcuffs hanging on the wall."

I stepped closer, there was a pair of police issued handcuffs with dried blood on the sides. "What do you think of those?" I asked pointing to the dried blood.

"Are they police issued?"

"It looks like they are." This was adding to the idea that it was one of our own. You could tell police issued cuffs from others like comparing a vintage Les Paul from one of those Korean made knock offs and these were certainly genuine. Logan reached around snapping a picture of them. They would have a serial number and this might just lead me to the guilty party. Maybe Logan was right. We have the case breaking clue we needed.

Boxes were tipped over leaving a wide mess of books and clothes everywhere. Scanning the area, I said, "It looks like we caught them in the process of looking for something. Stay here and make sure that everything left is secured while I go and investigate." I am not sure if leaving him behind was a good idea or not, but right now it was the only option I had. If we really caught someone in the act of removing evidence that might lead to a conviction which made keeping an eye on the storage locker was a must.

"OK I will call in forensics to go over things," Logan stated as he pulled out his cell.

I circled the shed looking to see if there were any escape routes or even better, somebody hiding around the corner, but it was empty. Luckily the back yard had a high white fence on three side with an open area on the only non-fenced side that we came in through. A small gate on the other side was leading towards the side of the house. I made my way along the back of the house scanning my surroundings, but I didn't see anyone. I knelt down looking in all directions, but there wasn't any place that I could see where anyone could hide. The yard only had one small oak and a picnic table over to the far side next to one of those big silver overpriced barbecues.

I stopped just before the corner and listened for the crunch of feet pounding on gravel, but all I could hear was silence. I stepped around the corner, gun in hand, but there was nobody there. At least nobody that I could see. Carefully I went around towards the opening that lead to the front yard. I just stood there searching the street, but there was nobody insight. I went to the street and looked in both directions. There wasn't anything suspicious or out of the ordinary. It was just another busy street in the not so good section of town.

I was walking back towards the back yard when I noticed blood on the front door. I ran towards it and stopped to look in the little window. There wasn't so much as a shadow to chase inside so I slowly opened the door and stepped in. The whole place was hauntingly quiet. I mean a college party place with no noise at all. It was out of place at best. Of course, it was school hours and there was a murder here, so I guess if I was in this position, I would avoid home too. I heard a creak from above me so I slowly slipped into the living room towards the curving narrow stairs.

I hated these stairs because I was always forced to bend in two to climb them, but there was somebody up there. The question was who and why? The stairs creaked with each step I took no matter how hard I tried to climb my way up in silence. I had just made my way to the top of the stairs walking slowly down the hall when I heard a door close. I ran towards the sound realizing that it had to coming from Rosie's room. Serial killers return to the scene of their crimes to relive it, something about ritual.

I think we all try and relive those happy exciting times of our lives. It's human nature. Old men tell stories about how handsome they were or how tough they were during the war. In a serial killer's life, the scene of the crime is their happy and exciting moment that they want to relive again and again until they kill again. It's my job to make sure this one doesn't get the chance to kill again.

I slowly opened the door and looked in. That's when I saw him just standing there staring out of the window. I watched him for a minute trying to figure out what exactly he was staring at. The memories that would excite him were inside the bedroom and in the bathroom where Rosie died. He was wearing a police uniform which shattered my heart and brought all my fears to life. It was one of our own. I slowly made my way into the room and with my gun right on him I said, "Place your hands behind your head and step slowly away from the window."

He slowly placed his hands behind his head stating, "This isn't what it looks like," as he stepped backwards and dropped to his knees. "Don't get trigger happy, I can explain everything."

I slapped the cuffs around his wrist muttering, "It's never

what it looks like." I yanked his arm back and grabbed his other hand placing the cuffs on him. "I can think of no reason why you need to be in this room."

"I am here on police business, honest to god."

"If there was any reason for you to be here, I would know." This was my investigation so I would know everything that was happening. The crime scene was released so we had no reason to be here. Nobody did. I was searching for blood on his clothes and hands, but there wasn't any. "What's your name?"

Looking up he murmured, "It's me, Harold. This isn't what it looks like."

"And what the hell does this look like?" I was having one of those moments when I had to ask myself if I just put a bullet in the back of his head would the world be a better place. He always seemed too weak and gentle to be a cop, let alone a killer. This kid fooled us all. All this time walking among us and I never really noticed him. He blended and even ran for coffee runs like he was one of the family. All this time he was hiding in plain sight and we even offered tips and training that eventually helped him allude us. It's like we trained a killer to be almost uncatchable.

"It looks like you caught me looking out a window at Lee's place." If Harold wasn't a bad cop, he damn well wasn't making a good case of it.

"So, what are you doing inside here?" I was still struggling to fight the sensation that smashing in the back of his head would be so much easier then booking him.

"Hiding!" Harold's body was trembling as he muttered, "I got scared and ran inside here to find shelter."

"Christ, you are a cop. Who do you need to hide from?" It was the worst excuse ever. I mean the kid has been trained to chase down criminals and disarm them. Our city counts on him to keep the streets safe and he expects me to believe that he ran into a crime scene because he was scared.

"Look out the window," he said.

I looked out the window and scanned the street in both directions. There was the usual traffic rushing towards the university, but nothing that should terrify Harold. "I don't see anything Harold. If you are looking to convince me of your innocence you're doing a piss poor job of it."

Rolling his eyes, Harold muttered, "look in front of the old Lapelle residence. White Kia sedan parked in front."

I leaned over and saw the car parked right in front of it. It looked new and shiny which wasn't something that you see in this part of town that often. It stood out but wasn't exactly something I would consider dangerous. "So, a rental car scared you?"

"Oh, yes that's it. I am afraid of a damn Kia. It's who is driving the car."

I was about to taunt him then I realized who was inside the car. "Charlie scared you?" It was more or less a stupid question because sometimes Charlie scared the hell out of me. He could be like a rabid pit bull and just as nasty. "So, what did Charlie do?"

Harold seemed terrified as he stared up at me, "I know you and Charlie go way back, but I have always seen you as law and justice comes first." I just nodded in shame. The truth is, I generally cave in the end and the idea of being driven to retirement seemed like a horrible price to pay for justice. "The sarge is on a rampage and he doesn't care about justice. He has already attacked Lee twice. Which brings me to the police business I was here on, I wanted to make sure Lee was alright. As I was leaving, I encountered Charlie and ran in here to avoid him. I knew how it would look to him, me being here and all."

"Twice?"

"Yes twice. I was walking away from Lee's place when the Sarge passed. He slammed on the breaks nearly causing an accident."

That Lee kid was a likable guy and I think Harold admired and envied him. The bad boy thing. Charlie would see Harold leaving the kids place as a betrayal. In his current state of mind Charlie would be intimidating to most men. He was hunting and hunters never let their prey escape. "You know you just ended your career? Checking on Lee sealed that deal." Going against Charlie was a career ender.

"I didn't realize it, but I can't do what the Sarge wants me to do. I tried but I can't." I was looking out the window and saw Lee walking down the street with groceries bags. If they gave a prize for bad timing, Lee would not only get a trophy, but a crown as well. He looked like shit. "Bruno there is something I need to tell you and you aren't going to like it."

I heard a series of thudding noises echo through the house. I screamed, "Son of a bitch, he was here the whole time." I burst out of the room and nearly killing myself as I forced my giant frame through the rabbit hole too fast. I charged ruthlessly pounding my way down the steps as I went crashing into the door as I hit the bottom of the stairs. My shoulder burned as I struggled to get back to my feet, but by that time, he was long gone, leaving only a blood stain behind him. I was sloppy and lost my monster in the process. Instead of using my skills and experience to catch the bad guy, I got caught up in what I wanted to see.

CHAPTER 18 – ASHLEY

The whole way to and from the corner store to get the cola all I could think about was Arthur. He was a monster by every definition of the word. Rosie once told Brown that she felt drained by him, like he was an emotional vampire sucking the life out of her heart. I think we all have our vampires in our lives. Whether its a guy, like me, chasing a naughty misunderstood girl like Rosie or a total asshole like Arthur, taking advantage of her tortured soul. We are all monsters and have monsters. I can't really explain it, but the fact that Arthur was probably dead bothered me more then I would have liked. It's not the fact that he was probably wrapped in plastic tossed into a dumpster, because if there was ever a man who deserved to end up in the trash, it was Arthur. The part that really busted my balls was the fact that I was going to be screwed over for his murder and I didn't do it. I don't mind doing the time, as they say, for something I did, but being locked up for something I didn't do was total bullshit. This was probably the only time in my life I was innocent and there was no way anybody was ever going to believe me. I was screwed and this time it was serious.

I couldn't let Arthur haunt my thoughts because I had eight bottles of cola to pour on the floor and blood stains to remove before the cops decided Arthur wasn't on the run. Like a magnet, they would be storming my door and boom, before I knew it, I would be locked up behind bars watching them throw the keys away. I needed to clean up my place to remove all the evidence that anyone could possibly find. Of course, the fact that my little dump was clean would be suspicious enough. It wasn't a choice, but a need. A survival thing because I was too small and pretty for Bloodvien prison. Seriously, I could hold my own, but the last thing I truly wanted was to make a new best friend, not because I needed a friend, but because we were locked in a small cell and he decided that he was in the mood for love.

That bad ass Sargent had to be parked down the street. Another case of karma setting me up to kiss the pavement again. I was still struggling with the bottles as he jumped out of the car and started walking towards me. He stuffed a silver pistol into his pants and pulled his jacket over it. He looked like one of those UPS drivers, only in blue rather then brown. The same blue pants that I saw before I was cold clocked from behind. Of course, he was the one. If a cop kills a dirt bag, they bypass his ass and come after the dirty trailer trash crook. "Having a party kid."

"Well I have so much to celebrate I thought what the hell. You know being recently single and all."

Placing his hands in his pockets, he chuckled, "I always thought that both people need to know that they are dating before you can call it a relationship. Maybe I am wrong though."

Now I am being heckled by a psycho who thinks that just because they gave him a badge and a title he was entitled. He would never understand how much I loved her or that she loved me. Love is complicated for most people, so how can normal people understand real love? I mean my way of loving, when I could never understand it myself. The thing I do know is that the emptiness inside me wasn't getting any smaller. I didn't expect my life to get better without her, but there was no way that I could have expected this. "Am I under arrest?"

Leaning against a little white Kia, he crossed his arms and

smiled, "Well I am not exactly on duty, but for you I will always make an exception."

Rolling my eyes, I muttered, "Now don't I feel special? I am a stalker being stalked." I noticed that he wore black scuffed up shoes. He had to be the guy who took or killed Arthur. It made sense. Mad man with a reason to kill. Now I guess he was here to finish me off too. You know when in doubt, kill them all, attitude.

"Have you seen Arthur? It seems that he vanished without a trace." Licking his lips, he continued, "That got me thinking that either he is guilty as sin or just maybe the guilty party decided to make sure that we were looking for Arthur while he gets off Scott free."

"Or maybe some killer cop took out good old Arthur and stuffed him in a garbage can and now you're thinking that just in case you killed the wrong man, you should take out the other suspect."

That amused him way too much. He was smiling one of those devilish grins that you see in horror movies. He was tapping on the hood of the Kia and said, "That is a good theory, but I think if Arthur ends up in a garbage bin, your door will be the first one I come knocking on."

"Should I call the cleaning lady first just to make sure you have another reason to come kicking my door in?"

"You have such a smart mouth kid. Has that smart mouth ever helped you in life?"

"Well it amuses me and the ladies think that it is rather charming."

He tapped my shoulder with his finger sending pain bursting through my whole body. "Don't be a smart ass. In case you forgot our last conversation and the results that it brought, I am looking for evidence against Arthur. Enough to clear your name and make me happy that I didn't just put a bullet between your eyes," as he poked me again.

I didn't have time to answer before we saw the front door of Rosie's house burst open and a bloody figure came running out the door. He was leaning forward pushing himself to run faster, almost stumbling, as he went. I never thought that I would be happy to see Arthur alive and kicking, but I was relieved to see him. I mean excited enough that my heart was pounding and I started to feel light headed. The cola bottles dropped, exploding as they bounced off the side walk sending a spray of mist like foam flying into the air.

The sergeant bellowed, "Son of a bitch," as he turned to face the house. The big crusty cop called Bruno came bursting through the door, gun in hand, in hot pursuit. It was like watching a headless chicken flopping around the slaughter house, only this chicken looked pissed off and carried a gun. A terrified look filled Arthur's face as he stumbled and hit the fence that trapped him from his escape.

In the movies, the bad guy flips over the fence with a cat like balance and reflexes the makes his daring escape possible. In real life, Arthur was a middle-aged want-to-be just struggling to make his way over it. The fence catches his shirt making him fall over and scraping his stomach as he tumbled downwards. Hitting the ground head first, I was certain that he was down for the count, but he surprised me as he stumbled up to his feet with a face full of blood. He was walking in circles with a stunned look in his eyes like he wanted to run but didn't have any idea where to run to. Whether it was just confusion or fear, I am not sure, but either way, he was screwed. How do you run away when there is no where to run to?

Arthur looked at Bruno, who was running towards the gate, obviously not wanting to repeat what he had just witnessed. Arthur burst out into the coming traffic still watching Bruno burst through the gate in his pursuit. Arthur's gaze was stuck on Bruno, otherwise he would have seen the sergeant yanking his gun out and aiming it at him with a giant smile on his face. I guess any reason to kill him was good enough in the sergeant's eyes. "I got you now you evil little prick," He bellowed as he prepared to fire.

Arthur finally realized that he was caught between a rock and a hard place. A cop on one side and a mad killer cop on the other side. He stopped right in the middle of the busy street, which normally I would say was just stupid, but maybe kissing the front of a Honda is better then facing either of them. I think if I was in his shoes, I would prefer to take a rusty bumper then a lead bullet. The Sargent grasped the gun in both hands muttering, "Freeze you little bastard." There was something in the way that he was holding the gun that made me think he was just seconds away from shooting him dead. Arthur stopped, raising his hands and twisting around trying to decide which way to run.

I don't know why I did it. I mean I have lived my whole life collecting stupid points. So many of them in fact, that I should have been given a hat and t-shirt that screams "yes I am the king." There was something about the way his eyes squinted and his finger slowly bounced on the trigger, not enough to fire the gun, but enough to convince me of his intent. I leapt forward pushing the gun upward hearing the thunderous boom as he fired into the air. I drove my knee into his stomach as I tried to keep the gun pointed into the air. I was grunting as I slammed his face into the hood of the car making a loud twanging noise as his face connected. The good old Sargent drove his elbow into my stomach forcing me to fold in two as he kicked me in the face. From the ground, I looked up to see a gun pointed into my face. Wiping the blood from his mouth he snapped, "you are under arrest."

The squeal of rubber on ash fault as somebody slammed on the breaks burst through the air around me. It was then replaced by the crackle of metal on metal. The look of shock that filled the sergeants face said it all. A fast-moving car had stolen his victory over Arthur and that left him with only one person to take his revenge out on, me.

CHAPTER 19 – BROWN

It was total chaos. The bloodhound Bruno was showing his age as he fell out of the house sliding on the ground like a sled flying down a hill in the middle of winter. It wasn't really his fault though. All dogs get old and a new younger mutt takes over the pack. It's the law of nature. Arthur was fleeing the scene, which is exactly what I wanted and it played out perfectly. They say that a first impression is the lasting impression, but I think it's the last one that truly becomes the memorable one. Especially Arthur's last impression. Covered in his own blood carrying some kind of book which obviously had something unsavory inside. I couldn't see what it was, but if he risked so much to get it, I am certain that it must be important. By important I mean incriminating as hell and that's exactly what I wanted.

Arthur fled into the oncoming traffic, which was a major divination from his usual self preservation way of thinking, or maybe it was exactly his way. Maybe facing oncoming traffic was preferable to facing the bloodhound. I never understood why people run from the cops. Where do they think they are going that the long arm of the law can't get them? People have this image of who they are and how the world sees them. Breaking that changes them in unexpected ways. Arthur was certainly a surprise. Maybe I underestimated his survival skills.

It was too late though. Plan A was almost complete and Arthur was the star of my plan.

The kid Ashley looked worse then I thought he would. He looks more like one of those zombies that you see on TV, but then again, he never was truly that handsome. Charlie certainly pounded him good and I am amazed that he is even out walking the streets, but then again, I think it was necessity, not any kind of internal strength that drove him. Charlie was watching Arthur like a cat stares at a mouse just before he strikes. It looked like he was going to shoot Arthur dead right then and there. That wasn't how I planned it, but that would work for me. It doesn't matter how it ends, as long as Arthur is the guy that pays the piper.

I was surprised to see the kid lunge at Charlie. The kid had balls, but I can't see any logical reason why he'd risk so much, especially to save his mortal enemy. He was smashing Charlie around like a pit bull fighting over a bone. He was a scrapper and I liked it. I mean choosing an apprentice is like having a baby and you don't want to have a broken one. No, you want the one that you can mold like clay into your own personal monster. I tried that before with a priest, but it didn't work out. Only an animal attacks without reason. Plus, 80% of the women I meet are better because I came into their lives. They grow as people and I am sure that even decades later, they look back and know I saved them. That priest, mad Mike though, he doesn't really try and save them. No, he marks them with a rosary tattoo then takes their lives like he is responsible for god's wraths. That's why you need to choose a protégé that is worthy.

A small little Honda was plowing down the street and swerved, barely missing Arthur. He froze there screaming as the car skidded past him and kept on going. Wide eyed Arthur just stared blank faced. He never noticed the little Chevy that was charging at him until it was way too late. The breaks screeched and the car seemed to bump along as the driver tried to stop it. Arthur spun around, but it was too late for him to get out of the way. Arthur folded in two as the car drilled into him forcing his body to skid across the hood and into the wind shield. His body went limp as it connected with a couple tons of glass and steal.

Motion and speed took over as flesh slammed into the glass sending blood spraying onto the street. I bet Arthur never expected that his day was going to end this way. Whether it was the hospital or a grave, it really didn't matter, Arthur couldn't talk his way out. As far as the cops could see, he was at the scene of a crime trying to dispose of evidence. I am not sure what was in the book, but I would know soon enough. The good thing about evidence is that it's easy to get your hands on if you know the right people. There had to be something incriminating in the book otherwise Arthur wouldn't have risked so much. Some times you need to force a man's hand if you want to win the game. Arthur just lost the game.

Lee seemed torn as he stared out into the street. He wasn't a predator like Charlie, but he was a defender in the truest sense. If you take away all the romanticized knight in shining armor persona and look at him logically, he was the man you wanted by your side. Even now, when Arthur was laying on the street broken and twisted, Lee was tempted to run out there and finish this. You can bet your ass that the kid stopping Charlie from shooting Arthur down right then and there wasn't him wanting to save Arthur's life, but him wanting to save the kill for himself. It's human nature. It's in Lee's nature.

I wish I could read Charlie's mind. The idea that destiny was stealing Arthur from him must have been almost unbearable to him. He had waited to find this guy for five years. It became personal the day Charlie found his only daughter carved up like a thanksgiving turkey. Arthur was looking his closure and a little blue Chevy took that all away. I liked the irony of it. Charlie looked lost as he stared at the body that was dying right in front of him. Was it enough that the man he hated and blamed for turning his heart to stone was dying in the streets rather then by his own hand? When a man stops believing in justice and starts searching for revenge, can he be satisfied with seeing the opportunity stolen even if the end result is the same? My father liked to call it tunnel vision. You see only one thing and can't see any other option even if it ends the with the same result. Any other outcome, no matter what it is, seems like a failure because you can't let go of what you wanted. Charlie's vision was him killing the man that killed his little princess even if her crown was twisted and tarnished like one of those cheap metal bracelets that fade and chip after a few days of owning them.

They say that you only hurt the ones you love and, in my experience, there has never been a truer word. Callie and Rosie were like twin souls. Soul mates if you will. Both were looking for approval in a self-destructive manner just like Jane. They couldn't look in the mirror and see somebody worthy of love. No not one of them saw their true value. They only saw a sexual creature that needed to fulfill a man's destructive wants. That was their down fall. They might have gone about it in slightly different ways, but the need was the same. The need was stronger than they were and more than I could bare. Day after day I watched them struggle as each tried to seduce men in the hopes that sex turned to love and the disappointment that always followed. They are free now. Free from the tears and heart break that always followed them.

Charlie's gaze came back to Lee, who despite his inner strength, seemed stuck on Arthur. With a quick snap, he smashed him onto the hood of the car and yanked his arms back. Charlie was playing cop, even if he lost the right. The cuffs were placed around Lee's wrists as his legs were forced open like it was an instructional video. I wouldn't have to intervene in this though. The Bloodhound still believed in true justice. He would see to it that Lee was protected. Bloodhound's are loyal that way. It's in their nature to smell out the rats and chase them down.

Charlie surprised me though. It was something out of character for him. Something that even I couldn't see. It was like watching a demon becoming human. The humanity returning to the monster that he had become. He lowered his gun and stepped into traffic holding his hand out as he went. There are always a million possible reasons why people do what they do and most of the time those reasons make sense to nobody except the one who holds on to them so tightly. I can only assume that Charlie wanted to save him so that he could enjoy the kill himself. That wasn't exactly how plan A was supposed to go, but it was still enough.

Charlie marched over to Arthur's body and knelt like you would expect a real hero to do. You know the kind of thing that you would see make the papers. Off duty cop saves alleged murder suspect. Yes, this one step would normally make him the talk of the town, if the town wasn't already talking about him. It was still an unexpected surprise though. He placed his fingers onto his neck checking for a pulse, but I kept waiting for him to choke him. He looked up as the sirens blared and the flickering blue and red exploded in to his vision. The minute I saw the disappointment in his eyes I knew that the hero the world would see was only an illusion. The world always needs illusions.

CHAPTER 20 – ASHLEY

The first time I ever found myself shackled in handcuffs I was fifteen years old and I thought the world would end. Not because of what I did, because stealing food when you are hungry isn't really stealing, it's a matter of survival, but it's the fact I got caught that scared me. The cops seemed like nice guys as they tried to relate to me on a human level. It was their way of reaching out to me on a personal level. At the time, I couldn't appreciate the effort that these two men were putting forth. I was too worried about what my foster parents would say when I was brought home. It wasn't a beating I was scared of, but the fear of being locked in my room and going hungry even longer. That's the life of an orphan, especially an orphan that witnessed his mother dying before his eyes. They call us non-placeable which basically means defective. Damaged goods.

I was still laying on the hood of the car watching the scene unfold in front of me. The EMTs came quicker than I expected, which is saying a lot considering my experience with those damn ambulance drivers. They arrived within minutes, which is never good considering the fact that generally I am pounding the hell out of somebody's face and don't want to stop. It only took them minutes to prep Arthur and slide him into the ambulance. It reminded me of one of those assembly lines you see on TV where they build cars. You know, it starts off with the cops searching for a pulse, followed by the ambulance showing up and the attendants jumping out and running over. After checks and stuff like that they plopped him on a stretcher and slid him into the back driving off leaving only streaked red lights as a reminder that they were even here.

At times like this the strangest thoughts flow throw my head. Seeing the man that had possessed everything that I wanted it life and that I now saw as my one true enemy, being taken away to some kind of critical care unit was torturous. It should have made me happy. However, that is the last thing that flowed through my mind. I saw the blood flowing down street and all I could think of was if I hadn't of dropped all that cola, I could have cleaned that up. I am sure the crowd gathering around me thought that I had lost my mind as I burst out laughing at the scene of an accident.

"He is under arrest for obstructing justice," the sergeant screamed as his hands flew through the air. I couldn't hear what the cop named Bruno was saying, but the way he was holding his hands out in front of him made it pretty clear it wasn't what the beast wanted to hear. "Under suspension!" he screamed. Pointing in my direction, he continually screamed, "The little bastard was aiding and abiding." As those words left his lips he pushed forward sending Bruno backwards while screaming, "I am not part of the investigation my ass. I put you on the case and I will yank you off in a heart beat! He is going to be booked."

The way that the good old sergeant was wailing his hands around and the way that Bruno seemed to be getting aggravated, I was certain that I was going to see cop on cop wrestling right here in the streets. I had to admit it was exciting to see. Instead of cop kicking my ass it was going to be cop kicking a cop's ass. If I was a betting man though, I would have to put my money on the mad man sergeant. Crazy bastards like him always seem to come out on top.

If you watch people close enough everybody has a tell. Bruno was stepping back at the start of their conversation like the Sargent was the alpha male of a wolf pack, but now he wasn't backing off anymore. No, he now kept one hand behind his back, while holding his other hand out in front of him keeping an arms length between them. The Sargent was too enraged to notice that Bruno's head dropped and he was bracing his feet. Pointing at me, the Sargent snapped, "He is staying in the cuffs."

This was the first time in the whole argument that I had been able to hear anything Bruno said. Each word he spoke was followed by his hand pushing down towards the ground. "You aren't in charge of this investigation and you caught him walking home with damn groceries. Groceries!"

The sergeant snapped, "He assaulted an officer of the law. It's still a crime as far as I know."

Bruno snapped, "You pulled an unregistered gun when you are suspended, so no, at this point you aren't an officer of the law. You are just like any other schoolyard bully acting like an uncontrollable thug." Stepping forward he pointed and said, "This ends now or I will arrest you here and now for obstruction of justice, among other things, and walk you to the cell myself."

The Sargent took a swing that clocked Bruno right in the face sending him back a couple of paces while he followed that up with a couple more. It looked like Bruno was about to tip over. Of course, I saw that in a pound for pound fight, Bruno was out matched by a superior fighter. It was like watching a street dog attacking one of those little tea cup dogs that rich people shove in their purse.

Everybody was too busy concentrating on the struggle to see Logan standing there with his hands on his hips looking as scared as a frightened child watching his parents fight. He looked too young to be a real cop, let alone part of a murder investigation. Seeing the two heroes of the Police force going at it like teenagers fighting over the hottest chick, must have been hard for him. The way he kept looking down the street, it was obvious that he was hoping a cruiser would pull up and help him, but he was screwed. He looked like he wanted to step out into the street, but he hesitated. He held a pair of cuffs in his hand, but I don't think he would dare put them on either of his superiors. That would-be career suicide for the little baby-faced cop. I mean jumping in between these two giants, let alone actually placing the cuffs on one of them, was unthought of.

The Sargent threw a wide punch allowing Bruno to grab hold, but when he went to slide the cuffs on him, he sucker punched him in the ribs. Experience allowed him to slam in a couple more punches before Bruno was able to throw him back a few paces. In desperation, Bruno lunged forward sending the Sargent falling backwards on his ass. I expected more from them. You know men who have spent their whole lives fighting bad guys should put on a better show or, at the very least, I was hoping to see more teeth falling onto the pavement.

The Sargent leapt up charging like a bull swinging his fists in the air in blind rage. I always thought how cool it would be to have two people fighting over me. You know, it's a guy thing. We always want to feel so special and important that two people will fight over me, but this wasn't the image I had in mind. In my mind, it was two blondes' in short skirts and a pool of mud, not two middle aged cops. Just my luck. This whole week was so bad if I had a diary, I am sure that it would makes me cry reading it over.

Logan seemed to suddenly grow a back bone as the fists flew back and forth and ran towards them. The sergeants fist flew back as he went to finish the battle with one well placed punch. Bruno was weaving backwards with blood dripping from his nose down his chin and onto the ground. Yes, I am certain that this last hit was going to end the battle and give me a free trip down town. It's that Goddamned karma again. It pushes a defender into your life, but he's a defective one so its just false hope inside a cheap suit.

Logan was right behind the Sargent as his fist stretched backwards and with cat like reflexes, he slapped the cuffs on him. It was rather impressive to see. As the cuffs clicked around his wrists Logan brought his arm over his shoulder and under his chin twisting him backwards as he flipped him over. With a slight hip check, Logan kept hold of his wrist as and jumped on him forcing his other arm behind his back. I would have to remember that move since I am sure that I would be meeting him in other circumstances in the near future.

I watched as the Sargent screamed and threatened both men, but neither seemed to care what he was saying. I guess he was suddenly finding himself on the other side of a thin line. You know, it's the us thugs and them cops line. Of course, he deserved to be on my side of the line. He wasn't any better then me and now the world knew it. Maybe karma was finally giving me break. It was about time.

Bruno was slowly making his way to his knees because of wobbly legs that wouldn't hold him quite yet. He kept wiping the blood off his chin as he struggled to make his way up. He was coughing and spitting as he knelt there holding his chest. Old men aren't meant for these kinds fights. I guess that's why they send a younger, stronger junior cop with them.

Logan was pulling the Sargent up as he screamed, "When I am done with you, you will be lucky if you aren't partnering with that simple Harold."

Logan slipped the .45 out of his pocket muttering, "And you will be lucky if you keep your pension Charlie. You just crossed that line between pain in the ass to total asshole," as he pushed him towards the side walk. It was nice to see a cop treating one of their own the same way they always treat me. Like a burden on society. Who knows? Maybe we can share a cell tonight since it was obvious that we both had reservations at the same hotel.

Bruno teetered over towards me looking beaten and enraged. It was the same look all cops get before they slap you around. It's what I call life experience and I have experienced that part of life too many times for my liking. He stood in front of me still a bit wobbly, "You OK kid?"

His eye was swollen and his lips had so many cracks that it looked like he just finished French kissing sand paper. Looking up, I grinned, "I am looking prettier then you are."

"Yes, well by the looks of your face, I am taking that as an insult." Well I haven't looked in the mirror, but I am sure that it was an insult of sorts. I looked like I was hit by the ugly stick over and over again.

He walked behind me and undid the handcuffs. As I heard the metal clicking it was a great feeling to be free of them. I was twisting my wrists trying to get the circulation back into my hands. "You hurt?" Bruno said watching me intently.

"I am fine. Just keep that mad bastard away from me." That wasn't a request, but a demand. I was tired of being hunted by a bad ass mad man who had no proof, just hate. Of course, one day the Sargent would turn around to find me standing behind him and he wouldn't like the outcome.

Pointing towards my place he muttered, "Go home now. In a few minutes, there will be a lot more cruisers then you can count and most won't be that friendly considering they still think that you killed Callie." I was still standing there holding my wrists as the first cruiser pulled up. There was something about the way they were looking at me that made me believe Bruno was right. It wouldn't take much for me to be shot accidentally on purpose.

I watched as Logan lead the Sargent towards the cop car and put him in the back seat. He was a proud man who held his head up and glared at me with such contempt. I didn't like the idea of having to keep my door locked and sleeping with one eye open for the rest of my life. "Don't worry about Charlie," Bruno muttered. "Charlie might not like the idea, but the proof will prove your innocence. We got our man and all I need to do is connect the dots. I am good at connecting those illusive dots."

I watched the cop car drive off taking my archenemy away to the police station. If this were a comic book, tomorrow he would be free and we'd start the fight all over again. "So, do I need to move away and get a new name?"

Laughing, Bruno muttered, "Not tonight at least." He handed me a twenty stating, "For the cola you dropped."

I know most people would say, "No" to the offer, too proud to take his money, but hell I am not that proud. I will take his money and still bitch about the fact that I dropped my pop. I made my way home trying to figure out how I was going to get the blood out of my carpet and relieved that if I couldn't, it wasn't an automatic prison sentence. I opened the door and couldn't believe what I saw.

CHAPTER 21 – BRUNO

I stood there in the shower for twenty minutes trying to wash the day away, but despite the fact the water drove the blood and dirt from my body, it couldn't erase the events from my memory. I stood there letting the hot water massage my aching neck while trying to put the pieces together. This whole case was like a used jigsaw puzzle. The pieces fit so perfectly, but the damn colors didn't match. There is nothing worse than having everything wrapped up in a nice bright bow, like a Christmas present, but realizing that they scratched out somebody else's name and put yours. I knew that it was there, but I couldn't put my finger on it.

My prime suspect Arthur was in critical, but stable condition. The doctors tried to explain exactly what was wrong with him, but the only thing I really got out of the conversation was the fact that he kissed the bumper of a car going 80 kilometers an hour and the effect wasn't what he expected it would be. Either way, he cracked his noggin too hard and there was some kind of bleeding in the brain. Through all of this though, my thought is that his wife must be some kind of Saint. This guy was sleeping with another woman yet, here this woman is at his bed side begging him not to die. They say love is blind, but they should have added it makes you stupid.

I walked into the station change room and it was colder

than even I expected, the other cops created a wide berth around me. As I got dressed and towel dried my hair, I mulled over everything that's been happening. It's a loyalty thing. Cops don't turn on cops no matter what they do and Charlie was the top dog here, so placing the cuffs on him was taken as an insult to everybody who wore a badge. If only Charlie wasn't so damn stubborn and emotionally involved in this case. He had blinders on and no matter what evidence might pop up, he was completely blind to it. The damn fool should know better. What was I supposed to do? Just turn my back on justice? Well at least Logan seemed to be on my side. I am still not sure he isn't somehow involved in things, but for the time being, he is the only ally I have. One friend is better than none, even if you can't turn your back on that friend for a minute.

I was on my way down to the evidence room to get the diary Arthur had dropped when Harold came slouching by. "So, we're able to verify my alibi?" he muttered like a sulking child as he walked by.

"Yes, I did." Grabbing his shoulder, I said, "Listen Harold there are things happening that you know and you have to admit, seeing you there looked suspicious." I didn't want to tell him that a lot of evidence pointed to one of us being involved and he stepped right into the spot light.

Pulling away he snapped, "I might not be the best cop in the building, but I am solid." He was stomping down the hall towards the cell block. "I don't take short cuts and I damn well can't be bullied, even by the Sergeant."

"Bullied," I snapped as I stopped and stared at him.

Turning around he pointed, "Yes bullied. He tells me that I am to keep my ear to the ground and try and get Lee to admit what he did, but report back to him, not you." Closing his fists, he muttered, "I won't be part of a witch hunt. I just wished that I could have been the one to clamp the cuffs on him."

"No, you don't," I replied. "That's career suicide."

"Only if you were wrong and Logan wasn't wrong when he did it."

"Logan won't last to the end of the year. I doubt I will

either."

Red faced Harold responded, "At least he stood up for justice." It's easier to stand up for your morals when it's only theory. The actual doing is where most people cave. Logan risked a lot and when everything is said and done, he will slowly be pushed out. I wonder how that fits into his career plan. Hell, I was trying to see where it left me. A friendless loner waiting for retirement.

Seeing Harold made me think of Charlie locked up in the holding cell. I was going to have to release him eventually and it was on my way to the evidence room, so I decided to just do it and get it over with. It's like a rectal exam. You hate the idea of a finger being shoved up there, but it's got to be done. As big of a pain in the ass that is, you know it might just save your life. I made my way through the metal doors that led to the holding cell. Charlie bellowed, "Harold call Bruno and tell him to get his old ass down here." I just kept walking towards him not looking forward to the upcoming conversation. Charlie might be one of my oldest friends, but he was still a well-respected officer. "Don't ignore me Harold or else your next job will be a crossing guard in front of the school."

"For Pete's sake Charlie stop the shit," I muttered as I strolled towards his cell. "You can't bully everybody that works under you because you are in a bad mood."

"A bad mood!" he snapped. "My daughter is murdered by a guy you can't catch and when you have all the evidence to get a conviction, you slip up." Holding the bars, he bellowed, "He almost got away because you couldn't get the job done."

"I couldn't get the job done!" I snapped. "Unlike you, I was following the evidence. You remember how that works don't you?" I was pointed towards him, "Remember when it was innocence until proven guilty?"

"You self-righteous bastard. If memory serves correct, we got the guilty bastard lying on his back in St. Michael's hospital right now. If he doesn't live long enough for a trial, it's on you. If the families of his victims don't get satisfaction, it's all on you."

"Satisfaction," I snapped. "You mean your satisfaction which amounts to his dying any other way then by your hands isn't good enough."

I decided to let him stew on it overnight.

I could hear Charlie screaming as I made my way towards the exit. "Aren't you going to let me out of here?" The echo of his fists slamming against the metal bars was chasing me as I went, "You son of a bitch Bruno, don't you dare leave me here. You owe me."

As I opened the door I gave him the bird saying, "Sweet dreams cup cake. I will see you in the morning."

The last thing I heard was Charlie screaming, "Fuck you Bruno. Fuck you!" Part of me wanted to say love you too, but I am certain that he would still be there in the morning and be in just as pissy a mood.

I decided to take the stairs down to the evidence room. It wasn't that I wanted the exercise, I just didn't want to have to take the elevator and deal with the damn stares of betrayal. You know the ones that don't look straight at you, but never leave you? Well that was the look I was getting from the newest rookie to oldest friend. I was the Judas of the Essex police force.

The evidence room was in the far back corner of a stuffy basement. Some cities have giant warehouse type storage areas that have millions of items from thousands of cases. Our city had too many crimes, but nothing like Toronto or Vancouver. I made my way to the little charge room where Donald the night guy works. I stepped in front of the gate. "Hey Donald, I am here for the evidence that was collected today."

Shaking his head, he muttered, "Can't help you Bruno, the hot shot already came and got it." Smiling he said, "Mark my words, that kids going to be your boss one day."

"How did he get the evidence when I said it was off limits to anyone, but me?"

"Ah well you know his family has roots here and he said that he'd have it back before you came to get it."

The look on his face said it all. He wasn't sorry that he

broke procedure just that he got caught. Men like him call it loyalty, but it's just a kiss ass thinking that Logan will keep climbing like a rocket. Even now they see him eagerly challenging the top dog, looking to be the leader of the pack. I couldn't really blame him for that, only the way they broke policy. It seems to me that this mister Brown was smack dab in the middle of everything and her diary might lead me to him or at least mention him. I needed to see her view of the world around her to understand where Arthur, Brown and the kid fit in her world. I had to forget about everything else and just follow the evidence.

I made my way through the hall way to Logan's desk. He was leaning back with his feet up, reading Rosie's diary. Part of me wanted to bitch slap him for going around me, but I needed him. If he wasn't mister Brown or a close personal friend of his, Logan had everything to lose by not solving the case and a dim future here, even if we did. "My god Bruno," was all he said while he looked at me over the book. His eyes were filled with sadness as they dropped back behind the pages glaring into the pages.

"You can't say my god Bruno and go back to reading. It's like saying you found something case breaking that you can't share."

Leaning forward he dropped the book on the table. "Everything about this girl is like a horror story Bruno. It starts a year ago."

Sitting next to his desk, "What exactly starts a year ago?" I don't know why, but I felt excited about it. Yes, I was shamed for feeling this way, but after seeing her online life hearing her personal thoughts would be mind blowing. It's like living your darkest desires through another's personal life.

"Well that is when it all started. I mean everything." Leaning back in his chair and taking a sip of his coffee, he then continued. "Have you ever heard of sugaring?"

"It's nothing to do with sweetener that's for sure." It was the newest fad. Basically, legalized prostitution. I had read about it a few months back. Basically, old horny men pay for young college students companionship. It was one of those things. You know what happens behind closed doors stays behind closed doors and nobody talks about it.

"No nothing close to that. Either way, Rosie joined this sugaring site and met with four men. Two of them are of interest."

Leaning forward I said, "Obviously, Arthur and who else? It cannot be Ashley because the kid doesn't have enough cash for this kind of life style." That was just pure common sense. The kid worked from home doing tech support for some no name computer company out of Toronto. It's another new fad. Why pay for an office when people can work from home in their underwear?

"No, it was this mysterious Mister Brown whose name keeps popping up." There was a sly grin on his face he added, "Maybe if we are lucky we can actually get a picture of him from his profile." That was probably the best news I had received all day. I don't believe in ghosts and the idea of chasing one wasn't making me feel any happier. The IT geeks couldn't locate the avatar he used on his chats because it was just a graphic he picked up from the internet. "Yes, the computer guys are already on it," he said as he took another sip.

"So, Mister Brown is her sugar daddy too?" Seems like the father figure wasn't much of a father.

"No not as far as I can tell." Skimming through the pages he pressed his fingers into the book. "Arthur was buying a sex toy. She knew it from the start and excepted that." Sliding his finger along the pages, he muttered, "It seems that Arthur had a special site that required a password to enter where he displayed pictures and videos. Not exactly a big shock, though is it?" It wasn't anything I didn't already know. The dude was such a pig every time I saw him, all I could smell was bacon.

"Here is the interesting part though." He slid his finger across the pages, "Last night I met Mister Brown in person for the first time. He wasn't exactly what I expected, but I immediately felt safe with him. He has this old-school charm and presence about him. He was fatherly and the whole time that I shared the meal, he never once asked me about what he would get for his money. No demands of expectations at all. He just asked about my dreams for the future and why I was interested in becoming a sugar baby. Such a sweet caring man." Oh, yes Mister Brown was seeming more like a saint every day. No man joins a site like that without having ulterior motives. No man is that fatherly with a sexy young single woman. No man.

"No here it gets even stranger."

You know how at the scene of an accident you stare? Morally you know that you could look away, but your mind won't let you do it? Damned if I know why, only that it's a fact of life. People just can't not look. It's the same with porn or sex. Yes, I have stumbled upon people doing it doggy style behind a dumpster and instead of arresting them, me and Charlie just ate our lunch and watched. We just couldn't stop watching. "At the end of our meal Mister Brown handed me five hundred dollars saying that if I ever needed a friend to call and then he gave me his number. As he was slipping his wallet back into his jacket pocket, I saw the badge fastened to his belt." The look in Logan's eyes said it all. Of course, I wasn't shocked after talking to the IT geeks, but Logan sure the hell was. "Can you believe it? This fatherly Mister Brown is a god damn cop." Shaking his head, he muttered, "This case keeps getting more and more complicated and twisted."

"I know," was all I could manage to think of to say. How to you tell a guy that up until a minute ago, he was one of my prime suspects? It's exactly the type of conversations most people want to have and I damn well know that I don't want to have it. "Does she give any other descriptions of him?"

Flipping through the pages, "Nothing that helps us. Later she adds that Arthur says that he wants her to belong only to him. That he insists she stop spending time with this Brown character."

"Is that it? There must be something incriminating against Arthur in there somewhere. Something that can help us determine who the hell this Brown is?"

"Nothing specific. This dude sounds like your average Joe, but I did find something about the Ashley kid."

I didn't really expect much more than the creepy guy who keeps staring at me, but evidence was evidence. "Ok what does she say about him?"

Flipping pages, he read, "Tonight we were out as usual when Arthur told me that I am no longer allowed to wear panties when we go out and he wanted me to wear my short dress. I told him that I didn't want to do that because ladies don't bring their private fantasies into public. He screamed that I wasn't a lady and he was paying good money to live out his fantasies." Staring up at me, Logan muttered, "She goes on about their argument and here is where it gets interesting." Skimming the pages, he stopped, "Lee showed up twenty minutes later. He just walked up and said that I was a lady, punching Arthur right in the face. It was probably the most the heroic and romantic event of my life." Smiling up at me, Logan asked, "you know what that means don't you?"

"That Arthur was using this poor kid to live out his fantasies."

Laughing Logan leaned back, "yes, but also that the kid was stalking her then too and it brings up a very interesting question. How did he know what Arthur said?"

That was a good point. Lee had her computer bugged so to speak, but was it possible to do it with a phone or place some kind of bug on her to listen to her conversations? Obviously, it was possible since the feds do it all the time, but was it possible for the kid to pull off? This was like real spy shit right out of the movies. "So, did you come across anything that would make Arthur risk so much? I mean he truly would be headed for a 6 x 9 cell if we found something interesting."

"Not so far, but I am not done reading yet," Logan said with a grin. "I think this is one of those cases when the truth is stranger than fiction." Laughing he added, "And a lot hotter."

"Show some respect." I stood up and decided to have another little talk with Charlie. As I walked away, I said, "Let me know what you find and don't let that damn book out of your sight. If we have a traitor in our midst, I doubt that he wants us to find out who he is."

"You got it," he said as he went back to reading.

"By the way, who was the third man she contacted on the sugar baby site?"

"Oh, some priest that Brown begged her to stay away from. The dude told her he was dangerous and called him mad Mike, but after that, she never mentions Mike the priest again."

"Keep him in mind when you are reading through the book."

I made my way back to the holding cell to see Charlie. I wasn't sure if he would be in a talkative mood, but I knew damn well that he would want to know about Mister Brown. I made my way towards his cell expecting him to start screaming the minute my feet hit the floor, but there was only silence. Strange I thought, but maybe he was sleeping. I hurried my pace and made it to his cell. The door was wide open and the cell was empty. Son of a bitch, they let him go.

CHAPTER 22 – ASHLEY

I can't remember ever being depressed before. I have been lonely and obviously so since I am not exactly mister popular, but I can't remember ever being depressed. I came home expecting to see my house resembling a slaughter house, but when I opened the front door, is was spotless. As much as I hate to admit it, I needed the life-threatening danger to help me push all the other troubles away. You know deep in the back of my mind, behind the figurative locked door, where all the other horrors get locked away is where I wanted those troubles to stay. I had been standing by the same window staring at the same window I had been staring at night after night for what seems like forever, pretending that nothing had changed. I know that Rosie was never coming home, but I didn't know what else to do with myself. I was lost. Rosie and her killer were dead. It's like every obsession I ever had was stolen in a minute.

Part of me wanted to go to the hospital to make sure that Arthur was indeed dead. Seeing is believing so they say and part of me wanted him to be alive. As much as I loved Rosie, I hated Arthur and right now I needed to hate somebody.

From my window I saw a car pull up and park in Rosie's spot. It was odd to see since for as long as I can remember only Arthur parked there, but he wouldn't be parking there anymore. I don't know why, but it seemed sad to me. I watched a figure jump out of the car and immediately prowl towards the back of the house until he vanished from site. I sat down waiting to see what was going to happen next, like it was reality TV. Life can be quite interesting if you watch the world around close enough and use your imagination. The light to Rosie's room flickered on then the blinds immediately closed choking out the light. Any other night, the sight would break my heart because of the images that came alive from it. Rosie's naked body being used and abused by another man when it was supposed to be me lovingly caressing her, but tonight it was a mystery. I hate mysteries.

A phone rang from the kitchen. It wasn't my phone because mine was sitting on the kitchen table and the ring was different. It took me a few minutes to find where it was coming from, but finally I found it hidden behind the fridge. It was like every aspect of my life was being twisted and invaded by the unknown. The caller ID on the phone said Sweet Rosie which was some kind of twisted joke that would likely get somebody killed. "Who is this?" I snarled.

"It's a friend," a muffled voice echoed. I saw the blinds across the street open and a figure standing in the window.

"I don't have any friends," I responded as I knelt down looking through the telescope trying to see who was in Rosie's room.

"Oh, I am the best friend that you will ever have," the voice said. The figure in the window seemed to be watching me. I hated being watched. I don't mind watching people, but ironically being watched creeps me out.

"What are you doing in Rosie's room?" I had never seen her room, at least not through my telescope or through a web cam. I always thought that eventually I would be invited in like a best friend or lover, but that will never happen now.

"It's not important. What's important is that we need to talk and this is the best way to do it." The blinds closed and he was lost from view, but based on his shadow, he seemed to be a fairly big guy. Too big for the Sargent that always seemed to pop up to slap me around.

"Do I know you?"

"No, but I know who you are and that's all that counts. I have been watching you for some time now."

This was something that not even I could have imaged. A stalker stalking a stalker. Try saying that fast a dozen times. It's impossible. "So, what is so interesting about me?" What kind of guy watches a guy from his dead girlfriend's window? Sick bastard.

The blinds flickered open as he responded, "Don't be so negative kid, I see potential in you."

"Why are you in Rosie's room? You shouldn't be in there." It was true. What kind of sick fuck enters a dead girls room? The blinds opened and closed again. I decided to go over and see who the hell my stalker was. I wasn't having a good day so maybe having this sicko close by was what I needed to blow off some rage. I snuck out the back door and slowly made my way down the fire escape.

"I thought that it was about time we talk."

"What do we have to talk about exactly? We aren't family, friends or anything else, so unless you are going to tell me that we are enemies, we have nothing to talk about." From the side of my sight line, I could see his silhouette in the window. I stood against the corner waiting for him to close the blinds again, but he didn't. He just stood there looking towards my window.

"Listen kid, you need to just stay home for the next couple of days. It's best for you if you find a hole somewhere and hide."

"I can't hide from the horrors of this world. All you can do is chase them down and kill them." I really don't know what the hell I was talking about. I was just babbling on trying to keep him on the line. He was still standing in the window so all I could do was wait until he stepped away from it, then I was going to charge in after him.

"Don't bullshit me boy, you are scared shitless. No Rosie to chase and love. No Arthur to blame and hunt for it. You are in way over your head. Stay away before good old Charlie comes looking for you."

He stepped away from the window and that's when I ran my ass over towards the house which was a task, considering Sandwich Street was always busy. As I dashed between the traffic I muttered, "And what does any of this have to do with you mister Brown."

He was silent which told me I was right. It made sense considering the mysterious figure had been talking to Rosie for a year and never missed a day. If I was lost and struggling, he damn well was too. "So, you know of me." Laughing he added, "Yes I should have figured as much. No better witness then your friendly neighborhood stalker."

I was at the front door and looking through the rocks trying to find the fake rock that contained the hidden key. In day light it seemed like the kind of things that screams out, 'rob me I am that stupid', but now in the darkness, it was hard as hell to find. "So, I assume that you are the one that broke into my place and hid the phone behind my fridge." I finally found the fake rock and slowly unlocked the door and slipped into the house.

"Yes, I wanted to have a little talk with you. By the way sorry I had to steal your laptops and tear down your pictures, but I have this thing about keeping my face out of the spot light."

"You took what," I snapped. "You stole my life. You took my happiest moments and memories." I was storming up the stairs screaming, "I am going to kill you when I get my hands on you. I will feel the life fading out of you as I wrap my hands around your throat."

Laughing he responded, "No that would not end well for you. I like you kid, but Brown likes Brown more. Remember that kid. If it comes to you or me, I will always win." Then the phone went dead.

I kicked in the door to Rosie's room prepared to kill Brown, but the room was empty. The son of a bitch was gone. I opened the closet and pushed all the clothes aside. He wasn't there and that pissed me off even more. "Where the hell are you Brown?" I screamed as I looked under the bed and even in the bathroom, but he was no where to be found.

I ran to the window in time to see Rosie's parking spot empty as a white car drove off, lost in traffic. "Son of a bitch," I screamed as I realized that he must have sneaked down the back stairs to make his escape. I was so stupid. I had him in my grasp, but he slipped away because of my ignorance. The car seemed familiar, but I couldn't place it. Where did I see the white car before? I knew I had, but I couldn't place it.

I looked down on the desk and saw a little note sitting on a bunch of Rosie's pictures. Older ones from when she was young and filled with innocence. "Sorry kid I needed to rip away those memories but needed to protect myself most of all. Take these and remember the young girl who had possibilities before life corrupted her." I took my fingers and slid the pictures around. Rosie was absolutely gorgeous, even back then. That is when it hit me. I knew where I had seen the car before. It was that god damn sergeant named Charlie. I had the name of the man I was going to kill. Now I just needed to find him.

CHAPTER 23 – BROWN

If you have tried to write a novel you have probably gotten to a point where you can't put the scenes bouncing around your head onto paper. Perhaps it was the part where the words you want to express just won't come through you and onto the page. They call it writers block. Now I have never written a book, but I understand the concept of it. That is how life gets sometimes. You have those ups and downs and when you feel inspiration or momentum strike, you can't stop because you never know when writers block will strike. That's exactly what I am doing. I reached out to Ashley as a first step in making peace and protecting him from the aftermath of Rosie's death. This kid could have a great future if he had the right teacher and I am that teacher.

Of course, the kid would be as challenging as Rosie ever was. Who knows? Maybe even more challenging. For his sake, I hope not though, because the kid was smart too. Too smart really. He knew my voice and maybe even my face. Who knows? Maybe he had everything stored in a cloud somewhere on the internet just waiting to be yanked back down. For his sake, I hope not because either he was going to be with me or against me. Things would be a lot better for him if he was with me.

The bloodhound would have realized by now that Charlie was set free. It took some doing, but I have some pull and finally arranged it. It wasn't anything as graceful as setting a caged bird free, no it was more like having a monster in the closet and opening the door so he can escape before turning the lights out. Charlie was my plan B after all. Even the greatest plan can swirl out of control and the Arthur plan had so many unexpected turns that I was beginning to lose faith in it.

I just sat there watching the light pass through the glass doors and push away the darkness of night. I watched the people in the waiting room reading out of date magazines or staring at the floor as they waited to be seen by an over paid doctor whose only thought is getting home after a long day. It's the reality of life in the ER. It got a lot worse since government cuts backs and the fact that they divided the hospitals. They call it specialization or something like that. I call it an extra ten-minute drive. If Arthur would have kissed the front of the car from the other side of town, that extra ten minutes might have killed him. Ten minutes can mean a lot.

Surprisingly the bloodhound didn't send anyone to watch over Arthur. It would have been a lot better for me if he had. Better for Charlie too because you watch over dangerous men, not forget them. The bloodhound had enough to lock him away, but he didn't. Oh, that Bruno was a smart one. He wasn't jumping through the hoops like I wanted him to. Charlie and Logan did more than I expected, but not the bloodhound. No, he was like one of those kids that gets blocks for Christmas and must examine every piece for imperfections before he plays with them. That's how the bloodhound was with evidence. Always examining every piece.

Charlie was predictable. Later than I expected, but very predictable. He was sneaking through the side doors at the far end of the hospital partially hidden by the over grown hedges. He was sliding along the building trying to stay in the shadows and hidden from the dull street lights that stood on either side. He wasn't exactly cat burglar material and clumsy as hell to boot. The only guy I know who can frolic through the park and trip over a leaf. Of course, that was back when princess Callie was still around. Back when he cared about helping people rather than being consumed by hating them. I always wondered if he even suspected that he walked right by Callie's killer every day since the day she died. I bet that would drive him madder than a hatter if he knew. Yes, I have been waiting for that shoe to drop for a long time now.

As he entered the door, I grabbed my spare phone and dialed reception, "Could you page Mrs. Andersen for me please?" I asked. Even the best chess piece needs a little help to get a check mate after all. I was certain that this little distraction would be all Charlie needed. Just a simple phone call to yank everybody away was all Charlie could desire.

"I will page her name," the voice responded. "I will need to place you on a brief hold while I do it."

"Thank you." It's always nice to be polite because people have a harder time remembering polite people then rude or cold people. "Yes of course I will wait." Once she placed me on hold, I hung up and powered down the phone. It was one of those American disposable phones that I picked up on my last trip to Detroit. I didn't want anyone trying to trace where the phone was because it would lead the bloodhound to me. By the time, they realized I hung up, it would be too late because Charlie would have already been to see Arthur. Now the question was what would Charlie do? Even I didn't know for sure if he would kill him or not, but I wanted to know.

The bus pulled up and stopped right in front of those double wide doors blocking my view. I know that millions of people around the world depend on public transportation, but it seems to me that in some way, those damn buses are always in the way. I waited impatiently expecting to see Charlie storming out of the hospital, but even if he did, that damn big red and white bus was in the way. Damn driver stepped out to have a smoke which, in itself was against the law. Smoking on hospital property was strictly prohibited. If I didn't want to keep a low profile, I would step out and bust his ass. Normally

I would move the car, but I couldn't risk it. People that move around a parking lot without reason get noticed and I didn't want to get noticed. I watched the driver get in the bus then slowly pull away.

I scanned the area in front of the hospital looking for Charlie but didn't see him anywhere. I was starting to think that he slipped out unnoticed when that damn bus was parked there. Part of the reward was watching everything unfold. Every task must come with its own prize at the end. Mine is watching how those I steer react to the plot as they follow along. The excitement that comes with watching my soldiers playing their roles so blindly. It isn't the reason I do it, but it certainly offers personal satisfaction and its own reward. Life is full of disappointments and this is just another one of them.

I saw the lights as a small little sports car pulled into the parking lot a few spaces away. Peering over I saw him jump out and head towards the emergency doors. Obviously, there was nothing exciting happening within because he was strolling, not running. I couldn't decide if I was happy about it or not since seeing Logan was yet another unexpected event of the night. That and the fact that he was staring in his own improv role. Seeing the excitement, I had caused in his life I expected soon there would two then three and before you know it the bloodhound comes strolling in. I didn't want the bloodhound sticking his nose into my business. Not yet at least. As Logan went into the room, disappearing behind the door, I thought that Arthur must have woken up. That was the thing that made sense. Logan was here to question him. By now Arthur was the prime suspect and my soon to be protégé was out of the spot light.

Charlie was standing in the door way peeking out like a mugger preparing to strike. You'd think a seasoned cop would know better than to wear a red hat. He wasn't bursting through the doors running for his life so I assume he didn't go through with it. I was on the fence about it. That's the whole reason I set him free. To see if there was really a killer inside him or not. Despite what most people think, killer instinct does exist inside all of us, but it's the situation that brings it out. Even in mourning, which he dragged out way too long, Charlie couldn't pull the trigger. Give him, a crook, with a .45 and he would not even hesitate to pull the trigger, but a defenseless little prick like Arthur just lying there and he can't do it. Human nature I guess.

I watched him slip out trying to avoid the cameras as he pushed his hands in his pockets, hunching over while trying to hide his face. Dumbass should have brought a pull over because the hood covers his face. About half way along the building, he started running full tilt. Maybe there wasn't so much integrity in him after all. Maybe Charlie's hate made him more savage then he'd like to admit. You gotta love human nature.

The front doors came bursting open and Logan appeared holding his gun in both hands. I wasn't very surprised to see that he was all business now. Pointing his gun around, he was looking from side to side, scouring everything in sight. I watched as he ran off in the same direction that Charlie ran off in. This night was certainly more eventful then even I expected and it seemed to me that Logan might have become the hero he always wanted to be, if only he had managed to run out a few minutes sooner.

CHAPTER 24 – BRUNO

Every case has a breaking point. Sometimes the break leads straight to a conviction and then there are the other breaks. The ones that makes the case crumble to dust and you are left holding your dick in your hand, wondering what you should do next. I was staring at the cruiser parked in front of the hospital trying to figure out what the hell I was going to do now. Arthur might seem like the perfect suspect on paper, but I had my doubts. On paper isn't always real life. I once knew this couple who seemed like the perfect couple on paper. He was probably the most romantic man I ever knew. Respected, admired and envied by most of the people that met him. Then there was the love of his life, Elyse. She looked and acted like the innocent girl next door. They loved each other whole heartedly and she adored him back on paper. Real life was different. She kept trying to change him and he kept asking himself if she was always so selfish. They ended everything two months after they moved in together. It's just another example that you can't always judge shit based on what you see on paper.

I got out of my car and started walking towards those double doors. Like most cops who have carried a badge longer than a minute, I knew that those glass double doors are steps away from a tombstone. I can't count the number of times I stepped through these doors to see idiots, victims and brothers in arms dying. That's why I rarely come to one unless I have no other choice. Of course, I already knew that Arthur was dead. The only thing I feared was the who did it. I didn't even really have to ask who it was because my gut told me that Charlie killed the poor bastard. I was here to confirm only.

"Bruno come with me," Logan muttered walking towards the me. "Security is getting me a copy of the surveillance videos."

"Did they have video pointing into Arthur's room?" I was well aware what he was getting to, even if I didn't want to admit it.

"You seem to be quite amused considering your best... well you know what I mean."

Yes, I damn well knew what he meant. My old partner and closest thing I had to a best friend and family, broke into a hospital to get revenge. I didn't have to like the evidence for it to be true. "So where were the camera's placed?"

"Main door, both side doors and the one at the back." Smiling Logan pointed, "I am thinking we will see one of two people sneaking in around 8:15 PM."

It didn't take an exact genius to figure that out. It had to be one of the two people who hated Arthur the most. I was betting on Charlie, but Lee was a good option. "Why 8:15?"

"That's when the call came in. Somebody wanted Arthur's wife out of his room and called at 8:15." We were making our way towards the back hallway where Arthur's room was when Logan added, "I showed up around 8:25 and he was already dead. So, I can only assume he got killed between 8:15 and 8:25."

"What the hell were you doing here?"

Smiling he added, "Following a clue."

Logan was one of those go getters who lived on coffee and pizza and I imagine he had already read the diary, the whole damn thing. "What clue is that?"

Almost giggling he added, "The wife knew." Rolling his eyes, he added, "The wife wasn't a victim, but a participant, so it made me wonder why send an email to a man's wife if the wife was aware of it and into it?"

"The wife knew! You mean she really knew about her husband and our victim?"

Laughing he shook his head, "She chose her. So now I have to ask myself who has the computer skills to hack three different email accounts and fake a three-way argument?"

"Hacker?" I knew what a hacker was, I just didn't see how he was jumping to this conclusion so fast.

"Oh, come on now. That Lee kid is a computer geek and if the wife already knew about her, why would Rosie bother emailing her?"

"Wasn't there an anonymous call about that?"

Nodding his head, "Yes and guess where the call came from?" Before I even had a chance to respond, he muttered, "From the pay phone at the station. It kind of feeds what we already knew, but the hacking thing makes Lee look pretty guilty."

More breaks. Too many breaks are never a good thing, especially in this case. I followed Logan as he headed down the hallway that lead to the server room or where the hospital might keep the video feeds. We stopped at a little orange door that said IT Department on a little black plastic name plate. Logan didn't even knock, but just opened the door and walked in. A small little, skinny and pimple faced guy in a faded green cap smiled and handed Logan two DVD's stating, "Here you go. I gave you from 7:30 to 9:00 PM from all four camera feeds. I would have given you more, but the video is 394 MB per fifteen-minute interval."

"How many people actually entered through any of the doors?" I didn't want to have to wait until we were back at the office to see. Leaning back in his chair he responded, "Twelve, but only two around 8:15 PM." Pointing at one screen he said, "This dude in a red hat at the side door," pointing to another screen, he smiled, "and this boxer type getting off the bus and walking in the front door, but by the looks of him, he was coming to see a doctor."

Logan muttered, "Son of a bitch," as he looked at me. "Both of our suspects were here at the same time." Son of a bitch was right. We were right back where we started. Two suspects, only now the body count increased to two. Yes, on paper both men looked guilty and now it was my job to chase them down. "What the hell do we do now?

"Find them," was all I could think of to say since one of them killed Arthur. The question was, which one? "Have you talked to the wife?"

It was one of those rare cases where Logan didn't smile, "No not yet."

I started walking away and chirped, "Talk to her while I try to find Charlie." Logan was good at charming people, so I am sure that if anyone was going to get Mrs. Andersen talking about any dirty little secrets that the family might have, it was going to be him. The ladies always liked the well dressed charming guys. I could easily intimidate her into spilling her guts using old school scare tactics, but Logan could charm her and charm always seems to get more.

In thirty minutes, I was out motoring down the highway towards Belle River. Charlie had a little ram shackle cabin there that he liked to call his hide away. It was nothing more that one of those tin sheds built in the bush thirty feet from a shoreline, hidden from view. He kept the land in his mother's maiden name for some reason, which, seemed like a truly great thing right now. I, like most people, wouldn't have even known that it existed or even have thought to search for his mother's maiden name if it weren't for a flat tire ten years ago. Back then, I was his most trusted friend. His go to guy. Times changed us both I guess.

The familiar buzzing of my phone caught my attention. "Logan what's up?" I didn't really care about what Arthur's widow might have to say right now because getting Charlie before he did something even stupider was a higher priority. Mind you, what could possibly be stupider then murder?

"You aren't going to like it," Logan responded. There was a pause after that and pauses were never good.

"What's up Logan? Don't screw around just come out and tell me," I muttered as I squeezed the steering wheel a little tighter preparing for the worst. When you are standing in the middle of a fire you must expect to get burned and right now, the world I thought I lived in was a wild fire.

"When Charlie was seen leaving the hospital, we searched his locker." It was an obvious step. Check his house, put an APB on him and his car, followed by checking his work place. "We found our Mister Brown."

"What exactly did you find?"

"One of these android tablets with a full chat and email history. I mean everything from the dating profile, notes about Rosie and the whole relationship."

I don't know why, but it didn't surprise me that they found everything in a locker as they were pretty sacred, every cop knew to stay away from another's personal space. No, it was just who's locker they found it in. Charlie wasn't exactly what you would call technically inclined when it came to these gadgets. He thought he was but wasn't. When we swapped over to smart phones, he hung up on me so much, by accident, it felt like we were dating and he was breaking up with me. Not to mention when we swapped over to those unbreakable laptops with the steal case. Our poor IT geeks got so frustrated, they installed one of those remote-control apps so they could walk him through shit repeatedly.

Logan whispered, "We are dusting for prints now though. Something just doesn't feel right about it." After a pause, he muttered, "I can only think of a handful of people who are here enough to do it and the guys in IT say that none of them were here during all the times that the tablet was used."

"How exactly do they trace that?" I asked. I knew the computer geeks could do wonderful things when it comes to tracking shit like that, but I never understood it.

Logan laughed, "How am I supposed to know? They said something about Mac addresses and protocols. It's like French to me." The office joke was Quebec was like a foreign country and anyone who could speak French, would be working in

Ottawa where you made a little more money and do a lot less work. Logan would never admit it, but I was sure he was trying to learn French. Being career minded and all.

I pulled into the drive way heading towards Charlie's cabin. It was one of those little farm path type of things that was barely used and looked more like a cave cut into the trees then an actual road. If there wasn't one of those deer crossing signs right next to the opening, I would never have found it. If Charlie was hiding anywhere, it was going to be here. The only question was if I was going to arrest him like procedure demanded or kill him and save him the dishonor and misery. I heard the crunching of pine cones under my tires as I slowly made my way down the quarter mile stretch.

CHAPTER 25 – ASHLEY

I don't know why I even went to the hospital, I just felt like I had to. I wanted to see the man who ruined me, laid out and broken. I wanted to feel the satisfaction of knowing that karma got him before I had to. It was about time too because karma's been slapping me around like a two-bit whore my whole life. The whole bus ride to the hospital I kept thinking that I needed to see Arthur laying there unconscious and in a lot of pain. I know the irony of it because when your brain shuts down its to protect you from the pain, but I like to think somewhere deep down your brain knows, that you still know and feel the pain. I wanted Arthur to feel the pain so that at least he would understand just a pin heads worth of the emotional turmoil that he brought to my life. There was the part of me that hated the fact that he was just lying there with his family holding his hand and weeping over his current state. He didn't deserve it. He didn't deserve any of it. Unlike most people who see hospitals as a sterile tomb where you go to die, I see it as warm caring place. He didn't deserve the warmth of love.

When I was a child, my mother's boyfriends would beat me for no other reason than I was there. You know the type, all they wanted was to make my mother scream and moan and I was just the burden that they were trapped with. When my mother was there, I was just ignored and when she was gone, they would abuse and beat me. That is where my feelings for the hospital came into play. My mom would bring me to the hospital and for those few hours I was the center of her world. She would drop everything to come to the hospital just to see me. Of course, she'd tell me not to tell the doctors what really happened saying that child services would take me away, but for those few hours she was so gentle and loving. For those few hours, I was the only one that counted. Not work, money or boyfriends mattered to her in those moments. Just mommies little soldier.

The minute I stepped off the bus I was already second guessing my decision to come here, but I needed it. I needed to see him either way. The great thing about hospitals is they are busy. I know a lot about hospitals and how to blend in unnoticed. It's easier for people to literally walk in unnoticed and sometimes that's enough to allow you to go anywhere that you want to go. That's exactly what I did. I wandered through the halls looking for Arthur.

I passed by Arthur's wife, but she didn't even notice me. Why would she really? I am a nobody in her eyes and I am sure that she is trying to decide what her next move is. After all, her husband is right in the middle of a murder case.

I watched her walk away from me. She looked sad and tired, but I guess she had good reason. Either way it was a good thing for me that she was leaving the room because people don't like to hear you tell them how you only showed up at the hospital to make sure the bastard was hurting. People always say that they want the cold hard truth, but most times it's polite bullshit they want.

I didn't even make it to Arthur's room when I saw him storming out. He was wearing a faded jacket with a cap pulled down trying to cover his face, but I knew that it was him. He was still wearing his dress shoes and no matter how he might try and squeeze himself inside his jacket, he was still the same monster he always was. I quickly stopped, pulled out my cell phone, turned my back and pretended to talk. The Good old

Sargent made it clear that if he couldn't find out for sure who killed his bimbo princess of a daughter he'd kill us both and I am certain he isn't the empty threat type. I watched him through the little round mirror, that was positioned just right, as he looked in both directions and then made his way in the opposite direction at a steady pace. I knew that walk too well. I mastered it a long time ago. Running away yet trying not to look like you are running away. I waited until he was gone and decided to go see Arthur. Since I now already knew where his room was.

I can't really say that I was casually walking towards the greenish brown door that lead to Arthur's room, but I sure as hell wasn't running either. Nothing good could come of this, that little inner voice of reason kept whispering, but I just had to do it. Like most people, my stupidity is much stronger than the common-sense part. I guess that's why they put labels like don't point the barrel at your face when you are cleaning your gun or the warning on a tree shredder not to stick your hand in to unblock the teeth.

So, I followed the advice of my stupid side and crept down the hall, ready to open the door, but still not sure what I would see. Maybe Arthur's severed head sitting between his legs or maybe him just lying there motionless, but still alive. I slowly pushed the door open and peeked into the room. I could only see the dull white sheet draped over his feet which reminded me of the morgue. You know the image you see in the movies of the dead dude laying there with the white sheet draped over his body. Of course, I always wondered if they looked and thought, 'damn what a hot body she had'. Yes, in life most things relate to sex or lead there, so that thought is firmly in my mind. For if I was the dude doing the autopsy, I would look.

I stepped into the room and saw Arthur just lying there with his hands down beside him and wires and hoses everywhere. It wasn't exactly how I expected it. He was just lying there with gashes and bruises on his face and some kind of plastic brace around his neck. The sheet only covered from the waist down and bare blotches he had on his chest where they must have shaved it to attach wires or something like that. I had always thought they placed little wires and sensors on those spots to monitor heart rate, pulse and things like that, but not in Arthur's case. No, I could hear the beeps from the monitor that stood beside the bed and a little red dot that rose and fell, but it was still eerie as hell.

I stood over him watching, thinking how calm and how peaceful he looked just lying there. I hated the fact that he seemed relaxed. So, peaceful while my whole world was in such turmoil. It just wasn't right. I placed my hands around his neck thinking how easy it would be just to choke the life out of him. How easy it would be to end his life, but I didn't want easy. I wanted him to feel my pain. The only way I could do that was walk away and hope that he got twenty years in a little cell to think about what he had done to Rosie.

Many people look at me and see a monster. It's true, by most standards, I am the monster, but I am not alone. No most people are just like me, only they keep the passionate, 'I will do anything for love side' locked away inside this little box so the world can't see it. I truly believe if more people loved like I do; the world would be a much better place. No woman would ever feel alone and unloved because they would never be.

It occurred to me that Arthur seemed lifeless as I removed my hands from around his neck. I think that there should be some kind of pulse, but I didn't feel anything. His chest wasn't even moving, which, even I know should be happening. I stared at the line on the little monitor rise and fall thinking that it should be flat if Arthur wasn't alive. I had watched enough TV shows to know that much. Not exactly sure how it works, only that it does. That's when I realized we weren't alone. Tucked in the corner, barely visible, in ugly green scrubs, was a little blonde girl. I could easily see her chest rise and fall and the wires that should be attached to Arthur, were attached to her.

I just bolted out of the room, almost running towards the

front doors. Charlie had fulfilled his promise to kill Arthur and that meant that I was next. I didn't let that thought linger in my mind though. I couldn't. I just slowed my pace, trying to calm myself. It's the panic on your face and running that makes you look suspicious and I needed to blend in so that when the cops came searching for suspicious characters, my face wouldn't come to mind.

A familiar voice was bouncing down the hallway as I made my way towards the exit. It was the cop Logan and I knew this couldn't be good. If he sees my little red neck ass in this situation, I was screwed. I just dropped down the list of Bruno's most wanted from number one to number two and if Logan saw me, boom I was back in the hot seat. I stepped into some storage room that had sheets and pillows wrapped inside plastic bags, they were neatly placed on shelves. I always thought that places like this had their own giant washing machines, but obviously, I was wrong. I listened as he passed, waiting for his voice to fade meaning that he was gone. I opened the door a few inches and looked towards Arthur's room. As Logan entered the room I burst out of the storage room hoping to make my escape undetected.

I didn't want to wait for the bus to arrive, since the further away from the hospital I was, the better it was for me. This was one of those few times I wished that I had learned to drive. I never saw driving as freedom though. I saw the car payments, insurance and gas prices as bondage. I saw the sheer cost of it as modern-day slavery, but today it seemed like freedom or at least the start of it. I was cutting across the parking lot when I realized that Logan wasn't the only cop lurking in the shadows. Harold's car was parked in the back corner between a big old jeep and a Lincoln town car. A red 1991 Pontiac firefly that seems to be held together with duct tape and a prayer stands out, even in the darkness.

Looking around I saw no real escape. At least not an immediate one that wouldn't capture the wrong attention. Looking back, I saw Logan marching out of the hospital gun in hand searching in every direction. Then finally, he started running along the side of the hospital, headed towards the soccer fields around back. I was trying to find my best escape route that would provide cover and a fast escape route. "Lee get over here," Harold's voice broke through the darkness.

Probably the last witness in the world was leaning out his window calling me over. Karma sure has a bitch of a sense of humor. If I had just stayed at home, karma wouldn't be kicking me in balls and giggling afterwards. "Lee get your ass in the car before Logan sees you." The fight or flight instinct was growing inside me like weeds in a garden, but there was nobody to really fight and I sure as hell couldn't out run the law. I slowly walked towards Harold's crappy little car half expecting him to yank out his handcuffs. Who knows? Maybe I might be the only guy who he ever gets to use them on. As I stepped closer to the car Harold rolled up the window and just stared at me like I was a naughty child and he was my dad picking me up at a party.

I opened the car door and jumped in the passenger seat expecting the worst. Holding up his hand, Harold snapped, "Don't tell me anything! If I don't know what you did, I can't be called to testify against you." Before I could even answer, he muttered, "I don't even know why I am here now helping except that you give me hope that a first impression isn't the true impression. I like to think that you really are just a sweet guy who is misunderstood and by misunderstood, I mean not a killer who happens to write beautiful love songs and poetry." I was about to say something when he held his hand up and said, "I am not done yet!" He shifted in his seat, "Tell me where you need to go and I will drop you off, but until things calm down we need to put space between us. I mean so much space it's like we had the worst break up ever."

I watched Logan come running out of the hospital entrance with his cell phone in his hand. Obviously, they found Arthur, the only question was if they were going to kick me to the top of the list. "Harold just take me a few blocks away and drop me off. It's safer for you."

"No," was all he said. "Lately all my spare time has been

spent watching over you."

I had spent all my time looking over my shoulder recently, but Harold's face wasn't one of the ones I was searching for. Hell, if there was ever a cop I wanted chasing me, it was him. He always seemed like the guy who you could distract with shiny objects, but here he was following me and I missed it completely. "Watching me?"

"Yes, I have been tailing you. Charlie made it clear that any little amount of proof was a death sentence for you. He didn't actually say it, but I can read between the lines, so I followed you."

"And what did you plan on doing if he came at me?"

"I don't know really. I hoped to stop him but wasn't sure how." He turned on his car and we drove away leaving everything behind. I leaned back in the seat wondering what I was going to do now.

We weren't even a mile down the road when a head popped up in the rear-view mirror and a light click popped in my ear. "I think that we need to take a little trip, deep into the woods."

CHAPTER 26 – BRUNO

We all have our secrets. I know everybody claims that they have no ugly skeletons in their closest, but we do. Some of us just seem to have a bigger collection of bones that we are trying to hide from the world. I hid my car behind a wood pile as to not spook Charlie. By spook him, I mean give him a chance to decide two murders under his belt wasn't any worse than one. There was a time when I would have just parked the car and sat on the front step with a beer waiting for him. There was a time when I had no reason to fear him because I knew him like a brother. Now, he was like one of those estranged third cousins, twice removed, we all hate to admit we have. In most cases, you find the bad guy and there's only a couple of outcomes, he either gets convicted or he gets off. Unlike most people, I don't examine how long the sentence is, only the guilty verdict. It's like simple math. Nothing was simple about this whole situation. It's more like fractions. This could go a few ways; Charlie confesses and I arrest him. Then there is the possibility that Charlie confesses and I kill him or he kills me. Then again, Charlie could be innocent and he still kills me or forces me to kill him. Fractions make the math complicated. There is always the possibility you will add it up wrong.

I made my way around the titling shack that Charlie called the camp, trying to find a window to jiggle open or an unlocked door. Of course, I could easily have smashed my way through the weathered soft boards that have stood here for generations, but that wasn't inconspicuous. Looking into the dusty, dirt stained windows, the whole place looked abandoned. If Charlie came here, he didn't enter the cabin or if he did, he ran away in a hurry. I couldn't blame him. I kept walking around the cabin looking for something to help me find him, but there was no evidence at all that he had ever been here. I was rounding the corner when my phone rang, that in itself might have given my position away. I pulled it out of my pocket and thought about the fact I had one bar of signal, which was amazing considering where I was. Being in the middle of nowhere, what more could you expect? "Hello," I said hearing a loud fierce crackle. There wasn't any response only the loud growling of static on the line. "Hello, are you there?" I muttered, not expecting an answer.

"Bruno, where are you?" Logan screamed, but the static was louder than he was. The last thing I wanted was Logan charging in until I had a chance to talk to Charlie. Two alphas can't really communicate, especially when one is the old alpha and the other wants the crown. "Where are you?"

"I am working a lead. Just find that Ashley kid." I truly didn't think that he was the man we were after, but he was still a lead that needed to be followed up on. There was a bunch of grumbling noises as he said something that I couldn't make out. "I can't hear you," I said.

"The kids gone," was the last thing he said before the call dropped. I thought that Lee missing could be a great thing or the worst, depending on how we looked at it. His running and hiding would keep Logan busy while I dealt with Charlie, but it would also make Lee look guilty. Part of me thought that letting the kid take the fall wasn't exactly the worst thing in the world, but that wasn't justice.

I heard the rumble of the engine long before I saw the dim lights tearing through the darkness. It wasn't Charlie's truck or the rental car that he was driving. From the corner of that shack, I watched the stream of lights bob up and down as the car approached. The foliage seemed to light up like a tunnel as it came closer and closer. If it wasn't Charlie coming home to hide, who was coming to hunt Charlie?

I unclipped the safety as I removed my gun from my holster and just rested my hand on the handle. It was there in case I needed it, but I hoped that there wasn't any reason for me to have to. I stayed there for some time just watching the car approach. I was trying to decide if there was any reason to be concerned. Kids have a habit of sneaking into secluded places where they can drink beer and make love. In the early days of my career that was how my Friday nights were spent, telling teens to put it back in their pants and trying not to laugh. The car coming down the lane was one of those small little compacts that were the rave in the 1990s, but by the sound of it, those were the cars glory days. I watched the car stop and then heard the engine putter and pop before finally going silent. The smell of exhaust filled the air and burned my nostrils as it invaded the clean country air. I waited for the occupants to get out of the car, but for whatever reason they just sat there. When people linger it's generally because they have no plan or are up to no good. Either way that couldn't be a good thing and made the hairs on the back of my neck stand. I couldn't see what they were doing, but something told me that they were waiting for something.

I waited for what seemed like forever for them to get out of the car. I was used to waiting, but never in the darkness listening to the crickets chirping and the wind forcing the trees to crackle as it pushed its way through the branches. Finally, I saw them get out of the car heading towards the cabin. "You don't need to do this sarge," a mouse like voice squeaked. "You don't need to add kidnapping to the list."

"Shut up Harold," Charlie muttered as he pushed him forcing Harold to stumble forward. "My career and life are already over so anything else that happens from this point on won't matter. " It was Charlie and it wasn't looking good at all. Desperate men do stupid things and I could almost smell the desperation floating in the air.

"Sarge you don't want to do this. You are a good man. Do you want your memory to be that of a mass murderer?" Harold pleaded. He seemed to be turning trying to face Charlie as he was pushed along, " Sarge, I mean Charlie, you don't want to be remembered as a mad man and cop killer, do you? Think about your legacy. How the world will remember you." Considering Harold was a lousy cop, he was following the process step by step like a pro. He was trying to make Charlie see him as a person not an object and the way you do that is to play on his pride. Few people want to be remembered as a monster and Charlie's career was important to him, so using that was exactly what he needed to do.

Slapping him roughly and knocking him to the ground, Charlie snapped, "Shut up Harold. I remember more about the psychology of dealing with hostage situations then you will ever know."

"You don't have to hurt Harold. You already took out Arthur and now you have me, so why not just let him go?" a voice snapped defiantly.

Charlie threw a wide swing sending him flying to the ground, "Don't sass me boy. You aren't in any position to mouth off." Charlie started kicking him around like a common thug screaming, "You good for nothing little bastard. I didn't kill the pervert, but you made sure that I am the one who will take the fall." He was waving his hands around as he was screaming in rage, which was never a good thing.

"If you ever drop that gun I am going to help you join Arthur," Lee snapped. "You have me, so let Harold go." Slowly he made his way to his feet muttering, "You claim justice then revenge, but you are just like any other school yard bully."

I heard the air burst from his lungs as Charlie booted him in the stomach screaming, "You stole everything I ever cared about from me!" Pointing towards Harold he bellowed, "And this little fuck is trying to help you cover it up and save your ass." I was amazed that Lee was still standing after all he has already been through today. Kid has spunk.

Harold whined, "I didn't help him cover up anything. I was

just trying to keep him from being shot."

Charlie was losing it. He booted Harold down to his knees muttering, "I think it's time we finish this," as he pointed the gun in Harold's face. Harold screamed and Charlie smacked him across the head with the butt of the gun, "Shut up and face it like a man."

Lee screamed, "He isn't involved in this. If you want your revenge because some bastard killed Daddy's little whore, shoot me and get it over with." The kid was defiantly tough and dumb as hell. Charlie was hysterically beating the hell out of the kid who just seemed too stupid to stay down and kept muttering threats, which just added to the flames of Charlie's rage. There was no way that this was going to end well for anyone, especially Lee. Especially now that Charlie saw no end in sight. Of course, it seemed like Lee wasn't seeing any good end in sight either since it appears Charlie had brought him here to die.

Stepping out from the corner of the shack, I pulled out my gun and slowly made my way through the darkness trying not to make any noise. Charlie had spent enough time in combat as well as carrying a badge not to take him seriously. I also knew to see him as a real threat. He was a better shot then me and in his current state of mind, I am certain he'd kill me too. I made my way through the weeds and brush watching his vicious attack on Harold and Lee who seemed so defenseless against his madness. I didn't want to have to shoot Charlie if I didn't have to so I crouched down behind a bush taking careful aim and yelled, "Charlie? It's Bruno, don't shoot I just want to talk."

Wiping around, he fired a shot into the night forcing me down onto the ground. Charlie was bellowing, "Stay where you are Bruno. You had your chance to fix this and you screwed it up, so now I have to fix it."

"Stop shooting at me you dumb ass," I bellowed. "I said talk, not fight." I didn't want to have to kill him. We had history and I didn't want to carry his face with me until I joined him in the grave. It would be like killing your brother. Well not my brother these days since he is a crazy bastard who has so many personalities that talking to him is like a soap opera, only you don't know who you are talking to.

Another two shots flew through the air as he screamed, "Don't you bullshit me Bruno. We both know that you are cop first, friend second and family always comes in last place." He was scanning into the night looking for me, stopping from place to place trying to find me. "Go Bruno. Let me be done with this business once and for all."

"Charlie, you know I can't just leave. What did Harold really do to deserve to die tonight? He isn't a killer, he is just a young lad who happened to be in the wrong place at the wrong time." I had to try and force him to see Harold as anything else other than a traitor. Harold wasn't a killer or a traitor. He was just a bad cop. Not a crooked one, just not very good at being one. "Killing Harold makes you as big a monster as Arthur was. Do you want to be remembered as a cop killer Charlie? This one action will erase all the good that you have done."

"Don't you dare start this shit with me Bruno. You owe me and I am collecting." Pointing his gun at Lee he muttered, "This little prick didn't just kill my Callie and the Rosie girl, he also ended Arthur's life. So how can I let him live? In good conscience, I can't let him live the rest of his days." Screaming he continued, "How can I live with myself if I do?"

Lee blurted out, "You killed him. I saw you leaving his room and went in right after to find his ass dead."

Charlie was putting the boots to him screaming, "I was there, but I didn't kill him." Still kicking him he muttered, "It was you."

I got up and stepped out muttering, "Bull shit Charlie. I saw the surveillance footage. You were in the room before Lee and you ran off."

Charlie turned with his arms apart apologetically whispering, "I was there, but he was already dead. If I didn't kill him and Lee didn't kill him, who else did?"

"Charlie, we know about the chats. I have read them and so has Logan. It's too late to turn back now."

Screaming Charlie snorted, "What chats?"

"Charlie, we found the tablet in your locker. You can change the name, but not the location where you were talking from." I was gambling now. Throwing all the evidence I had at him hoping he'd see some light in the darkness of his soul.

"You are in on it too. That useless Harold befriends one waste of life and Logan defends the other. Everybody turns their back on me and justice." He was running at me firing his gun as he went screaming, "You traitorous bastard. You are in on this too. You bastard," as he emptied the clip in his gun.

CHAPTER 27 – ASHLEY

It was like stepping into the old west as Charlie burst into the night towards Bruno screaming, "You traitorous bastard." Each shot sent a small bright explosive flame into the darkness with a booming echo that broke the tranquility of the night. I just laid there on the ground no longer concerned about the blood dripping down my chin or the little bursts of throbbing pain that seem to go from my temple to my toes. I just laid there curled up in a ball trembling as my heart pounded so fast and hard that each beat seemed to shake my whole body. I am not sure when the gun fire stopped only that suddenly everything went silent. I had always seen myself fighting until the very end in these types of situations, but now I realized that my fear choked my courage until all that was left was a dried-up skeleton of the man I thought I was. Deep inside the warrior was a coward who screams and hides in the face of danger.

"Run and hide in the trees," Harold whispered as he dragged his body through the dirt. "You don't win gun fights if you don't have a gun," he muttered as he pointed towards the trees. My whole life I always had something funny and charming to say, but today my mind was empty as I just stared into the darkness. I was fearing those that lingered in the shadows. "Get out of here, now," Harold fiercely muttered still pointing towards the trees.

I watched him slither away, inch by inch, until he was lost to me. Harold had the luxury of knowing that he was a coward so running away wasn't something that he'd regret and let haunt him endlessly. Me, on the other hand, I would let it chase me down and scream yellow belly at me until I hated my reflection. Harold was a lucky little bastard that way. He could run away like that. I envied him.

In the distance, I could hear Charlie roaring like a made beast, but I didn't dare get up and look over at him. He wasn't exactly the kind of animal I wanted to face and certainly not in my current state. My hands were trembling so bad that I couldn't even make a fist let alone throw one. "I don't want to kill you," Bruno bellowed.

"You know damn well that I had nothing to with killing my daughter you Judas. You know me, so how can you even think such a thing?"

"All the evidence points to you Charlie. Explain how it happened then?" Bruno sounded like he was a heart beat from crying as he cried out, "Just give me something, Charlie? Anything?"

There was still a breaking, clunking noise that followed as they grunted and groaned. Even now, I could hear the echoes of hatred and heart break bouncing between them.

"Get over here Lee," Harold muttered as he crawled back over. "You are going to get yourself killed." My mind knew that he was right, but my body wouldn't obey my commands. I was paralyzed in place, trapped between my fears and my thoughts. Tugging on my arm, he said, "That crazy bastard killed one man already and I am not hanging around to be number two or three." Harold might be a bigger coward then me, but he certainly had a clear mind.

So how he managed to drag me along with him as he made his way back to the shadows was lost on me. We crawled away as Bruno and Charlie continued their battle. "Can you at least try and keep up," Harold exclaimed as he forced me along with him. "He isn't going to stay distracted forever." He had a good point. The mad man wouldn't be arguing with Bruno for much longer. If he did kill his friend, I had no doubts that we would be next.

When we were safely tucked in the bushes, Harold pointed at me chirping, "Stay here," as he ducked, got up and walked further into the foliage. "Don't run into the forest. Even if you hear me scream or even worse hear more gun fire." I stood there staring into the night as Harold slipped away and disappeared into the darkness that surrounded us. Maybe there was a hero deep inside him or at least more to him then I thought was there.

Harold ducked down and crawled across the waist high weeds and trees, slowly making his way towards the cabin. I couldn't see him anymore as the darkness was heavy. The crackling of breaking branches gave me a clear idea of exactly where he was and the direction that he was going. He might be brave, but certainly not the sharpest hero. I should have been there with him leading the way, but I wasn't. No, I was hiding in the trees trying to keep my hands from shaking and the lump in my throat from choking me. Fear can be worse than any beating when you can't control it and it owns you like a slave.

As the clouds passed over us and in the dim flicker of moon light, I saw Harold kneeling just in front of the ancient cabin. He kept bouncing like he was about to pounce at whoever might be stomping past him. Of course, it was obvious that if Charlie came booming out of the darkness Harold was screwed, but I guess for him, duty came first. Duty always comes first. Some people live that way, others, like me, are trapped by it.

A loud ear breaking boom followed by a bright flash of light that broke through the darkness as Harold jumped to the ground from his crouched position on the cabins porch. Somebody howled, "You shot me! I can't believe you actually shot me." There was an eerie silence that followed then a second bang that seemed to make the ground shake and a haunting squealing sound rose.

A figure stepped out into the moon light, but I couldn't see who it was only that he looked massive compared to Harold's little bulky frame. At first, I sighed with such relief realizing that the giant from the shadows was Bruno. It was like seeing a cow boy in a white hat coming to save me against the rugged villain trying to steal my farm. They both just stood there staring at each other for what seemed like forever. When the knot inside my stomach loosened and my knees stopped shaking, I stepped out of the trees not realizing what was about to happen.

Harold turned and burst into a full run, screaming, "Lee run!" as he went. I just stood there dumbfounded as I watching him race towards me breaking the small trees and bushes as he went. "Charlie isn't the killer," he screamed as he leapt through the air arms swinging wide through the shadows.

Lost, I kept walking towards him thinking, "What the hell! Bruno is one of the good guys. You told me so." My pace slowed as I stepped closer in his direction trying to figure out exactly who the killer was.

Harold was still bursting right at me as fast as he could run always looking over his shoulder bellowing, "For god sakes Lee get your ass out of here." Common sense might tell us when somebody screams run away, you do it. I mean, after witnessing a gun fight you get your ass out of dodge as fast as your legs can carry you, but that's not how life works. I was still looking from Harold over to Bruno trying to figure out what the hell was going on. If Charlie wasn't the killer, who the hell was? Harold was still screaming, "Run," as he leapt straight at me, flying through the air.

Harold was just steps away and still screaming when he went wide eyed and his mouth fell open forcing a croaking sound out of his mouth while spraying me in blood. His chest flew forward and his body twisted as he reached out to me before falling face first into the ground. I watched in horror as he slid right into my feet. His whole body shook like one of the headless chickens that jump around spraying blood all over the place at the slaughter house. I dropped to me knees screaming,

"Harold are you ok?" He didn't respond, but his body just trembled as blood dripped from his lips. Grabbing his head, I looked at him muttering, "Harold speak to me," but the only thing he did was wheeze as his eyes seemed to get dimmer with each passing second.

I placed my hand on his shoulder and felt something warm flowing from him. It didn't take long for me to realize that he didn't just crumble at my feet but was driven down as an axe sliced through the air and dug deep into his shoulder. I ran my fingers along the handle thinking how easy it would be to just yank it out. I wanted to pull it out, but I honestly thought that it would cause more harm than good. When you are talking muscles and bones, I think ripping a blade out would make the damage worse, though I didn't know for sure as it was medical crap that I was unaware of.

A voice burst out from the darkness, "You can't save his life Lee, things have gone too far now. It's time to follow plan B. The only question is, are you going to fall with the rest of the sheep or become the wolf that you were meant to be?"

I looked up and realized that his voice was a familiar one. I stood up and snapped, "I knew that we would meet one day Brown. We just had to."

CHAPTER 28 – BROWN

I watched Lee stumble around trying to regain his composure. His world had been redefined today seeing a coward become a hero and his own self-image shattered. Everybody has their own way of seeing themselves and they try to live up to that person, even if the image only exists in their mind. Lee sees himself as a rugged loner who's quest for love makes him a true defender. Someone who faces danger like it's his calling in life and it's that belief he will defend to the last breath. Today his courage was replaced by fear and it shattered his idea of who he really is. "Yes, eventually we had to meet in person. I wanted us to meet under different circumstances, but life sometimes pulls us in a different direction then we plan on."

Lee's eyes kept flipping from me to the incapacitated Harold who just laid there groaning in pain. It was unfortunate because I didn't have anything against him, but he got in my way. Now that my plans were in ruins and he had seen my face, I couldn't let him live. He saw me kill Charlie and I couldn't afford to leave any witnesses alive that I didn't control. Harold was on the straight and narrow. A man that didn't look in the mirror and see an illusion. No, he knew himself more than most people could even imagine and when it came down to it, the only way to save myself was going to be if I killed him.

"I don't think that you will like the result of our meeting," Lee muttered as he stood up. His whole body trembled. He was almost bouncing with rage and seemed to be preparing to charge right for me. He's fists were clenched as he stepped a little closer still not realizing who I really was. He looked like the world had been beating him with a stick his whole life and yet he was still as defiant as a Pit-bull.

It's a good thing he didn't yet because if he turns away from the path I set before him and sees my true face, I would be forced to kill him too. Holding my hand out I said, "Don't step any closer," in my calmest voice. "We need to come to an understanding first."

Placing his hands on his waist Lee bounced, "Oh yes we do. I have something's I am wondering about and you will answer my questions." He was still bouncing from side to side trembling in rage as he waited.

It made sense that he wanted answers since he wasn't stupid after all. He might be compulsive and misunderstood, but he had a brilliant mind if you only took the time to really listen. "I don't think we are at the place yet where you can ask any question and demand an answer. I don't want to lie you Lee, so let's build up to your questions." Lee's knuckles cracked as he twisted his muscles and stretched. "Hold it there cowboy, you don't want to open this can of worms." Strange how Charlie broke him with a little gun and a few words. Yet, now when he was facing a true danger, he was consumed with such defiance. I stepped back trying to give me just a little more room because if we couldn't come to an understanding and he saw my real face, things would go bad for him in a hurry.

"Why did you kill Harold?" Pointing at the broken body, he muttered, "Really? Was it necessary to slice him up like that?"

It had never occurred to me that Lee would befriend his jailor. A lone wolf doesn't run with the pack, but I guess, at times, they find another lone wolf to walk with. Of course, I didn't realize that Harold saw Lee as human. That Harold saw him as more than the weird little monster that he was. I had to be delicate with these answers otherwise I might just be forced to kill him and I didn't want to kill Lee if I didn't have too. "Stay where you are for now. This will end better for you if you do."

Those cold eyes were glaring at me as he measured me. Men like him always measure those around them, like a carpenter with his measuring tape. The way his legs trembled and his hands shook, he was scared. At first, I thought it was rage that made him tremble, but it was fear burning inside him and all he could do was play the part of the warrior hoping that there wasn't a battle coming his way. "No there is no way this ends well for me." Stepping forward he placed himself between me and Harold like a wall. "There is no version of this that ends well me because I see you now."

I thought that the shadows would protect my true face. That the darkness would save my secret and keep me safe, but it was too late now. If Lee wouldn't join me in my life's mission, he was going to have to join Rosie in the afterlife. It was simple math. Either he walks beside me or he lies under me because I am not spending the rest of my life looking over my shoulder. Today he might be scared, but tomorrow he would be mad. "You have all the power Lee. You can choose the path you follow and where you lead those that will follow you." Stepping back again I added, "I am offering you this and more if you can only open your mind and see my vision. If you can only join my quest."

This time Lee stepped back until he had a foot on either side of Harold, "And what quest is that exactly?" I was still trying to grasp my mind around the emotional connection he had made with Harold. It was more than friendship I think. Brotherhood is a better term.

Tapping my bloody fingers together, I chirped with excitement thinking that if I could only help him understand my mission, he would be the perfect ally. When I was too old to complete my work, he would step up and take my place saving souls and eating the sins of the those too weak to do it themselves. "I save those who can't save themselves." His cold eyes were staring through me in disbelief. "I search out those who can't see their own value and I build them until they can face the world on their own." It was a fact after all. I was a builder of self-worth and lead those that needed my help to personal salvation. "Just think of what I can offer you Lee. I can be more than the father figure that you desperately need, but I can be your mentor."

"I don't have any daddy issues so there is nothing you have to offer me," he snorted as he stared down at Harold. Pointing down he added, "Besides, lying right here on the ground is the closest thing I have to a friend."

He was too caught up on the now to see the possibilities I offered. I liked him, but I had forgotten just how young he was. Emotionally, he was like a child. He was grasping too hard to the idea of what was now rather then what was to come. "What if I could completely change your life? Not just the way the world looks at you, but how you look at the world?"

His fists relaxed as he stared me. It was a small gesture at best, considering he still looked like he was about to make a mad dash towards the forest and what he saw as safety, but it certainly was a start. Even Moses had to start hearing a message from God before he could truly serve him. That's where we were standing right now. Lee had just heard the first message from a higher power. Lee was still flickering between me and Harold caught between the past and the future. "It doesn't matter how the world sees me. I am happy being me."

That is the problem with lies. The more you say them, the more you believe them. That's exactly what Lee was doing. Repeating the lie that he didn't care how the world saw him, so that in his heart, he would start believing it. Rosie was the same way. She told herself that Arthur loved her. That if she satisfied him in every way, she would always have him. She might have been right about the always have him part, but he would have never loved her. Not truly. The only thing that she would get from that life is getting knocked up by accident and then her children would repeat that cycle. That's why she had to die. To save her from herself. To save another generation from being slaves to an idea. It's the idea that lead to her death. The idea of love.

"Let's not start our partnership on a foundation of lies and twisted truths. I would like us to be honest right from the start."

"Partnership?"

Lee was a bright kid, but youth offers little in common sense or the ability to see the big picture. I couldn't help but smile at how naive he seemed here and now. "Yes, a partnership. I have souls to save and you are one of the few worthy enough to carry the torch when I retire.

Stepping forward again, he asked, "I am a lover, not a killer."

"We both know that is a lie. I like to call what you have as the killer instinct. It's still in its infancy, but we both know it's there. Without me you will make the 6 o'clock news. I know your secrets Lee. You are as much a killer as anyone. I know that there is blood on your hands."

Almost bouncing he muttered, "Everybody has blood on their hands." Wiping his brow, he added, "You just seem to have more. Much more."

He was being stubborn and that stubbornness was blinding him to the truth. It was blinding him to the purity I was offering. Save them one way or another. It's that simple. "What if I told you that if I could have saved Rosie with you by my side?" Holding my finger up, I whispered, "What if is power."

He whined, "Rosie's dead. She will turn to dust and nothing can save her. Nothing."

Obviously, it was too soon to mention Rosie. The wound still too fresh, but I needed him to open his eyes. To see just how magical what I offered really was. The power to save souls, even those undeserving creatures like Rosie. I still missed her, but she refused to see the light and the only way that I could save her soul was to end her life. "Her body was her undoing. Her down fall. Too much pride in her beauty and sexuality."

He stepped forward again, "her undoing?" His hands

trembled and he was preparing to come at me with revenge in his heart and fists flying. I had to calm him if I was going to save him. I didn't want to have to break him, after all, he has come so far. Many children from broken homes, that have been chased by so many tragedies, grow up to become such a burden on society. Lee is misguided, but he has so many possibilities. "Rosie was beautiful. Brilliant even. She didn't need to be saved, she needed to be loved."

"She could never be truly loved. It's not in her nature."

Lee screamed, "She was loved. She was truly loved, desired and pro... " He just stopped in midsentence unable to push the words out. His head dropped as he thought about it. He wanted to say protected, but he couldn't save her. Only I could.

"She couldn't accept your love. You cannot change who she is at her core. She was searching for something that she couldn't have. Her desire for an emotional attachment was twisted and turned into abuse." That was the realization that he had to accept."No matter if it was me or somebody else, twenty years from now Rosie was going to die. Whether it be by my blade, disease or a ruthless lover taking the pleasure or pain too far, Rosie had to die. The only real difference is that I saved her from damnation. I saved her from decades of self-loathing and abuse."

"She loved me!" he screamed as he charged towards me. "She just couldn't admit it yet. In time, she would have seen that I was the best thing for her. That I was the only one who truly loved her like she deserved." I couldn't see his face, but I am certain tears ran down his cheeks. He was still mourning her loss. It was only natural, so I will over look his outburst. His blindness towards her. "She was meant to be mine. My soulmate. My one love."

In my calmest voice, I whispered, "She loved you? How could she when she couldn't even love herself?" I placed my hands together trying to allow him to see that I didn't want to harm him. That I was his savior too and he had no reason to fear me. "I spent a whole year trying to save her. A year of my precious time wasted on this foolish broken girl. I gave her advice and encouragement yet, she was too broken to heed my advice. Sometimes you need to hack away the dead flesh to save the whole leg."

"She wasn't damaged or broken! She was misguided, but she was loved. Her turmoil would have been calmed in time. I would have waited for as long as it took." He was sincere in this. Blind love isn't so rare, but true love is quite extraordinary. That's why I chose him. Not because of the blindness, but the purity of his heart.

"I saved her from herself Lee. Without my help, she was damned." It's an exhausting task trying to show an unbeliever the light, but I think Lee was slowly seeing the truth. Well in time he would come around. "In time, you will understand." I looked down at Harold's motionless body. He was the last piece of the past. That last connection to Lee's old life. I needed to kill that connection if I was going to save him. I didn't have a plan for this. I expected this meeting to come months from now. Of course, nothing went as planned these days. Too many unknowns and not enough control. Either way, Harold had seen my real face and because of it, Harold must die.

"You had to kill her to save her?" he snapped. He was wide eyed and shook with rage. "All this time you were the one that killed my precious Rosie. It was you and there is not excuse for it." He was charging forward trembling in rage, "you killed the love of my life and now you are going to die."

He was consumed with pure hatred. Such a primitive human emotion. I would need to break this emotion if I was going to save him. If I was going to teach him to assist me then replace me. "Kill Harold, he is dying anyway. You will be a lot gentler then I will be."

Lee's face dropped like a stone. "I will gladly kill you, but I am not killing Harold." This was an expected response. He was still in the process of becoming worthy of my tutelage. This would be his first struggle, but he would impress me. He had to, after all, I knew him better then he did.

I pulled out my gun and pointed it at him. I only had one bullet left but it was enough to get this done. I hadn't imagined it coming to this, but it's the way things turned out. "Kill him or I will kill you here and now. Either way, he dies, but my way means you die too."

"I am not doing it," he replied staring down at Harold's body. "I won't kill an innocent man," he said stubbornly.

Crying like a baby, Harold surprisingly croaked, "Just do it Lee. It's not murder if you are forced at gun point. Just do it quickly because I don't want to suffer." He was barely able to move, but his course whisper was still clear enough. "Just make it quick Lee. I can't suffer any more pain." It was a bit surprising he even had the presence of mind to speak up. He had lain motionless for so long.

"No, I won't do it," Lee blurted out. "I won't kill a man because of some sick twisted game."

Harold cried out with his last ounce of strength, "Do it Lee. I saw how he saved Rosie and I don't want to go through that type of pain. Take the axe from my back and put it right in the back of my head. Make it quick."

I kept my eyes on him and commanded, "Do it otherwise I will." As Harold laid there crying, Lee looked at me then back to him. He was running his hands around the axe examining it intensely. It was good to see compassion in him. It was character and men need character. Anyone can kill, but the truly great ones don't enjoy it and certainly they aren't cruel about it. I never enjoyed the killing. Not even tonight when I was forced to take Charlie's life. I didn't hate him despite all his flaws. I did it out of necessity. It was the same with Rosie and Callie before her. I tried to save them and make them better people. To make them more complete, but the world broke them beyond repair. I tried both times as I took their lives. The heart break of my failure was a great burden that I would be forced to carry, but it had to be done. There was no other choice.

Harold wailed as Lee ripped the axe from his flesh and the blood began to flow. He was committed now and he knew it.

Harold would bleed to death and die either way. I truly wished Harold remained a coward and ran away. His sudden courage was an unwelcome surprise. He shouldn't have seen my real face because once he did, his fate was sealed. I survive to continue my work because nobody ever sees my true face. I liked Harold, but I loved my freedom even more. Raising the blood dripping axe over his head Lee whispered, "I am sorry Harold. I truly am."

CHAPTER 29 – ASHLEY

As a kid, I watched old black and white westerns where the guys in black hats used to pull up their handkerchiefs over their faces when they robbed banks. Of course, I always knew who the bad guys were in those movies. It was because of the color of their hats, but in the real world, nobody wears hats. You never really know who the bad guys are. Brown had part of his face covered trying to hide his identity from me. Just like the robbers in those old westerns, covering his face was a sign that he was up to no good and now he was trying to force me to be like him. Was Brown testing me? If it was a test, I wanted to fail miserably. I was good at failing tests and this test I had to fail.

My hands were shaking so bad that I was certain I was going to drop the axe that I held in my hands. The axe felt heavier than I expected, but then again, I didn't expect that I would be mere minutes away from killing a man. I had imagined days like this. I had always thought that I would just swing the blade or slash with the knife without any second thought. In those fantasies, the person on the receiving end was a monster like me. Harold wasn't a monster, but a victim. He wasn't like us. Brown was so twisted that his mind was like an over tightened spring and he could snap at any minute. We were all twisted in our own way. Me, Charlie, Brown and even the relentless good guy Bruno, but Harold was different. He was human surrounded by savage beasts.

If I dropped the axe here and now, my life would be changed forever. There would be no coming back from this. It's a strange thing to look up and see a broken reflection of what you can become or who you can be and not like the image. If I followed this path; took this next step, it wouldn't be evolution, but the last step in my own personal fall from grace, if any still exists. I didn't want to keep falling. Harold whispered, "Just do it Lee. You have no choice. It's kill or be killed."

Even though I couldn't see his face, I knew Brown was smiling under his mask. "Kill or be killed. It's accurate and I like it," he muttered. "So, kill." My whole life I didn't have a choice. I had more control then most, but I didn't have many choices. I wasn't born this way, but time pushed me onto a path that lead right here and I wanted a choice. I needed a choice. "You are starting to disappoint me kid. You need to be strong, even when you don't want to be."

I lowered the axe and stood up staring down at Harold's blood covered body. "I am strong."

Brown lifted the gun muttering, "That's not the choice I hoped you would make." He kept it aimed on me as he looked around like he was pondering his next move.

I was surprised to see sadness in his eyes, like a disappointed father catching his son stealing from the change jar. I knew that look. I had spent enough time in foster homes to know that look. "I am not like you. I won't kill Harold." I tossed the axe into the brush thinking that it's better to die anonymous then to have the whole world remember me as the ultimate predator. The TV is full of documentaries of men like me who gave in to their killer instinct rather than stand up and say, 'I refuse to give into it'.

He laughed, "Oh either way Harold's going to die. He must. Look at him, he is bleeding out. Killing him would have been a favour."

Harold's body was trembling, but I think that he was too

weak to do anything. He closed his eyes and prayed. People do that in their last minutes. They pray to an unseen God hoping that there is more in the next life then they got in this one. "I know, but not by my hand. It can't be by my hand."

A flash of light broke through the darkness as a loud bang echoed into the night, then was lost forever. I felt the spray of something warm hitting my body as Harold's body quaked then went motionless. I just stood there staring down at poor Harold. Blood flowed from what was left of the back of his head and I could see his fingers scraping and digging into the ground. Nerves I guess. My heart exploded like a bomb as the realization hit me. I was covered in Harold's blood and he was gone forever. "You killed him," I screamed as I charged towards Brown. "You actually killed him." I was still trying to wrap my head around the idea that it took just ten seconds to end a life and it took decades to make it. Most people think life starts at conception and I guess they are right, but I think we evolve as we grow with memories, emotions and sensations. In my mind, we are always starting a new life each day that we wake up.

My emotions were stronger then me, or at least I wasn't thinking, because blindly I charged at Brown without any thought. It was like hitting a wall though because I didn't send him flying back onto the ground. No, I just bounced off him like a ball ricocheting off a wall. I snapped back stumbling over Harold's lifeless body slamming into the ground. As my head pounded into the dirt, the air was driven from my lungs and I just laid there trying to wipe the tears from my eyes. The back of my head was throbbing, I just laid there trying to catch my breath. I knew I was covered in Harold's blood, but I didn't want to think about it. I couldn't allow myself to think about how much was lost today or the fact that in killing Harold, Brown pushed me into isolation.

He stepped over me like a giant, grabbing hold of my collar with one of those massive iron hands. "You aren't seeing the big picture. No not at all," as he yanked me upwards. "Harold is just a small piece of a much bigger puzzle. You and I are the big pieces. If I had you by my side, I never would have had to forcibly saved Rosie."

The image of Rosie lying there naked on a metal slab in the middle of a cold room made me want to cry inside. She wasn't broken. She didn't need to be saved and she didn't need to die. All she needed was to be loved. To have a man who would grab her unexpectedly and kiss her for no other reason than he wants to taste her lips. This beast didn't save her or me. He stole her life and, in the process, he stole the love from my heart and life.

"Help me save the next the Rosie. There are so many of them out in the world. Lee join me and we can save them from themselves. We can give their lives meaning and value." As I stared up at him I saw the madness staring back at me. What is the value of a life and who decides what is value and what isn't?

"I don't care about the next Rosie," I muttered. "I cared about my Rosie."

I could feel the warmth from his breath touching my skin as he asked, "Don't you want to be a savior? To save those hopeless creatures that can't save themselves?" He was so self-righteous standing over me like a king.

Grinding my teeth together I bellowed, "You aren't a savior. You are the monster that I refuse to become."

Laughing he slapped me across the face, "You already are a monster. The only question is whether you want to be the kind that makes the nightly news or the kind that actually makes a difference in the world?"

His attention was stolen for just a second by some noise in the distance, but a second was all I needed. With all the force I had in me, I threw my fist upward hearing my knuckles crack as it connected with his face. He groaned and broke his grip letting me fall to the ground as he covered his face. As he stumbled backwards I kicked his knee with all the force that I could muster and heard him scream out as he fell to the ground. As he lifted his head, I screamed out, "This is for my Rosie," and booted him in the face. His head shot up and I kicked him again hearing a loud pop as the cartilage in his nose was breaking away from the bone. He rolled over still holding his face screaming, "That wasn't something you should have done. No, not at all." Even in this dim moon light I saw the small flicker of silver as he yanked the little blade out.

In my mind, I was rolling onto my stomach, then made a fast dash into the forest and towards safety, but that was just the image in my head. The reality was that I was slowly flipping over, stumbling to my feet as I made my escape. I was clumsy at best and my feet skidded as I tried to bounce up into a full run and that's when he got me. At first, I didn't even realize what happened. It felt like I had twisted my ankle or pulled a muscle, but slowly it started going numb and I could feel the blood dripping down my leg. I hobbled my way into the trees not even sure if he was following me or not. I just kept running until I was hidden in the thick foliage.

Brown's loud voice bellowed, "You can run, but I will find you Lee. I will find you. I always get my man." At the tree line, I stopped and turned looking for him, but he was already gone. I was certain I had snapped his knee, but now it didn't seem like it. No, he had vanished. Of course, like all monsters, he would be back to hunt and kill another day.

I don't know why I did it, but I screamed out, "Then come and get me. I am waiting right here." That was the kind of statement idiots make when they are too stupid to run away. After letting those words explode out, I knew that I was an idiot. I might as well have just painted a giant neon target on my back.

I heard a clanking sound coming from behind the wood pile and realized Brown was getting something from a car. This couldn't be good. No this was not going to end well for me. I watched Brown step out from behind the wood pile carrying something in his hands. From my vantage point it was hard to see exactly what he had, but I am positive that it couldn't be anything good for me. Brown screamed out, "You can hide, but I will find you. I always find the poor souls that need to be saved."

I watched him walk in my direction then realized just how screwed I was. He was carrying one of those pump action shotguns and every bullet was meant for me. My mother used to say I came from a long line of war heroes because every war had at least one Truelove in it and not one of them died in combat. Of course, I always joked that the reason we lived was because us cowards could out run bullets and I think Brown was going to test that theory.

I watched him slowly make his way through the weeds and grass, heading in my direction. He kept waving the gun from side to side as he scanned the area, but he was heading straight for me. Brown was going to find and kill me, that was a certainty. "I will find you," was all he said as he charged in my direction.

In the background, I saw the dim lights of a car burning through the darkness like a demon's eyes searching for me. I had no false hope that whoever it was driving down the cow path lane was coming to save me or would even be any help. If anything, this was Brown's assistant coming to help him tie up all the loose ends. In many ways, I was that last loose end.

CHAPTER 30 – BROWN

I saw the head lights long before I heard the rumble of the engine. The light were projector lights and threw off a unique glow that stood out from any other. Logan had one of those car kits that you hear about. You know the kind of thing that older retired men buy to fill their time. Logan's was a 1934 ford replica that he had built for him. He would never admit it, but he dropped a lot of coin in it. This was an unexpected distraction that I hadn't of thought of, but I could twist this in my favor. Logan was useful so I didn't want to have to kill him unless there was no other avenue. Having a mole in the department that could be steered in any direction I wanted, was a useful thing.

I turned back towards the forest trying to gauge where my prey might be running off to. I couldn't get distracted from my real mission, besides its best to let Logan come to me and play my role in this play we call life. I heard the click of the shotgun shell entering the chamber as I pumped the shotgun. "Come on now Lee, don't make me hunt you down. This will be a lot easier on both of us if you just surrender." As I walked towards the tree line, I heard the engines rumble die down to an idle rather than the booming rumble. It wouldn't be long until Logan was helping me hunt down my naughty protégé. Of course, he would want to arrest him and take him in, but I couldn't allow that.

I heard the clank of the door closing and the scuffling of branches rubbing against his pants as he walked in my direction. Obviously, he had his gun out and was trying to decide what had happened. This is where my acting skills come into play and gullible Logan falls for it hook, line and sinker, every time. I was almost at the tree line when I finally heard his loud stomping behind me. In a crackly voice, he asked, "What the hell happened here?"

Still walking towards the trees, I didn't even look back. I just muttered, "A complete cluster fuck. Charlie went bat shit crazy and went after the Ashley kid."

"What's that got to do with Harold? He has a giant hole in the back of his head. Did Charlie kill him?" Logan asked as he stepped closer.

"No, it was the Ashley kid. Seems like Harold and him came after Charlie and then the kid turned on Harold. It's a complete mess."

The snapping of his footsteps behind me stopped and there was this awkward silence. I wanted to keep chasing Lee, but I was going to have to deal with Logan before it was too late. It made me wish that Logan wasn't such a good cop. "None of this suits his MO. Charlie I can see. Hell, after taking out Arthur, I knew that he was going to be hunting for the kid. You know, when in doubt kill them both type of thing."

Logan was too suspicious about the kid doing it. I guess being an educated man he was too involved now. Probably profiled the kid so much until he understood his way of thinking. I had to bring him in on the hunt at least until we had him trapped. The kid couldn't be allowed to be arrested. He would bring too many doubts to the table. The right questions would lead to more investigation and that might lead straight to me. Rosie's death was starting to get expensive, but saving souls always has a steep price. "I didn't see the kid do it, but I know that he has a gun."

"This doesn't suit the profile. This whole case doesn't suit any profile. We need him alive so he can bring some light to the table. If we are ever going to get to the truth, we need him, but Harold being involved does make sense. Seeing that the Brown chats came from the precinct." He was walking behind me with his gun extended. "I even bet if we check the work logs we will find that Harold was working when the Brown chats were taking place."

"And if the kid discovered Harold did it, what do you think that he would do?" Sometimes you need to spoon feed even the smartest cookies.

He was silent for a minute as he let everything sink in. "Son of a bitch!" he screamed, "It all makes sense now." Stepping a head of me, "I can't believe that we missed it. Ashley spent so much time with Harold while being locked up that he started pushing himself into his life. Do you think Harold really killed Rosie?"

Yes, that's what I needed to hear. Logan was being lead straight to the conclusion I wanted him to jump to. The evidence might not be all tight and tidy like I usually like, but if the kid bit the bullet, nobody would question it. That's the great thing about lazy police work. Once the toe tags go on everybody just goes with the flow and stops asking questions. "That's the direction things seem to be going in."

"Let's get the kid and then sort this shit out,' he muttered as he slowly entered the trees. He stopped and mumbled, "I already called for backup. ETA is twenty minutes behind me." He pulled out a small cell phone, "Thanks to GPS I can track him right from my phone. IT geeks set it up for me."

This was another unexpected event. Twenty minutes wasn't much time to tie up all my loose ends, especially when the body count was climbing like stairs. "So, that's how you tracked us here?"

"Yep. It doesn't matter where he tries to run to. If he has his cell phone on, we can track him no matter where he runs off." Logan stopped and turned smiling. "Technology can be as amazing as it is scary."

"Then let's get him before more guns get here. The more fingers on triggers the better chance our killer will become a target." Logan just nodded thinking that we were teammates not opponents and that's exactly how I wanted. I needed all his attention on Lee and not pondering the details of the case that must be driving him crazy.

I followed him through the trees and he kept staring at his cell phone pointing in various directions. Of course, it made tracking him a lot easier, but it wasn't a good thing. In the good old day's cops went in different directions chasing the suspect until they found him. Those good old days were good for this kind of business. Good because it allowed guys like me to protect themselves and call it self-defence and nobody was the wiser, but now we could track him like we had a map that lead straight to him. How was I going to kill the kid and not have to take out Logan at the same time? Logan stopped turning off his phone and held a hand up motioning for me to stop. He whispered, "He's right over there. Hang back in case he runs this way."

It wasn't exactly proper protocol. The rookie taking the lead in a pursuit and I am sure that the bloodhound would scream and curse over it, but I was going to let him chase the kid down. Obviously with him following a map straight to him I wasn't going to be able to just shoot the kid, but maybe this might give me a valid excuse to drop him. You know, mad criminal attacks rookie cop and the only way to save the rookie was to shoot him dead. It wasn't my preferred way of dealing with this, but I was quickly running out of valid options.

I watched Logan slowly creep through the brush as he tracked him. Each step made a low snapping echo breaking the silence of the forest. I stood there watching him filled with excitement as he slowly made his way towards Lee. This was a new way of catching the bad guy and I would need to use this technique in the future. Of course, I originally thought that I would be able to use Lee's modern stalker skills in my work, but I would have to adjust that plan since Lee was minutes from being located and in turn, minutes to an accidental shooting.

I watched Logan scout a small area always looking around

with a puzzled look on his face. Kneeling he pulled his phone out of his pocket lighting up a small hole in the darkness around him. He looked at the phone and slowly turned in a circular motion, "It says he is right here," he whispered as he turned around. "He should be standing right beside me, but I can't see him." I was about to respond when he leaned into the bushes and pulled something up off the ground. Opening it a second light flickered, "Son of a bitch he tossed the phone."

That's when it happened. From out of the bushes a figure jumped out swinging a baseball sized branch screaming something that I couldn't understand. Logan dropped to the ground as he was beaten down by Ashley. He was screaming and grunting as he swung the branch down screaming, "You two were in on it the whole time."

We were running out of time. In ten minutes, more patrol cars would invade the solitude of this sanctuary and my chance to wipe away all those loose ends would be lost forever. This little show of power worked in my favor though. I could kill the kid with a justified reason behind it. Ashley was pounding down again and again trying to over power law and order.

I heard the sirens blaring in the back ground as the reinforcements came charging in. They were earlier then Logan said they would be and I had to end this. I lifted my gun and fired two shots in Ashley's direction. I heard him yell out in agony as he fell into the brush behind him. I wanted it to be a kill shot, but shotgun kills are rare especially with thick branches and leaves between me and my target. Of course, if he wasn't dead, he wasn't going to be running any races anytime soon. It's hard to run or hide with a couple dozen little balls digging into your flesh. I was running in his direction, but by the time I got there, he was long gone. Logan was laying there unconscious, but still alive. He would have a collection of new scars, but nothing truly life threatening. He would never know how truly close he came to dying or that this beating saved his life.

I grabbed one of the cell phones lying on the ground and used the light to scan the leaves and found exactly what I was looking for. The leaves were covered in fresh blood and broken branches marking Lee's escape route. I followed the trail that Ashley left behind and knew he wouldn't have gotten far. Too much blood was left behind for him to make it far. As any hunter can tell you, an injured animal might storm away, but not for a great distance. No, he would be stumbling around almost dropping within fifty feet and even if he made if further, he had the lake to contend with. No Ashley was trapped and had no way to escape.

I was following the trail through the trees and fallen timber thinking what a waste. This kid was tougher then he looked. I was already forty feet into the forest and he was no where to be seen. Of course, he was quickly running out of ground. Despite what people think, swimming with lead in your shoulder doesn't work. It's like trying to clap with only one hand. Looks awkward and doesn't quite sound right. Hitting the edge of the tree line I saw him standing there still holding his stick in his hand trying to swing it single handed. Still defiant as hell I thought. Even in his last minutes he wouldn't go quietly. I stepped out of the trees, "It's over kid. You threw the dice and lost."

Bouncing from side to side he muttered, "I see you now. It was there the whole time. Right underneath my nose." I couldn't see his face, but I am certain that it was covered in shock and dismay. He had seen me and didn't even realize it. Yes, I am sure there's nothing more in this world he wants beyond choking the life out of me. "The killer was never caught by you because you are the killer."

Holding my gun tighter I laughed. He finally saw the light at the end of the tunnel, but of course he was like a deer paralyzed in them too. This must be so confusing for him. He was wrapping his mind around a stereo type that he only knew from TV movies and now he was being touched by the real thing. "Oh, you are talking about the bloodhound Bruno."

Still swinging the stick in his hand, he screamed, "Don't act like you aren't a sick bastard Bruno. You are going to kill me anyway, but don't insult my intelligence."

"Oh, so you want the truth now, do you?" He wouldn't understand the complexity of it. He would not be able to handle the idea that two men were trapped inside one body like a horrific science experiment gone array. "The bloodhound is truly trying to catch the killer. He stays up at nights going threw the case files. He mourns poor little Callie's death and hates himself because her killer is the only one that got away."

"Got away? You killed them. Charlie's daughter and my Rosie," he snapped.

I burst out laughing. "You don't get it Ashley. Bruno didn't kill them, I did. The bloodhound doesn't understand people like I do. He just follows protocol and the evidence like a dog on a leash. I can see all the possibilities and only I can save them. Those I can't save, I set free."

"You are Bruno," he snapped.

He was too closed minded to see the truth. Most people are. "I am not like Bruno. I am the stronger, darker side. I am the strength that cannot be contained."

Stepping into the water he just shook his head in disbelief as he looked around the water. He seemed to be lost as he looked back at me, "Don't play me like a fool. Don't insult my intelligence."

"I am not insulting you. I wanted you to join me. To understand me, but it's too late for that now." It was true. I admired his strength and loyalty. He would never be able to understand our complexity. I see the bloodhound, but the bloodhound doesn't know me. That I haunt his dreams and even though he keeps chasing me, I am the shadow that always alludes him. "We are joined souls me and Bruno. The good and evil so to speak, except the evil forces that he's so desperately trying to catch is his shadow."

"What?" he muttered in confusion. A glimmer of hope came over him as the sirens grew louder. The idea that somebody was just a heart beat away from saving him. It happens a lot. In the last moments of their lives they get this glimmer of hope even if hope doesn't exist. He was looking at the lights from the cop cars as they made their way towards us, but they weren't going to be here in time to save him. No one could.

I lifted my gun and fired a shot. At this distance, I couldn't miss and he couldn't survive a direct hit. He just dropped face first into the water as the pepper of pellets bit into his flesh. I felt remorse as I walked over towards the water. I didn't want to kill him, but I had to. He was a missing piece to a puzzle, but if you look hard enough there are always other puzzles and pieces. It's was hard to find them, but not impossible. I pumped the shotgun watching the shell pop out into the water. One shell left and soon I would be free of suspicion and able to continue my work. My work was more important then any life was.

CHAPTER 31 – BRUNO

A body was floating in the water as I walked towards the lake. The water hitting the shore made a hollow thudding sound and the wind whistled as it whipped past me. Obviously, another murder, but I couldn't remember when I was called here or how I even got here. The first time this happened it scared the hell out of me. It's like sleep walking and waking up right in the middle of the worst things possible. The first time was the day Callie died. I was sleeping and my phone woke me up. In the middle of the confusion, I realized that I was two blocks away from the murder scene and couldn't remember how I even got there.

The smell of gun smoke was still floating in the air even though there was a strong wind passing by. Shots were fired and by the warmth of the shotgun barrel, I had been the one who fired. The real question now was who I shot and why did I shoot him? God, I hope it wasn't Charlie. The way he's been acting lately it might have come down to kill him or be killed by him. I was afraid to look, but I knew I had to do it. If I killed Charlie I needed to see the look on his face. It wasn't anything to do with respect, but closure. When you kill a man, you should see the result, even if you couldn't remember why you did it.

I finally forced myself to the water's edge and grabbed onto the victim's foot dragging him onto the shore. The body wasn't stiff so I don't think he's been dead for very long. The problem with cold lake water is that it screws up determining time of death. Well for us flat foots. The pros in the lab can always give us an accurate time line. I stood there combing through my pockets looking for my little flash light so I could see his face for identification. With the light in my hand, I turned it on and shined it into his face. OMG it was that Lee kid. How did he get to Charlie's cabin and why the hell did I shoot him?

I leaned over and felt for a pulse. Thank god, he still had one, but by the way he was bleeding out, if he didn't get emergency care soon, he was going to die. His muscles were shaking and trembling as I tried to apply pressure to the wounds. The problem was that there were so many of them. I had no way to get all of them. Damn the kid was shot at close and personal range, which meant there had to be a gun somewhere. That's the only reason why I would shoot anyone. Pure self-defense so I had to find that once back up came and by the sounds of the sirens, they're only a minute away tops.

I scanned the water's edge with my flash light trying to find the gun. Dragging a lake is almost impossible so I damn well hoped that it landed close to the shore. As I scanned the shore, I finally gave up and went back to the kid who was barely hanging onto life. Time wasn't in his favor and there was nothing I could do.

The kid started coughing and I could see a small mist like explosion of blood each time he did. I leaned over and whispered, "Don't worry kid help is on its way." Yes, it was probably a giant ass lie and he was most likely going to die, but you need to keep them calm if at all possible. Stress causes the heart to speed up and that in turn forces the blood out even faster. Patting his blood-stained shoulder, I said, "Everything is going to be fine."

As he was struggling to breath he croaked, "Fuck you Brown or Bruno or whatever your name is." He was struggling to raise his fists, but the blood loss made him too weak to finish it.

The word Brown was ringing in my ears like a bell as I grabbed hold of his collar and snapped, "Brown! Where the hell is he?" I was snapping him up and down screaming, "Where's Brown?"

The kid's eyes were dropping as he started to slip into unconsciousness. The last words he chirped was, "You are Brown." It took a minute for me to understand what he was saying. You are Brown. How the hell was I Brown? I had never even heard of him until a few days ago, what was so important about comparing us that it was the kids last word?

I stood up looking behind me. I could see the flashing lights parked in on the other side of the trees. The boys arrived just a few minutes too late. I was still flashing my light across the top of the water when I saw something reflecting the light. I walked over expecting to find a hand gun. There just had to be one. It was the only thing that made sense. I was a good cop and good cops don't just shoot innocent people. Reaching into the cold water I fumbled trying to find the gun, but there was nothing to be found.

"You can't find what's not their bloodhound," a voice taunted me. I jumped up looking all around but couldn't find the source. "Look me in the eyes bloodhound. I think our meeting has been put off far too long now."

I stumbled around trying to find him but couldn't find Brown even though I knew that he was just out of reach somewhere. "Where the hell are you Brown?" I screamed.

The clouds drifted through the sky above me opening a curtain allowing the moon light to come tumbling below like a giant spot light. On the water, I saw something drifting along the waves. I looked now and don't know how to explain what I saw. Cold eyes were glaring at me and a twisted evil grin filled my face. It was me, but not me. It's like staring at a dark shadow of yourself. Tapping the side of his head he snickered, "I am right inside your noggin cowboy. Hanging out right between that little fat kid that everybody teased and the hero you always thought you were. I am right where I have always been and where I belong."

"You are not inside my head," I screamed. "You are a killer, aren't you?"

Laughing he added, "I am the stronger personality. I am the one who takes the damaged little flowers you can't help and turns them up into tall shining roses."

I snapped, "Roses. You call what you did to Rosie as making her into a healthy rose!?" The image of Rosie's dead body just lying there in the tub surrounded by bloody water came to mind. It was just like the day it happened. I hated the memory, but like all nightmares, it just wouldn't fade away.

"No Rosie wasn't a good flower. That's why I treated her like the weed she is."

I snapped, "You didn't just kill her. You tortured her."

"They say love hurts and I loved you enough to hurt her. It's the only way to save her soul. It's the only way to save them. You know, through blood and pain."

I screamed, "Them!"

I once heard that our dreams and nightmares are reflections of those images that we have encountered and for the first time, I understood my nightmares. It was always those empty haunting eyes that got me. Those possibilities that were choked out like rain falling on a flame. It was my eyes that watched Rosie that night, but it wasn't my soul that controlled the body. No, this was the invader Brown.

Rosie was standing by the window watching Ashley being loaded into the back of a cop car. This wasn't anything new since Arthur was always abusive and Ashley always came to her rescue or at least he tried, but she was blinded by that dream. If only she could see that the physical act wasn't the same as the emotional connection. We watched her through the little crack in the door. One body and two souls. Brown the savior and me the observer. I was a passenger in my own body while Brown drove. As the memory went through my mind, I wondered just how many times I had been over powered by his sheer will power. How many times did I wake up feeling lost and exhausted unaware that my dark side had stolen control?

She moved her legs forcing her hips to twist as she

continued watching out the little window in front of her desk. Most people would see the way her body curved and moved in its own rhythm and struggle not to reach out and touch her, but not us. No, we saw her for what she really was. Underneath the fancy black silk panties and matching bra was something distasteful. Ugly even. Despite all the time and energy that was wasted trying to make her whole, she was nothing more than forbidden fruit. Beautiful and sexy on the outside, but as ugly as a leper on the inside.

Her phone rang. Still staring out the window she picked it up saying, "Hi baby." We didn't need to hear who it was because the only person she called baby was Arthur. He was a true wolf. In the public eye the perfect man. Successful enough that he always money on hand, a father figure that went to all his kid's events and he even sent flowers to his wife a couple times a month. That was the version he allowed the world to see. The version he hid from family and friends was an abusive control freak who lived out his fantasies of power. How many times did she call us crying about how much he hurt her? The next day she always went back to him. It was a cycle that we couldn't stop. We had thought about killing him, but experience told us that she would only find another more abusive master.

"Yes, I saw them take Lee away." She leaned over and watched the police car pull away. "No, I don't know why he is always after you. No, I didn't tell him anything bad about you, ever." After a brief pause her head dropped, "I told them what you wanted me to say." Wide eyed she just mumbled, "No baby I don't want to upset you or ruin your life." The buzzing on the phone went on for too long before she finally whined, "No I don't want to hurt you."

This type of conversation went on for some time. We had never actually heard her beg before. Up until today, it had always been her saying things but never begging, but we weren't surprised by this. It was the cycle of self-destruction that we had tried to pull her away from. The path that she always told us she needed to leave, but never did. The closest thing that she would ever come to being truly loved was sitting in the back of the cruiser. To save him, we needed to save her, only her salvation was written in pain and blood. Her pain and her blood. We loved this child, but we need him.

Finally, she said, "Will we be together forever?" She smiled at the response then said, "I love you too baby." She stepped away and said, "Yes I promised if you sent me my allowance I would send it. Yes, I am going to do it now. One just for you." With that she opened her closet door revealing a full-sized mirror and started to get undressed. We watched as she started sliding out of her clothes revealing her slutty undergarments. How many times had we warned her that this type of behavior would not lead to the love and family that she wanted? That she would be used over and over like the slut that she allowed herself to be treated like? We watched her snap a few pics and then send them to Arthur. It was a cycle that she would never break, no matter how much time we wasted on her.

The night was quiet now with all her roommates working or studying late into the night. That's why we chose tonight to save this helpless sinful child. No distractions or witnesses. Tonight, was just the three of us alone so that we could save her. As she slipped on a white housecoat, grabbing a towel and soap, humming a classical tune that we had heard before, she headed to the bathroom. It was her nightly routine. She thought that her nightly routine of soaking in the tub was cleanliness, but we knew all her little secrets and not everything she did in there was wholesome. We slipped into one of the other rooms and waited. At times like this you must wait for the best time and setting.

We heard the water tumbling into the tub and we waited. Rosie was humming that same song endlessly. If only she knew that the next song she sang was going to be amongst Angels. Through the little crack in the door we could see her naked body as she slowly undressed. She was vain about her body and enjoyed the idea of being watched by those around her. It was a flaw in her character. One of many flaws that existed and those who took the time to truly see her, took advantage of it.

We stepped closer towards the door. A low squeak rang out with each step we took. From the little crack in the door we could see her smile and slip under the white foaming suds. Her eyes sparkled as she tried to determine who was watching her. After a moment, she lifted her body up just a little higher allowing her nipples to poke through and an even bigger grin filled her face. Such a naughty child she was and now we would punish her.

Opening the door her smile dropped as she whispered, "What are you doing here?" She dropped beneath the water whispering, "You can't see me like this!"

"Don't worry Rosie. Remember I said I would save and protect you always."

Her lips quivered as she whined, "Yes."

Pulling the knife from our pocket, we whispered, "Tonight's the night we save your soul and release you from your body."

It was the sound of Rosie's screams ringing in my ears that brought me back to reality even though I didn't want to come back, but then again, being trapped in that nightmare wasn't any better. I just stood there letting everything sink into my mind with the wind blowing through my hair. It was a lot to take in. Being the very monster that I have spent my whole career chasing. Not just any monster, but a predator who kills innocent women and friends. I didn't have a lot of friends. Most people blame the job, but the truth, is that it's not the job. It's me. I have always been that guy who feels alone even when I am in the center of the biggest crowd.

Brown's voiced boomed, "We will get away with this bloodhound. Nobody will suspect us if you play your part right. We are untouchable." Untouchable was another way of saying that we were getting away with murder. Not just one murder either. How many had we killed? How many times had Brown become the dominate personality and the alpha male? I didn't know the answer and I wasn't sure I wanted to either. "Oh, come on Bloodhound. There are no more secrets between us. It's a good thing really. We are the perfect partners. I am the closest thing to a soul mate that you'll ever get."

He called us soul mates. This wasn't what I had in mind when I thought about forever. Two sides of the same coin. The light and the darkness inside me shattered into two separate pieces. As long as Brown survived, the world wasn't a better place. The problem was if I survived, so did Brown. I dropped to my knees whispering, " I have been chasing you for so long Brown. Tonight, I finally caught you."

I took the shotgun and placed it into my mouth. It was time to put this monster down. Brown bellowed, "What do you think you are doing? We still have so many people to save."

Brown kept screaming in my ears as I slowly felt my finger snap down on the trigger thinking, "I am saving people. All of them."

EPILOGUE

I woke up to blinding light and the sweet smell of perfume. It was the unmistakable smell of Black Opium. I am not sure who makes it, only that I always found it alluring. As my eyes focused and the room started to take shape around me, I knew where I was. I was in the hospital. Instinct made me stretch and then the damn burning started which made it feel like my skin shrank. I just laid there trying to push the pain from my mind as I tried to fit the pieces together.

The last I remember is floating on the water thinking that I had used up the last of my lives. I was like an old tomcat that way. Every time I think my end is here, boom, I wake up in a hospital room. This time was different though. No, this time I was just another victim. Realizing that Brown and Bruno were the same person put me here. I was a victim of love and it almost killed me.

"I am happy to see that you are alive Mister Truelove," a soft voice whispered. "I didn't know how long you would be under."

Turning, I saw a little nurse writing in a clip board. "How long have I been under?"

Looking at her watch she said, "Oh about 36 hours or so. Don't worry about that now. You need lots of rest and relaxation. When you came in you had more holes in you then a sprinkler." She was a little stout woman with red curly hair. As she made her way towards the door she stopped and mumbled, "It's a shame that you didn't wake up ten minutes earlier."

"Why is that?" I asked expecting to hear that the cops were here earlier.

"Oh, because your friends widow was just here. Such a caring woman. Even in her grief-stricken state she comes by to check on you."

"What friend?"

"The police offer who died in the line of duty of course. Harold something." I had forgotten that Harold was dead. Murdered by that bastard Brown. I was going to miss him even if we weren't really friends. I guess though that his widow was going to miss him more. We had something in common. One man stole the love of my life and took her husband from her. "If you look beside the flowers she dropped off, you will find a note that she left.

I looked over and saw one of those red lily type flowers with metal wrapping paper around the base. It wasn't anything special really and not an expensive bouquet, but it was the first time anyone ever took the time to send me flowers in the hospital. The first time ever. I slowly reached over and grabbed the note that she had left. It took some time to open since every muscle burned with even the thought of moving, but eventually I got it open.

Mister Truelove,

I know that being the last person to see my husband alive must be a hard burden to carry. Maybe even an impossible one to get past. I just wanted you to know that Harold was very fond of you and even thought of you as a friend. You should not carry any guilt over this catastrophe. He died in the line of duty following his conscience and saving a friend. I can think of no more honorable a reason for him to trade his life. Move past this life changing event as best you can and know that you are not responsible for any of it.

I will pray for your fast recovery and good health.

Rachelle

Such a sweet woman I thought. Even in a time like this she took the time to think of me. Women like that are rare and I think that maybe she was reaching out to me in her own way. We both carry the loss of a loved one and can help each other move on. Besides a single widow woman might just need a man to protect her and take care of her. I set the note on the table and the name Rachelle lingered through my mind. Such a soft sounding name. Sexy Rachelle. I would need to look her up when I got out of here.

ABOUT THE AUTHOR

Robert Skuce thought that he was too pretty and small for prison so he decided to write about it instead. After dabbling in different genres, he found himself at home as a thriller/crime writer. A man, who was born and raised in Eastern Ontario, Canada, in a small town, he decided to try his hand at creative novel writing. Turned out, he loved it and kept writing to improve his craft and is now the writer he is today. He enjoys a good mystery and once in a while he likes to go back to horror when it was simpler and less complicated then you find in this day and age.

Currently living in Southern Ontario with his wife and four kids, he enjoys long walks, time with his family and lazy afternoons getting caught up on television. He loves playing with computers and is the household personal IT technician. When he goes out, you can find him exploring the different restaurants his city has to offer and driving in the country side. He is always looking for new places to be the basis of his books. He photographs abandoned buildings and unique parts of town in order to create a sense of realism in his books.

Filled with ideas and personalities that are unique, he is always coming up with a new and twist-filled story that will make its way to the pages everyone can enjoy. Captivating his readers with the difficulty in his books and leaving them trying to figure out who did it, will make you want to keep reading to see what Robert Skuce will come up with next!